Praise for the Cold Case Investigations

The Murder Book

An Amazon and Barnes and Noble Bestseller

"A simply riveting read from cover to cover."

—*Midwest Book Review*

"Fans of contemporary police procedurals will want to see more of the plucky Lauren."

—*Publishers Weekly*

"A pulse-racing pace, well-chosen details of Buffalo's mixed industrial landscape and characters to bleed for make this a stunningly good second book. Highly recommended."

—*Kingdom Books*

"I loved the friendship between Buffalo Police's Lauren Riley and Shane Reece, and long to see The Murder Book as a movie."

—*Crime Thriller Hound*

A Cold Day in Hell

"Recommend this one to anyone who loves courtroom dramas where lawyers tear into witnesses like pit bulls. And to anyone hot for a police procedural where tired cops make mistakes but slowly, relentlessly—and with morbid humor—get the job done. Redmond delivers both in one package ... The real attraction here is a key-hole view into a world that turns our expectations upside down—a world where a bullying, quasi-fascist cop can be the only one with a handle on reality. Keep your eyes on Redmond, a retired cop who knows how to write."

—*Booklist*

A

MEANS

TO

AN

END

A MEANS TO AN END

A Cold Case Investigation

LISSA MARIE REDMOND

MIDNIGHT INK
WOODBURY, MINNESOTA

FIRST EDITION
First Printing, 2019

Book format by Samantha Penn
Cover design by Kevin R. Brown
Editing by Nicole Nugent

Midnight Ink, an imprint of Llewellyn Worldwide Ltd.

Library of Congress Cataloging-in-Publication Data
Names: Redmond, Lissa Marie, author.
Title: A means to an end : a cold case investigation / Lissa Marie Redmond.
Description: First edition. | Woodbury, Minnesota : Midnight Ink, [2019] |
 Series: A cold case investigation ; #3
Identifiers: LCCN 2019012023 (print) | LCCN 2019013525 (ebook) | ISBN
 9780738755670 () | ISBN 9780738754284 (alk. paper)
Subjects: | GSAFD: Mystery fiction. | Suspense fiction.
Classification: LCC PS3618.E4352 (ebook) | LCC PS3618.E4352 M43 2019 (print)
 | DDC 813/.6—dc23
LC record available at https://lccn.loc.gov/2019012023

Midnight Ink
Llewellyn Worldwide Ltd.
2143 Wooddale Drive
Woodbury, MN 55125-2989
www.midnightinkbooks.com

Printed in the United States of America

For my grandfather, Joseph Kogut,
the greatest storyteller who ever lived.

Author's Note

I was born and raised in Buffalo, New York. I have never lived anywhere else and hope my great love for the city shines through. This book takes place in Buffalo, but it is a work of fiction. In the spirit of full disclosure, I took many liberties with locations in this novel. The gated community Lauren lives in does not exist. Garden Valley resembles a neighboring town south of the city, but you won't find it on a map. Real roles—such as mayor, Erie County district attorney, and the police commissioner—are populated with fictional people who in no way resemble any living person. I took great pains to create fictional characters to populate the very real Buffalo that I love. Hopefully my fellow Buffalonians will forgive the literary license I took.

"The murder isn't over until the killer stops deriving pleasure from the crime."

The eyeless skull stared off into the trees as Buffalo Police Cold Case detective Lauren Riley bent at the knee, resting her back end on her heel to get a better look. Behind her, outside the crime scene tape, a couple of deputy sheriffs talked to a trooper as they waited for the state police crime scene technicians to show up. Maneuvering herself in front of the skull's lifeless gaze, Lauren snapped a picture with her cell phone.

"Come again?" Shane Reese asked his partner, staring down at the remains of a body. It appeared to be a female to Lauren. It was hard to tell with that much decomposition. The clothing was really the only clue to the gender, except for the long, stringy hair clinging to the last of the tissue on the scalp.

"It's just something I learned at that crime scene assessment seminar you didn't want to go to over the summer."

Used to blacktop and concrete, Lauren was out of her element in the woods roughly sixty-three miles south of the city. It wasn't bitterly cold out, the weather was actually quite mild, but a wicked wind ripped through the barren trees, stinging her face and ears. The spot was desolate, a quarter mile off the New York State Thruway, deep into the scraggy tree line. Whoever had dumped the body had carried it a long way to make sure it was hidden. The clearing was small, maybe twenty feet by twenty. The state police had marked a path from the road with crime scene tape threaded between the trees, then roped the whole clearing off in a wide circle.

Lauren had been careful not to step on any evidence, to maintain a proper distance, but she craned forward, trying to commit to memory the details in front of her. Tucking a loose strand of blond hair back up into the black knit hat she wore, she tried to make out what the dark splotches on the chest of the jacket could be. Blood? Dirt? She squinted against the wind. Crime scene photos were great, but nothing replaced actually being at the scene.

The body lay in two pieces, the upper half lying face up, a denim jacket barely holding it together. The lower half was approximately five feet away, torn at the waist and dragged, possibly by animals. The skull had detached from the neck and was tilted to the left side. A skirt covered the pelvic area, but the leg bones were totally exposed and strewn about. The original color of the skirt was impossible to tell, as it was now a muddy dark brown from exposure to the elements. Lauren suspected it was pleather, that plastic material they called vegan leather now, but that too was just a guess. The victim's shoes were mostly intact, the heeled mules adding more evidence that this was, indeed, a female.

There had been a thaw, not unusual for Western New York, whose weather was famous for fluctuating wildly, especially this early in the month of March. Two hunters had come across the body while hunting rabbits. The day before, the temperature had gotten into the midforties. It was colder today, and there were still dirty patches of snow throughout the clearing, but the sound of running water from somewhere nearby told Lauren that it had melted enough to uncover the body.

The young hunters were now sitting in the Chautauqua County Sheriff's Office, giving their statements. Lauren wondered what they must have thought when they saw the skull staring past them, the way it was staring past her now. The dank smell of mud and decaying leaves filled her nose, but it was muted, the remaining snow absorbing the scents. The body itself was past the time for the tell-tale stench; it had been out there, exposed to the elements, for a long time. Except for the leather-like skin holding what was left of her scalp in place, all of the soft tissue was gone, although there might be some under the skirt or jacket. The medical examiner would cut away the clothes at the autopsy and see what was left.

Lauren made note of a bulge in the denim jacket's front pocket, which appeared to be the shape of a cell phone. Hearing a shrill hiss, she looked up. Nasty little black birds were cawing at the police personnel from their perches in the skeletal tree branches surrounding the body, pissed off someone was encroaching on their territory.

"What the hell are you two doing here?"

Lauren turned to see Cam Bates from the Garden Valley Police Department striding past the crime scene tape strung between two thin trees. He wasn't dressed for the weather, wearing only a thin jacket and some gloves. Lauren knew from previous encounters with Bates that he had almost made it to the pros playing hockey until a knee injury sidelined him in college. In his early thirties, Cam Bates had the lean muscular body of an athlete not yet gone to seed. He was

3

one of those guys who still played league hockey, still walked around with a wad of chewing tobacco in his lip, and still thought he was a super star.

"As of January first, the Buffalo Police brass gave the Cold Case squad all adult missing persons cases. Our special offense squad was getting overwhelmed. They should have done it years ago," Reese told him, pulling himself to his full height. While Lauren ignored Bates completely, Reese wasn't about to be bullied by a suburban cop with an attitude. "The State Police called us because they think the body might be Brianna McIntyre. She went missing from a coffee shop on Chippewa Street last May."

Folding his arms across his chest, Reese locked eyes with Bates. "I should be asking you—why the hell is Garden Valley here? Last I checked a map, you were located twenty miles south of the city line."

"I called him." One of the investigators for the State Police stepped up. He was a small man, with olive skin, thick black hair, and deep-set dark eyes. "I'm senior investigator Manny Perez. I was one of the first to respond when Amber Anderson's body was found"—his round face pinched up as he nodded his head toward a large, jagged stump—"not even fifty yards from this spot." Amber Anderson had gone missing from Garden Valley almost two years ago. Her body had been recovered sixteen months ago, dumped and decomposed, right there. The case was still unsolved.

"How can we know for sure this is your missing person?" Bates asked, angling himself to see past Lauren, who was still hunched down, blocking his view. For someone as skinny as she was, she could be awfully opaque when she wanted to be.

"We can't, not until the DNA and dental results come back, but we have this." The Chautauqua County sheriff who was in charge of the crime scene held up a plastic evidence bag. Inside was a very weather-beaten wallet. "It was found about ten feet from the body," he said, pointing, "by that exposed rock. The hunters who found the body didn't know enough to leave this where it was. They handed the wallet to the first officer who arrived on the scene. Driver's license and credit cards all belong to Brianna McIntyre."

The sheriff walked forward and handed the bag to Lauren, who carefully examined its contents through the clear plastic. The driver's license picture mirrored the missing person's poster in the file: a twenty-two-year-old strawberry blonde with freckles peppered across her face. She had gone to meet a man from a dating site and never came home.

Lauren's stomach clenched as she thought of her own two daughters, not much younger than the victim. "Thank you," she told the deputy, turning the wallet over in her gloved hand, looking for any hint as to what happened the night Brianna disappeared.

"Now that we all know how *we* got here," the same sheriff's deputy said, "why don't we concentrate on the body and how *she* got here?"

Reaching back, Lauren handed the wallet to the deputy with a small, knowing smile. His crime scene was now crowded with four separate police departments and he was fighting to maintain control as the evidence techs from the Chautauqua County Forensic Investigation Team came in with what looked like oversized tackle boxes and black nylon totes to do their thing.

Lauren knew how the body had gotten there. Twenty-year-old David Spencer had murdered her and dumped her there, just like he had murdered and dumped his ex-girlfriend, Amber Anderson. While the young psychopath had been on her radar for other crimes and Lauren had also been looking into Brianna's disappearance, there had been no reason to tie the two of them together.

5

Until now.

Lauren stood up, gave Reese a nod, and they made their way back under the tape. He had his leather folio unzipped in his hand, opened to the yellow legal pad. He had made a rough crime scene sketch: body, trees, rock, stump, trees. Along the bottom, he had scrawled the notation: *not to scale.*

"I didn't want to ask in the middle of the pissing contest," Lauren said, looking back at Manny Perez and Cam Bates huddled together, comparing notes, "but who's going to do the family notification?"

"Good question." Reese clapped his folio together and zipped it closed. Even his cheeks were a ruddy red against the wind. With green eyes and flawless brown skin, Reese yanked his own knit hat down over the tips of his ears, which were starting to look raw. One of the black birds startled in the tree above, causing them both to jump. "I hate nature," he added, buttoning the top button of his black wool pea coat. "This is why I live in the city."

"I didn't see any obvious bullet holes to the skull," Lauren said, adjusting her own outerwear. Four months before, she had been stabbed in her office by another cop, collapsing her lung. Though she was still not fully recovered, she had insisted on coming back to work full time.

Reserved to the point she was often considered aloof, Lauren Riley had appreciated turning forty in February. She liked the anonymity of her now-average looks and loved the fact her dating prospects had dried up. Her life felt so much less complicated on her own. Naturally thin all her life, she had lost even more weight after the stabbing, making her appear gaunt. She'd gone from a blue-eyed, honey-blond waif, complete with a sprinkling of warm brown freckles across her nose, to just a shell of herself in a matter of weeks. Her hair was darker now, limper. Her skin had taken on a sallow tinge that highlighted the creases around her eyes. She'd gone from strikingly beautiful to barely average with one stab of a knife. Rather than mourn the loss of her good looks, Lauren took pride in it as the price of surviving.

Lauren turned to the sheriff's deputy in charge. She considered asking him about the notification, but he was pointing something out to Cam Bates on the ground. The deputy was someone she hadn't met on the job before. Lauren estimated him to be in his late forties, with neatly cut dark brown hair and a kind, serious face. Watching him work his scene, she didn't want to interrupt his flow. Instead she turned to Reese, who told her, "The autopsy will tell. I'm betting a broken hyoid bone, if the animals haven't damaged the body too much to tell."

"Let's head over to the sheriff's department." Lauren's eyes followed the crime scene photographer as he snapped shot after shot of the torn upper torso. "There's nothing left to see here."

2

Despite its homey 1950s red brick façade, the Chautauqua County Sheriff's Office was a lot more modern than Lauren thought it was going to be. She wasn't kidding when she joked about not being a country girl to Reese, but she had forgotten one very important thing about the area: it was home to the famed Chautauqua Institution, a world-renowned center for arts, culture, and learning. That was big, big money. Any crime, no matter how small, was going to be handled with the upmost professionalism and care; at least that's what the poster hanging in their detectives' squad room said. Lauren sat at an empty desk across from Reese, studying the layout of this alien place. Clean open work spaces. New, modern chrome-edged furniture and natural light pouring in from the windows were as foreign to Lauren as deer tracks and bear shit.

"I'm Manny Perez, senior investigator," Reese mocked in a high-pitched voice as he reclined in one of the office chairs, fingers laced behind his head. "I like to throw my weight and low testosterone around at other people's crime scenes."

"It's not nice to argue at someone else's party," Lauren reminded him.

"And thank you for not scaring our hosts with tales of the demonic David Spencer."

"You don't think he did this? You think some other guy killed Amber and Brianna? Dumped both their bodies out here?"

"I think we should wait for all the evidence before we jump off the conclusion cliff."

Lauren's face got hot. "After everything that's happened, you know he did this."

"I think he *most likely* did this. Let's do our jobs and find some good solid evidence and maybe then put him away for good."

He was right, she knew, but that just made her angrier. Lauren liked to think of their partnership as a codependent, verbally combative collaboration. She'd been borderline obsessed with David Spencer since they'd found ex-cop Ricky Schultz's body in his basement with a cryptic message left on his computer screen just for her. And while the department had handed that investigation over to other Homicide detectives, she'd worked it from the wings since she came back from her medical leave.

"This squad room is great." Reese tried to swivel around, but the chair hit the desk with a *clang*. "I love the décor in this place."

"You want to transfer out here?" Lauren asked, thumbing through a travel brochure someone had left on the desk. A picture of a smiling family boating on Chautauqua Lake graced the cover with the words DISCOVER CHAUTAUQUA COUNTY! blazed in green letters across the top.

"I think our skill set is better suited for the city," he replied, sipping the Tim Hortons coffee they had stopped and grabbed on the way over to the department. Maybe the rest of the country ran on Dunkin' Donuts or fueled up at Starbucks, but in the Buffalo area Tim Hortons coffee and donuts reigned supreme.

"And what skills would those be?"

He glanced around the immaculately clean office. The secretary who led them there had politely sat them down and retreated. "The ability to deal with urban problems. This here is a whole other set of rules."

"You think so?" She dropped the brochure back down. "I think people are the same all over."

"I do not think so. I mean, yeah, to an extent. I'm sure they have their drugs and domestics and drunk drivers just like we do. But the vibe is different. Can't you feel it?"

"I think your hat is too tight on your head."

Tugging on his knit cap, he flashed her his brilliant smile. "You're just saying that because I shaved my head and you don't like it."

She couldn't deny it. "You look like a biracial Yul Brynner."

"I'll take that as a compliment. Yul Brynner was smooth as fu—"

"Sorry about the wait." The deputy who headed up the scene finally came banging through the office door, cutting off Reese's profanity-laden comparison to the late actor. He pulled his winter police hat off, tousling his dark brown hair and slung it on the coat hanger next to the door. "The medical examiner and his assistant just finished up."

"No worries." Reese stood with an outstretched hand. "Detective Shane Reese, Buffalo Police Department."

Lauren got to her feet as the two men shook, then offered her own hand. "Lauren Riley."

His hand was warm and smooth around hers. She noted the gloves stuffed into his coat pocket. He must have peeled them off right before he came in. "Deputy Sheriff Jack Nolan. Good to meet you both." Releasing Lauren's hand, his eyebrows pulled together. "I know you." Hazel eyes searched her face. "Where do I know you from?"

Reese ran interference for her. "She's got that kind of face. People say that to her all the time. Anyway, we brought a copy of the Brianna McIntyre file with us if you want to make some copies."

Nolan snapped his fingers in recognition. "You're the one who got stabbed." Seeing the look on Lauren's face, he quickly tried to recover. "I'm sorry. Forget I said that. Probably a sore subject. It's just that it was all over the news."

It had been. Live-streamed for a week straight until a coup in some country Lauren had never heard of stole the cable news cameras away. Waving a hand in dismissal, she told him, "It's fine. You should see the stares I get when I go to the grocery store." That was a lie. Except to go to work and on PT-prescribed walks before most people were even out of bed, she barely left her house. The drive-thru at the fast food place a mile from her house was keeping her alive. That and whatever she and Reese grabbed during their shift. It was no wonder she was a physical ruin.

Jack Nolan unzipped his heavy police jacket and draped it over the back of a chair. Lauren surmised it was his chair, at his desk, due to the framed photo of him standing with his arm around a teenage boy who looked exactly like him, only thirty years younger. "Let's try this again. I'd love to see the file you have on Brianna McIntyre."

Reese handed over the paperwork while Nolan cleared a space for them to gather around his desk. Pulling up the chair she had been sitting in, Lauren sat shoulder-to-shoulder with the sheriff while Reese dragged an older wooden chair from against the wall to sit across from the two of them.

The first thing Nolan pulled out of the file was an 8x10 photo of the missing girl that her mother had provided. The generic blue background practically screamed that it had been taken at a discount department store somewhere, probably as some sort of family portrait package. She was resting her chin on her fist, smiling right into the camera, strawberry blond hair falling down around her face in thick curls.

"Her mother, Angela McIntyre, said that picture was taken two years ago. The only difference was the length of her hair," Lauren explained. "She said Brianna had grown it out."

Nolan placed it face up on his desk and pulled out the official missing persons report. She watched as he carefully read it over, jotting some notes on a random piece of paper left on his desk. "She was last seen in a coffee shop?" he asked, looking up.

"According to her friend, she was supposed to meet a guy she met on an online dating site at the shop. It was early, seven o'clock. The last text the friend got was that the guy was late. That was at..." Reese's face scrunched up as he tried to think of the exact time. "Seven ten, I believe."

"And you canvassed the coffee shop?" Nolan dipped his hand into the file and pulled more papers out.

"Not us. The original detectives. This is their canvass report here," Lauren tapped one of the papers in his hand. "It was happy hour on a Friday. That particular coffee shop is right on Chippewa Street in the party district. It used to be a bar until the owners lost their liquor license last year for serving minors. It doesn't serve alcohol, but it hasn't changed much," she explained. "It was packed that night. They have a happy hour on Friday nights with coffee specials. No one on the staff remembered her specifically. Her friends said she didn't frequent that place, so it must have been the guy's suggestion."

"Her cell phone records?"

"Her last text and the last ping off the tower put her in the coffee shop. But it looked like she had her phone in her jacket pocket at the crime scene." Lauren reached over and pulled the cell phone records from the stack to show him.

"The medical examiner removed an object from her jacket pocket before moving the body. It was a cell phone," Nolan replied, "but the battery was missing."

"The killer made sure right away she couldn't be tracked by her phone. It shows pre-planning," Reese commented.

Nolan was flipping through the pages of phone records. "This unknown number that's highlighted. Is this our online boyfriend?"

Lauren nodded. "We think so, but it's a burner. Prepaid cell phone. It looks like he called and texted her for three days before they met. He was very persistent."

"And the online dating site? Did you look at this guy's profile?"

"Fake," Lauren said. "Pictures of a male model from Germany. It was created at an Internet café on Main Street, near the University of Buffalo's south campus. Whoever did this was very careful not to have anything fall back on him."

She wanted to tell Nolan that David Ryan Spencer was very careful. She wanted to tell him she had gotten a very smart little monster off on a murder charge and now he was running amuck. She wanted to say it was his ex-girlfriend's body they had found in the same spot over a year ago. But she held her tongue. Reese was right. The body hadn't even been identified yet. No use in sucking Jack Nolan into her paranoid obsession with David Spencer until she had to. It was bad enough poor Reese had to deal with it on a daily basis.

"Her car was found parked in the lot behind the coffee shop. Doesn't look like she ever got back in it once she parked," Reese added.

"This was in May of last year though, right? You think she's been there since May? Out in the open all summer like that and no one's found the body until now?"

Lauren shrugged. "It's hard to say. Even the medical examiner will probably have a hard time giving a rough estimate of how long she's been out there, given all the freezes and thaws we've had. Not to mention the hot summer months." *Not as hot as the summer before though,* Lauren thought. *That was record-breaking heat that David worked his black magic in.*

"No ex-boyfriends? No stalkers? No one lurking in her past?"

"An ex-boyfriend who goes to school in California whose whereabouts on the day of the crime are well documented. Kids these days post everything they do on social media. We can track what Brianna did all day long, every day, for months just by looking at her feeds. She gets to the coffee shop, sends a few texts, and everything just stops. It's like she was erased."

"You have everything she posted that day, right?" Nolan asked.

Reese picked up the studio portrait. "We could've put a hundred different selfies from the day she went missing on the posters, and some of the ones her mother had printed up do have them on the bottom, but she was showing cleavage or making a duck face or posing in a bathroom mirror." He handed the picture to Nolan, who looked it over.

"Millennials live their lives on the Internet." Nolan motioned to the picture on his desk. "My sixteen-year-old son posts ten pictures of himself on Instagram every day. He lives in Colorado with his mom, but I never have to wonder what he's doing."

"Thankfully, Brianna's mom found a notebook in her room with all her passwords written down. We've been monitoring her social media accounts." Lauren produced a typed-up cheat sheet they had taken down to their computer analysis techs at the Erie County computer crime lab. "Our lab guys should be able to juice it up and get in. We'd have been in big trouble with the phone if we didn't have her security code."

"What do you do with a victim or suspect's phone if they won't give you the code?" Nolan asked. "We don't get a lot of homicides out here."

Reese shrugged. "If the victim is dead? With certain brands of phones, nothing. Once it's locked, it's locked. If it has a six-digit passcode, even the FBI can't get in. Not for a long, long time, sometimes never. You have to reconstruct their movements through their friends' phones. All of those text messages? They're from the phone records of her best friend, Olivia Lange, and a few others. We can get the cell tower data, but in this case, it just puts her at the coffee shop."

Nolan sat back in his chair, looking at the records Reese had provided. "What do we know about the victim? Does she have any connections out here?"

"As far as we know right now, no. She lived in North Buffalo. Worked at an Italian restaurant on Hertel Avenue, which is also in North Buffalo. She was taking accounting classes at Erie Community College City Campus," Lauren replied. "She had only recently started using dating websites and the one she was on is actually one of the less skeevy ones. The man 'likes' the woman's picture, and if she 'likes' his, his profile will appear and it's up to her to make contact with him."

"I'm so glad I meet my women the old-fashioned way. In bars," Reese said.

"You and me both, brother," Nolan assured him. He had the dating site profile in his hand now. "I wouldn't even know how to go about doing all this." His eyes flickered over the fake profile's stats and measurements. "It's like a casting call."

"It's the perfect way for a killer to anonymously attract a victim." Lauren wanted to point out to Reese that he met women in bars, restaurants, bowling alleys, insurance agency waiting rooms—pretty much wherever women were—but it was not the time for witty banter between them.

"We called the DA's office on the way here. They're sending out their victim's advocate to speak to the mom. Carl Church's people are making arrangements with your county attorney and coroner to have the body sent to the morgue at the Erie County Medical Center. The press is going to be all over this."

"Thanks for that." Nolan got up, gathering the file back together. "Mind if I make copies of these?"

"Go ahead," Lauren told him. She watched as he crossed over to a fancy new copier in the corner. Their copier had run out of black toner yesterday morning, so they were printing everything in blue until the copy guy could get there and install a new one. They'd run to an office store and buy a new cartridge themselves, but the model was so old stores didn't carry that brand anymore.

"Are you going to talk to the mom?" Nolan called over his shoulder as he fed in the pages.

"Yes," Lauren told him, "but probably tomorrow. It's going to be hard on her because she won't be able to bury the body until we get it back from the forensic anthropologists our medical examiner's office uses down in Pennsylvania." Lauren pictured Mrs. McIntyre sitting on the brown microfiber couch in her North Buffalo living room, eyes vacant, nose running, hearing but not hearing what the victim's advocate was telling her. She could feel her stomach knot up again at the thought of having to endure that news. The mom had clung to the hope that as long as Brianna was missing, there was a chance she'd be found alive somewhere. Now there would only be grief and questions. Every mother's worst nightmare.

"Would you mind sending me an email copy of your notes from that interview?" Nolan asked.

"Not a problem. I'll send you the entire digital file." Lauren liked the calm and easy demeanor Nolan had. As opposed to Reese, who'd found a scrap piece of paper and was ripping it into tiny shreds, making a little white pile on the desk. Her hand shot out and clamped over his. Giving her his best apologetic look, he brushed the mess into his hand and quickly dumped it in the trash can next to him before Nolan could see. Ripping things up was one of Reese's nervous ticks when he got excited.

"I'll email you copies of everything from our end if you leave me your cards." Nolan crossed back over to them, handing back the paperwork. Reese grabbed it and put it back inside the file folder as Lauren fished her business card out.

"Our extension is the same." Lauren wrote Reese's name and cell number on the back of her card. "You shouldn't have any trouble reaching us."

Nolan took the card. "Oh, and hey," he said, suddenly sounding a little sheepish, "sorry about the whole 'you look familiar' thing."

Standing up, Lauren gave him a tight smile. "Not a problem. Don't worry about it."

They all shook hands again and Lauren noted Nolan's was still warm.

Funny, she thought as she and Reese made their way out of the building, *I feel cold as ice.*

3

Lauren's head was filled with more questions than answers when she pulled up to her house that night.

Located in one of the only gated communities in the city of Buffalo, Lauren had been awarded the house free and clear after her divorce from her second husband, Mark Hathaway.

She never once felt guilty for taking it; Mark was from a family of old money and a successful real estate attorney. He could buy ten more houses just like it if he wanted to.

Lauren and Mark had a brief and disastrous affair during her handling of the David Spencer case. It fell apart just slightly faster than their marriage had. Still, her daughters looked to Mark as a father figure, and she had never discouraged that. Their own father had abandoned her when she was pregnant with their second daughter, Erin, and died not long after that in an accident. Lauren realized after her and Mark's affair had ended that he would always be a part of her life;

she would just never get the happily-ever-after she had once wanted so badly for them.

She parked her new Ford Escape in the driveway. It still had that new car smell she loved clinging to the interior. Her last Ford had ended up mangled in a wreck with a stolen cab after the now-famous wild car chase in December. Dents you can hammer out; bullet holes not so much. So it got totaled and she got a new SUV.

Checking out her flower beds as she came up her front walk, Lauren noticed no tulips, no daffodils, and only a few sad-looking purple crocuses. Spring was definitely on hold.

Looking down the street as she separated her house key from the twenty other keys on her ring, Lauren noticed the lights were on at her friend Dayla's place. She was in no mood to talk to her, or anyone else for that matter. She'd text her the next day when she got a few minutes. There was no such thing as a short conversation with Dayla Oliver.

Lauren unlocked her door and stepped into her foyer, breathing deeply. She'd made banana nut bread the night before and the aroma still hung in the air. Now that her daughters were both away at school, she rarely baked, but last night she'd seen the overripe bananas on her kitchen counter, got out her mom's cookbook, and baked herself some bread. That would be her dinner.

Dumping her tote bag on the chair in the foyer like she'd always told her daughters not to do, she wandered into the living room. Her iPad was set up on the coffee table. She had fallen asleep the night before watching Netflix and hadn't bothered to put it away when she finally dragged herself upstairs to bed.

Outside her front window she saw two neighborhood boys run by holding hockey sticks. One of them almost slipped on a patch of ice, causing the other thirteen-year-old to point and howl with laughter before they ran on. She loved the night noises of her city neighbor-hood—the rumble of trucks, the sounds of her neighbors taking their dogs for walks, the occasional siren. It was so different from the quiet in the woods that seemed to engulf you. The city had a pulse you could hear beating, night and day.

She plunked herself down on a floral couch that was beginning to look dated and hit the touch screen so she could check out the news stations.

The recovery of the body was the lead story on several of the local news outlets. None of them speculated it was Brianna McIntyre. Yet. Right now, all the press had was that possible human remains were discovered. By tomorrow morning someone would surely leak more information to the press, especially since Brianna's wallet was found with the body. There had been too many people at the recovery site for that detail not to come out.

The sense of urgency she had tried to keep tamped down at the scene came surging back up.

David Spencer was smart, calculating, and manipulative. He'd morphed into something very dangerous since she first met him the summer before last, in the holding center awaiting his arraignment on charges for the murder of Katherine Vine. Gone was any boy-next-door innocence, even if it was faked. It'd been replaced with a cunning, hand-some man capable of terrible things.

Lauren needed to get him off the streets. She'd been waging a one-person war against him, and she was losing. She had to take this further before anyone else got hurt. *Truth be told, I shouldn't have waited for another body to show up,* she thought. *This is on me.*

She snapped her iPad closed.

Now I have to bring in reinforcements.

21

4

"If what you suspect is true, we need to speak to the other agencies involved and talk about forming a task force."

One day after Brianna McIntyre's body had been found, Lauren asked for a private meeting with Buffalo Police Commissioner Barbara Bennett. Unlike other big city departments, Buffalo was more like a small town, or even a big room. Everyone was connected to each other in some way. People joked there were only two degrees of separation, but even that was a stretch. Although there was a definite chain of command, officers and detectives were known to skip the middle man and go right to the top. Bennett wasn't used to that kind of open-door policy her first few months on the job, but she quickly realized that somehow it worked for the Buffalo Police department and kept her door open.

"It is true. All I want are the resources to prove it."

Bennett's smile reached her chocolate brown eyes. "I like you, Lauren. You remind me a lot of myself when I was on the streets, before I took a supervisor's position. No one could tell me anything once I got something stuck in my head."

Lauren's morning meeting with Brianna's mother had been gut-wrenching. The poor woman sat on her couch sobbing the entire time she and Reese had been at her house while her sister comforted her. Mrs. McIntyre kept asking over and over again, "But you're not sure? You don't know for sure that it's Brianna. It *could* be someone else."

Unfortunately, no matter how many times they repeated that while they could not say with one hundred percent certainty the body was Brianna's, the evidence found at the scene definitely supported that conclusion, Mrs. McIntyre clung to the hope that it was all a huge mistake. Lauren thought of how she would react if one of her own daughters had gone missing and knew she'd do the exact same thing. A mother never gives up hope on her baby.

Which only fueled Lauren's resolve to put David Spencer away for the rest of his murderous, psychotic life.

Commissioner Bennett's office was stacked high with boxes in anticipation of headquarters' move. The walls of Buffalo's first black female police commissioner were full of pictures of her during various stages of her career: in uniform while on patrol, plainclothes as a detective, an older man with graying hair pinning on her lieutenant's badge, getting an award for bravery from her original department in Georgia. On and on, until you got to the picture of her in Buffalo, surrounded by what appeared to be her entire family, getting sworn in as police commissioner. Sprinkled in between the work pictures were crayon drawings of flowers, grammar school pictures of smiling kids with missing front teeth, and a formal portrait of Bennett and her wife on their wedding day with their mothers or grandmothers and maybe some brothers or cousins, all posed under a great tree, smiling into the photographer's lens, a perfect picture of family love.

"We can't wait. He's escalating—"

The commissioner held up her hand, silencing her. "You've pled your case. And I believe you." Lauren took a deep breath and the commissioner continued, "You need to slow it down. I know you're still on an adrenaline rush from Vince Schultz's crazy chase. I know seeing Ricky Schultz murdered like that hit home, especially after what happened to Joe Wheeler, but we've got to get the other agencies on board or you're just going to be spinning your wheels. If you're going to pursue David Spencer, we need all the information in one place, with all the agencies involved working together."

Vince Schultz had been the cop who had collapsed her lung in an effort to conceal a cold case homicide committed by his younger brother. Vince was still on the job when he stabbed Lauren and stole her Murder Book, which had been the hand-written and typed log of all the Cold Case homicide files from the last fifty years. It had never been recovered. Vince and the youngest brother, Sam, were arrested, but their older brother, Ricky, was found murdered in his home before the district attorney could lay charges on him.

The mess that ensued after her stabbing and Ricky's homicide had made national headlines. Thankfully, the news media had a short attention span.

Joe Wheeler was Lauren's ex-fiancé who was beaten to death with a tire iron in his driveway during the investigation into her stabbing. To top it all off, he was also the Garden Valley detective who had arrested David Spencer for murdering a wealthy local socialite.

"Garden Valley PD thinks Ricky or Vince Schultz killed Joe Wheeler. Chief Ritz has all but closed that case." Bennett paused to let that sink in, then added in her slightly southern accented voice, "Although Lincoln Lewis is convinced you had something to do with it." Lincoln Lewis had been the Schultz brothers' defense attorney. He still represented the two living siblings. Lewis was also convinced Lauren had a hand in Ricky's death somehow, and he had been very vocal about it to the news media, the district attorney's office, her department, and whoever else would listen to him.

Sinking back in her mahogany chair, the commissioner pushed away from her desk a little so she could cross her legs, and then she crossed her arms over her chest. "I know the Garden Valley Police Department were willing to work with us when you and Reese were their main suspects. We combed both Vince and Ricky's residences and found not one iota of evidence that suggests either of them had anything to do with Joe Wheeler's death. It'll take a little convincing, but I'm sure Carl Church and I can at least bring Garden Valley to the table to hear us out. And they'd want to be in on the investigation. Nothing hurts worse than not being asked to the dance."

"Five murders—three women, two cops. What could be more convincing than that?" Lauren demanded, the red rushing to her cheeks.

"This is complicated," Bennett said. Picking up a copy of the timeline Lauren had created to illustrate her cause, the commissioner ticked off the reasons on her fingers one by one. "In the first case, that of Katherine Vine, the suspect, David Spencer, has been acquitted, thanks to you. And don't think Carl Church has forgotten that. In the second case, Amber Anderson, the cause of death is unknown because of decomposition. However, you believe she is actually the first victim because she went missing months before Vine's murder." She held up a third finger, "Your ex-boyfriend, Joe Wheeler, was bludgeoned to death with a tire iron." She stuck her thumb out like she was hitch hiking. "And Ricky Schultz, the cop you couldn't arrest, was stabbed in the exact spot on his body where you were stabbed. The only connection in all of those cases is you. Did I miss anything?"

"My connection to all of them is David Spencer."

She let the timeline fall onto the neat report Lauren had created. "And this girl that was recovered yesterday? Any link to David Spencer that you know of?"

Lauren realized she was clutching a ball point pen in her fist, her knuckles white. "She might as well have been dumped on top of Amber Anderson's grave. If that's not a message, I don't know what is."

Bennett slapped her palms on the dark polished wood of the desk, piled high with smaller boxes on top of boxes. "I'll ask for one investigator from each agency for sixty days, with the option to terminate or extend after a review of the process at two months."

Lauren exhaled audibly. "Thank you."

Bennett waved that comment off. "Don't thank me yet. Garden Valley, the State Police, and the Chautauqua County Sheriff's Department all have to be on board. Don't forget about Carl Church. He's going to take some persuading," she reminded her. "And there's the matter of the departmental charges lodged against you."

She and Reese had run their own covert operation with a retired police lieutenant in an effort to grab a sample of Sam Schultz's DNA to match him to the old shooting. It had led to a high-speed car chase, shots fired, and an epic car crash. Since Sam Schultz now sat in jail for the murder of an eighteen-year-old kid, Lauren had not one regret about any of it.

"Reese and I are both going to plead guilty and take the thirty days unpaid suspension."

Bennett nodded, seemingly satisfied with that answer. "Your union president told me yesterday that hearings are backed up until June at this point. If you're still on the task force at that time, you'll have to bow out."

"Understood."

Bennett twisted the gold wedding ring on her left hand. "I'm going out on a huge limb here. There are a lot of folks, including Church, who are saying you are the reason David Spencer is walking around in the first place."

"I know." Lauren owned that. "And they're right. I set that little monster free and I have to be the one to pen him back up."

Bennett cocked an eyebrow. "Did you tell Detective Reese about this meeting?"

"He's spent enough time protecting me. It's time I protected him."

Glancing down at a group of papers paper clipped together off to her right, Bennett picked them up, examined them, then put them into a box on her desk marked: TIME SHEETS. "He's going to want to be on the task force."

Lauren knew Reese would want to be on the task force. After all he'd done for her, he deserved it. But this was her fight. She'd already pulled him into her obsession too much. And she needed to know that someone was still working their cold cases. She couldn't trust them to just anyone. That's how most of them had ended up cold in the first place. "You said it yourself, one investigator per agency."

The commissioner shook her head slightly. "I hope you know what you're getting yourself into."

I never do. Lauren's thoughts were bitter and angry as she dropped the plastic pen into a ceramic cup on Bennett's desk, feeling the circulation returning to her fingers. *That's my problem. But David Spencer isn't going to stop. Not now. Not when he has my full attention.*

5

The day after her meeting with Commissioner Bennett, Lauren was back in the Cold Case office, surrounded by the chaos of the movers trying to box her fragile case files to move them to the new headquarters building. Standing in the doorway, watching the movers in their dust-covered overalls fumble with dollies, swearing at each other, and manhandling her precious files, her OCD hit catastrophic levels. Her blood pressure rose with every dropped box, every errant piece of paper that floated to the ground; she was sure she'd stroke out if she stayed in the office much longer.

"Relax," Reese admonished from his desk by the far wall, "at least they aren't touching the files in here for two more days."

She turned away from the disaster, hugging her arms to her chest. "I can't watch this anymore."

"Sit down, drink your coffee, and concentrate on the case we're working. Remember that case? Brianna McIntyre? Ring a bell?"

She made her way to her desk and dropped into her cheap office chair. She'd had a better one that she'd bought for herself, but when she came back from her forced medical leave it had disappeared and she'd had to scrounge a new one. Cops were notorious office product thieves. Her chair would turn up at the new building—the city would never buy new furniture when they had loads of craptastic stuff to reuse—and she'd have to steal it back.

"Did you talk to the friend?" Lauren asked. Her chair squeaked ominously beneath her as she tried to swivel.

"Yes." Reese quickly scanned a list in front of him. Lauren had gotten him into making lists to keep him on track. He was a brilliant detective, the best Lauren had ever worked with, but his mind tended to wander in five different directions at any given moment. "Olivia Lange is coming in at one o'clock for an interview. Brianna sent the last text message from her phone to her."

"You have the copies of the cell phone records?" She knew he did. In his pyramid of files piled on his desk. Somewhere.

He held up a stack of papers. "Way ahead of you."

Smiling at her partner, she nodded. "Good."

The landline buzzed at her elbow. Lauren checked the caller ID before picking up. It was a county number, no way to know for sure whose specific line it belonged to. Once again, the feeling of dread knotted her stomach. "Cold Case, Detective Riley. How can I help you?"

There was a slight pause on the other end, as if the person was preparing what they wanted to say before they blurted it out. "Detective Riley? This is Maureen from over at the DA's office. Mr. Church would like to know if you have a free minute to come over and talk to him."

Maureen was Erie County District Attorney Carl Church's new secretary. She'd obviously heard around the office about his and Lauren's history. Lauren took a deep breath, like her physical therapist taught her, and answered, "Sure, Maureen. When can he squeeze me in? I have an appointment at one."

"Right now, if you could." *Maureen has got to get tougher or she'll get eaten alive over there,* Lauren thought, hearing the hesitation in her voice. Church was known for hiring young local graduates, giving them a chance. Sometimes it worked out fine; other times not so much. Poor Maureen was definitely on the fence. You couldn't be afraid to speak to a detective when the entire hostile world was out there, demanding answers for every decision Church made. His last secretary, Camilla, had become a polite pit bull after a year on the job. Last Lauren heard, she had taken a job with the Buffalo Bills organization. Lauren had to give it to Church; if he saw potential in you, he gave you opportunity. He had seen it in Lauren when she first made detective, and they had worked amazingly well together until she took the David Spencer case. She was still dealing with the fallout from it.

"I'll walk right over," she told Maureen, and hung up before she could stutter a goodbye.

"Who was that?" Reese asked, paging through the phone records with a highlighter.

"Church wants to see me."

He stopped highlighting and looked up. "Why?"

"I don't know." At least she didn't have to outright lie to Reese, although she suspected the truth.

"You want me to come?" Reese gave the Jim Kelly bobblehead doll he swiped from their captain's desk a flick, sending the little head into spasms. Captain Maniechwicz's office had been packed up two days ago, but not before Reese took his beloved doll. He kept putting Jim in various places around the office, taking his picture and sending it to the captain. Whether the captain thought this was funny or not was unknown. The squad didn't call him the Invisible Man for nothing.

She shook her head as she removed her Glock from the left side drawer in her metal desk. "I'm good. He probably wants an update on Brianna."

His eyebrows knit together like they did when he thought something was suspect. "Then why just you?"

The gun made a satisfying click as she snapped it into the holster clipped to her belt on her right hip. "Don't get paranoid. Everything is just getting back to normal."

"That's why I'm paranoid," he said, staring at her hard. He was no dummy. He knew her tells and knew when she wasn't letting him in on everything. She had to make a quick exit or she'd spill the whole task force idea to him.

"Hold down the fort. I'll be back before Olivia gets here." Lauren snagged her coat off the rack near the door. It was still warm out for early March, but the weather in Buffalo changed by the hour.

"And Riley," Reese called as she was about to walk out the door, "don't try to fix anything on your own, okay? We're partners."

She paused, slipping an arm into the warm black wool. She almost didn't say anything, then nodded. "Okay," she told him, closing the door behind her.

Silently, she cursed him as she walked down the stairs for knowing her so damn well.

6

"I've been the district attorney for a long time." Carl Church steepled his fingers under his chin as he gazed at Lauren from across his huge desk. "And this is one of the most unusual requests I've ever had to consider."

Lauren tried to keep her face neutral as she returned his gaze. Church never changed much, always had on the charcoal-colored suit with the power tie. He had reverted to his shaved, bald head after letting it grow out a little over the winter. With his smooth, dark skin, demeanor of a former marine, and serious attitude, there were never any surprises with Church.

At least, there hadn't been until she'd broken his trust and stood on the other side of the courtroom against him. A year and a half ago Church had prosecuted David Spencer and she had worked for Spencer's defense team. Hell, she and his lawyer, Frank Violanti, *were* his defense team. They had gotten Spencer off, a fact Lauren regretted every day. Her relationship with Church had been non-existent during the year between the acquittal and her stabbing in police headquarters.

Thrown back together four months ago by the bizarre circumstances of the three Schultz brothers, Lauren and Church had mended fences as she lay in the hospital. Together they had managed to put two of the guilty brothers in jail, including Sam, the brother who had been campaigning against Church for DA. Would their tentative truce be enough to convince Church to back her now?

Maybe if she apologized and groveled. *No,* she thought, *he'd see that as a sign of weakness. And he despises weakness. Better to just lay it all out.*

"I know now that I was wrong to take the David Spencer case."

The skin around his deep, brown eyes crinkled in amusement. "That's almost an apology. I'm touched."

Taking a deep breath, she plunged forward. "I know I was wrong. I should have trusted your decision in prosecuting the Katherine Vine case last year. I let my former relationship with Joe Wheeler cloud my judgment. And I let a very dangerous young man sweet talk me into believing him over the evidence."

The heavy wooden wing chair she was sitting in hurt her back. She shifted around under Church's gaze, the large American flag he kept at attention on a small wooden pole framing him in the background. *He looks like a frigging campaign poster,* she thought as she tried to gauge his reaction. *And justice for all.*

"I read the task force proposal you gave to Commissioner Bennett. I read your timeline. I was primarily interested in the fact that David Spencer brought flowers to you at the hospital, and in the conversation you had with him when you went to his residence. Then the line you threw at Spencer shows up weeks later at Ricky Schultz's homicide scene. You're sure the exchange you had with David Spencer in his driveway were the exact words written on Ricky Schultz's computer screen?"

"I am." The words scrolling across the screen as Ricky sat in front of it with a knife sticking from his side was burned into her retinas. It was a direct message to her: YOU CAN FIND OUT JUST ABOUT ANYTHING ON ANYONE ON THE INTERNET. It was a comment she'd tossed at David Spencer when he'd questioned how she had found out where he lived. She suppressed a shudder as she remembered the cocky smile he gave her when he told her he liked that line, he was going to write it down.

He might as well have written it in Ricky's blood.

Shaking the image from her head, she regained her focus. Church was speaking. "And his attorney, Frank Violanti, can confirm this conversation took place?"

She nodded. "Violanti called me the same day. He told me I had upset David Spencer."

A wry smile spread across Church's face. "I'm sure he'd categorize it differently. He'll say you were harassing his client."

"I was," she admitted bluntly, "and I think it set in motion the deaths of Joe Wheeler and Ricky Schultz."

"That's a very strong opinion of your pull over David Spencer."

It was hot in Church's office. She yanked at the scarf around her neck, feeling the sweat beading up on her temples. Ever since she'd been stabbed and had her lung collapsed, it seemed like her internal temperature gauge was off. She found herself alternately freezing and frying at any given time. *Unless I'm going through the change, but forty is a little young.* She stuffed her gloves in her coat pocket. "Look at me, Carl." She motioned to her stick thin body, her drawn face. "I'm a wreck. Whatever it is that David Spencer has for me, I doubt it's lust."

"You're the one who used to be the sex offense detective. Is it ever about lust?"

No, she thought, *it's about power. And control. And dominance.* She didn't need to say that to Church; he was just reminding her of the answer. "Whatever is driving him, we have to rein him in. Now. Brianna McIntyre went missing in May. That was six months before I got stabbed. He's a predator. Plain and simple."

Church tapped the keyboard on his laptop perched to his left side. "You've made a pretty compelling case for a task force. Multiple victims over multiple jurisdictions. Acceleration. Direct connections to at least three of the victims." He studied whatever it was on his screen for another moment, then returned to Lauren. "I should say yes to the task force and no to you being a part of it. That would be the right thing to do. The prudent thing. Because you're right"—his eyes traveled her, up and down—"you're not exactly in top physical condition. I doubt you should even be back to work. But I know you're stubborn and you pushed to get cleared."

"I am stubborn," she admitted. "There was a time when you would have said that was what made me a good detective."

"You are a good detective, Riley. But you know what else you are?"

He waited for her to answer this time.

"No," she finally replied.

"Bait."

The complete honesty in his voice was like a slap in the face. She sucked a ragged breath in as he continued, hands now clasped in front of him, punched out toward her. His smile was wide, like he had just heard the Buffalo Bills were going to the Super Bowl again.

"Good luck on the task force. I hope you nail that little fucker. Before he gets to you, of course."

7

Lauren's heart pounded in her chest as she crossed the street that separated the Erie County Court building from current police headquarters. Ankle deep in slush from the mild weather, she wrestled with what she was going to tell Reese. *He's going to tell me this is not how partners work,* she thought as she had to scale the small snowbank at the curb to get to the mostly shoveled and slightly salted sidewalk. *He's going to accuse me of going behind his back, of being obsessed, of taking things too far. That Carl Church is using me and doesn't care what happens to me.*

He'll be right.

The last thing Lauren wanted was to lose Reese as a partner. When she got stabbed, he never left her side at the hospital, and he moved into her house with his dog to watch over her. Reese had become more family than co-worker. *And this is how I repay that? By going behind his back. By purposely leaving him out. By shutting out the only man in my life who has ever been nothing but good to me.*

She swallowed back the bitterness, swiping her ID card against the door reader. With a loud click it popped open and she made her way back up to the third-floor offices of the Homicide squad. Her physical therapist told her to take the stairs, but since her injury she got winded easily and was just now getting her strength back due to early morning walks, so she stuck to taking the world's slowest elevator. The building only had four floors, but you would think the car had to descend and ascend great distances, with maximum energy exerted, from the way it slowly rumbled to a stop at each and every floor. In a way, Lauren thought she might miss the shaky old elevator, along with the rest of the building. It was true; as much as she had complained about it over the years, she was definitely going to miss the building when they moved. It had always made her feel like Buffalo cops had to do more with less, that they didn't need a fancy building or modern equipment to clear crimes.

They were old school; they hit the streets and worked the leads the way detectives had, well, since Buffalo first had detectives. She'd even started to compile a new Murder Book to replace the one that was stolen from her office and never recovered. She imagined one of the Schultz brothers must have tossed the green three-ring binder in a dumpster somewhere. The Homicide squad had searched for it at all three of their residences but found no trace of the book. Fifty years' worth of murder details lost forever. At least now she was entering the information into a database instead of just relying on old-fashioned paper. And she'd been backing it up constantly. She was working backward from last year's cases, and she had no idea how long it would take her once she reached the point where records existed only in their dusty file cabinets.

She swiped into the Homicide wing and smelled the coffee someone had scorched and left on the burner. She dipped into the kitchen area, grabbed the carafe off the machine, and hit the off button. She was delaying the inevitable, she knew, as she rinsed out the pot. From down the hall she heard Craig Garcia yell, "Hey, Vatasha! Is that you? Did you get the plate number?"

She didn't answer. Garcia wasn't her favorite person and she wasn't his. She put the pot upside down on the drying rack and headed over to the Cold Case office. Garcia stuck his head out of his office door, saw Lauren, and retreated without a word. Their mutual dislike for each other was well known around the office. At least now they avoided each other like grown-ups instead of engaging in verbal combat every time they saw each other.

Reese and Olivia Lange were already in the tiny interview room off in the far corner of the Cold Case office. It wasn't wired for video, so it couldn't be used for suspect interviews, but for witnesses like Olivia, it worked just fine. It had a window that overlooked the courtyard, if you wanted to call the roof of the first floor a courtyard, and a view of the Narcotics office on the fourth floor, when they had their shades up. It was the sunniest spot in the office, and since it had its own radiator, the warmest.

It was only big enough to fit a desk that backed to the window and two narrow chairs. Lauren slipped in mid-question. Ignoring the faux pas on her part, Reese smiled up at Lauren. "How did everything go with Church?"

"You have to grow your hair back." Lauren sank against the wall, leaning on her left hip, grateful to be out of Church's torture device. "You can't have the same haircut as the DA and expect me to be nice to you."

He ran a hand along his smooth scalp, marred only by the scar from the staples he received a few months ago. "I think I look good," he assured her.

"How about I shave my head too?"

"You could." He considered. "But you'd look like a plucked chicken. Or a featherless Big Bird. You know, because you're tall and skinny and yellow? Big Bird?"

She laughed in spite of herself. "Fine then, keep it. Have fun shaving your dome every day."

"You just can't handle all the—"

"Are you two married?" the girl Reese had been talking to interrupted.

"I'm sorry," Reese apologized, realizing they had both forgotten for a second they had company. "People ask us that all the time, Olivia," Reese said. And they did. Their relationship was so familiar and they spent so much time together, they often got asked if they were a couple. "But no. This is my work partner, Lauren Riley."

Lauren smiled at the blond-highlighted girl and sat in the chair next to her, offering a hand to shake. "Detective Riley. Nice to meet you, Olivia."

"You're the one who forked that guy in the face." Olivia's eyes widened in recognition. She still held onto Lauren's hand as she told Lauren, "Me and my friends must have watched that video a thousand times. When the guy filming says, 'Damn!'" She looked over at Reese to see if he thought it was as funny as she did. "We would die laughing. You forked him so hard." Then she quoted the kid who filmed the video, "'Damn!'"

"Not my finest moment." Lauren smiled, releasing herself from Olivia's grip. A thick girl in her early twenties, Olivia had two black lines tracing her upper eyelids that swept out to form a sort of wing on each side. She was wearing a yellow and brown uniform with her name printed on a plastic badge over her heart.

"No way," she disagreed, "you were so badass. I can't believe you're the detective on Bree's case." Lauren noticed Olivia had her cell phone in its rhinestone-studded case clutched in her other hand, glossy green nails curling over the screen. "Everybody loves that video."

Lauren had come to realize through her daughters that YouTube stars were every bit as famous to millennials as anyone in the movies or on television. In fact, most of the people who recognized her were the kids under thirty who had watched, shared, and reposted that stupid video clip over three hundred thousand times. Poor Brianna McIntyre had already been murdered when they had thrown down with Vince Schultz. She wondered if any of the prisoners Vince was now living with at the state prison recognized him from that viral video.

"Getting back to Bree's case," Reese redirected Olivia, "why don't you tell us about what was going on with her? Did she use dating sites a lot?"

Olivia's round face pinched up as she shook her head. "No. She was with Chuckie for like, three years, before he went to California. She was planning on moving out there when her semester was over, but he dumped her. She took it hard, gained a bunch of weight. I kept telling her to stay off the hook-up sites, you know? I told her to get on one of the real ones that actually matches you up with people using an algorithm or whatever. That's how I met my boyfriend."

"On the same site she was using?"

She looked down at the jewel-encrusted phone in her hand. "I told her it was better. Because the girl makes contact with the guy and he doesn't get any of your information unless you give it to him. It seemed really safe." Now she turned her eyes upward to stop the tears that had welled up from spilling over. "I can't believe this. I can't."

Reese pushed a box of tissues across the desk to her. Pulling one out, she dabbed at her eyes, careful not to ruin her elaborate make up job. "Did she tell you anything about the guy she was supposed to meet?"

"She sent me one of his profile pictures. She said he was really nice. They texted back and forth for like, three days, and then he called her. They talked every day for a week. He wasn't gross, asking for nudes or anything like that. She said he sounded like someone who might actually want to date and not just hook up."

As Olivia dabbed at her eyes some more, Lauren marveled at the thought that not sending or asking for nude pictures made you quality dating material in their world.

"Is this the picture she sent you?" Reese held up a copy of a picture taken from the cell phone dump the original detectives had done on Olivia's phone in an effort to locate Brianna. They had taken her phone for two days and noted that she had called the office twelve times to see when she could come pick it up. Then had her mother call twice.

"That's it. Look at him, I mean, come on." The picture showed a handsome man in his early twenties with dark hair, neatly parted to the side, and wire rim glasses that framed two laughing blue eyes. He was standing in front of a body of water, maybe the ocean, a breeze rippling his hair a little. He looked smart and cute and gentle. Someone who would never hurt you. "At least you know who to arrest."

Reese tapped the picture with his finger. "This man lives in Germany and used to be a model. This picture was downloaded from the Internet. He's not the person who talked to Bree," Reese informed her, trying to be clear.

"Are you sure?" Desperation crept into her voice. "She didn't say he had an accent, but maybe it's him."

Reese shut down that line of thinking. "The original detectives spoke with this guy. Those pictures are over ten years old. He absolutely did not leave Germany at the time of her disappearance. He's married with two small kids, working at a bank now. He has no idea who even owns the rights to the photo now, but you know as well as I do, once something is out there, it's out there forever."

"So you don't know who did it." Olivia's voice got small and strained.

"Whoever she was meeting set up a fake profile." Lauren said. "Everything was fake."

"What about his phone number? Can't you find him from that?"

"It was a prepaid cell phone," Reese jumped in. "Probably dumped that same night."

"No," Olivia said with certainty, her mascara puddled under her eyes despite her best efforts. "The guy who made the profile never showed up. He stiffed her. See"—she scrolled through her phone, then held the screen to Lauren's face—"that's the last text I got from her."

HE WAS SUPPOSED TO BE HERE A HALF HOUR AGO. I THINK I JUST GOT GHOSTED.

Underneath that was a selfie of her sitting in a coffee shop next to a window, making a frowny face into the phone.

"He could have waited outside, to see if she'd show," Lauren reasoned, "then followed her to her car."

"Or it could have been some random dude who saw her and grabbed her on Chippewa Street. What you're saying is, you don't know." The tears ran freely now, her careful make up destroyed as she buried her face in a fresh tissue pulled from the box.

Neither Reese nor Lauren said it, but they exchanged glances over the weeping girl that sadly confirmed: no, we don't know, not for sure.

Lauren couldn't let Olivia know who she believed did it, either. Any leak of David Spencer's name at that point would sink the task force before it started. She couldn't even ask if Brianna or Olivia knew David Spencer without letting the cat out of the bag. And it was getting to be a big frigging bag.

"We are checking into every possible lead and that starts with you." Lauren's voice took on the gentle, soothing tone she used to use when one of her daughters was upset and crying. Olivia was so young to be going through something so terrifying. She wanted to drape her arm around the distraught girl but fought back the urge. Instead she tried to get her to focus. "As far as we can tell, you are the last person she had contact with before she disappeared. Can you tell us anything she told you about this man, anything at all, that might help us?"

A mascara-blackened tear dripped off her chin and splashed on her chest, making a dark splotch on her uniform. She took a deep, sniffling breath and said, "The only thing I remember is her texting me saying he didn't have any kids and that he worked in real estate."

Reese pounced on that. "Did she say what kind of real estate? Did he work for a company? Was he an agent?"

Now Olivia was the one who laughed through her tears. "On those dating sites 'working in real estate' can mean the guy's a roofer. Everyone tries to make themselves sound so extra. You have to expect nobody's a hundred percent for real."

Still, Reese jotted that down. On the fake profile page, the person had listed himself as self-employed. Sometimes little things turned out to be big things. "They talked on the phone. What did she tell you about their conversations?" Lauren asked.

"Just that he really seemed interested in her. He asked her a ton of questions. He wanted to take her to one of those escape rooms. You know? The ones where you have to solve the clues in an hour to open the door? She said maybe on the second date."

Escape rooms had popped up all over Buffalo and the suburbs in the last two years. Her daughters had tried to get her to go to one the last time they both visited in February. She had been tempted to try it but knew if she couldn't get out in an hour, she'd never hear the end of it from her girls. Or from Reese.

The interview lasted another hour before Reese and Lauren walked Olivia Lange out of the building. They hadn't learned much more than what the original detectives had learned. Their next stop was going to be the coffee shop, but Reese had some questions for Lauren when they got back up to the office.

"What was the deal with Church calling you over there?"

Lauren made her way across the cluttered office to her computer. Shuffling the mouse around on the spongy pad, she stared intently at the city logo screen saver. "You know," she answered vaguely as her homepage popped up. "Stuff."

"Stop stalling, Riley." His voice rose a notch. "I know when you're holding out on me. Spill it. Now."

The room seemed claustrophobic in that moment. Lauren took in a deep breath and let her hands fall away from the keyboard. "There's going to be a task force assembled to look at the connections between the four unsolved murders and David Spencer."

Propping himself against his desk, he asked, "That's a good thing, right? What you wanted?"

"It is." She studied the pale, almost transparent skin covering her left hand, the blue veins that ran along the ropy tendons. One tiny, insidious age spot had taken up residence just south of her thumb. She put her other hand over it. "But it's small. Only one officer each from Buffalo, the State Police, Garden Valley, and the Chautauqua County

Sheriff's Office. I think they'll throw in someone from the State Attorney General's office to oversee it."

"One officer each," he repeated, just to make sure she knew he understood exactly what she was telling him.

"That's what I was told."

"And that one officer from Buffalo ain't me."

She shook her head without tearing her gaze from her hands. "No."

It was his silence she couldn't stand, that brought her eyes up to his face. He was waiting for her to say something else, a classic interrogation technique. People felt compelled to say something to fill the void. The best she could do was: "I'm sorry."

He spun around, grabbing his coffee mug off his desk, and headed for the door. "Never apologize for something you're not really sorry for," was all he said as he walked out of the office.

8

Reese had a lot more reason to be mad at Lauren than he knew. She had been keeping secrets from him.

Since the body of Ricky Schultz had been found stabbed and posed in front of his computer, Lauren had taken it upon herself to research every aspect of David Spencer's life using her expensive private investigator databases. That included unofficial surveillance of him, his girlfriend, their house, and the properties she owned and maintained. Lauren was more than borderline obsessed, and she knew it. Now that they'd found the body of Brianna McIntyre, she was more convinced than ever that David Spencer was the most dangerous person she'd ever dealt with. And the guilt she felt at helping him get acquitted in Katherine Vine's murder ate away at her daily.

She had already sat outside his house out in Clarence a few times, trying to learn his routine. She'd watched Melissa, his sequined older girlfriend, sparkle her way down the driveway and hop in her BMW heading off to property auctions. Lauren had followed David to a house they were renovating on the East Side of Buffalo, watching as he joined the small knot of men in the driveway, who kept motioning to the tarp on the roof. She'd watched long enough to get the plates on the work trucks and white vans parked there, then drove off. Surveillance was tricky, and if you got sloppy, you could blow the whole operation.

After Reese had left the office, Lauren closed up shop and headed home for the day, but only to change her clothes and pack her personal surveillance equipment. During another midnight records search in her home office, a new property had come onto her radar. It wasn't officially owned by Melissa St. John or her LLC, but it was listed as owned by her brother, Hank.

With all the adrenaline of the day's events pumping through her veins, she decided to check it out rather than sit back and stew about whether Reese would show up for work the next day. Or put a transfer in. Or just dump her as a partner while she was on special assignment and hook up with someone else in the Homicide squad. All of those options seemed to be on the table for him at the moment. She decided to obsess about something else for the moment.

Dressed in a black hoodie, black jeans, and her black work boots, she loaded up her appropriately dark-colored Ford Escape with a nylon duffle bag, her camera, a Glock holstered in the small of her back, a .25 on her ankle, and a couple bottles of water. It could be a long night of surveillance.

The traffic was light as she made her way to Buffalo's Old First Ward. The original ancestral home of Buffalo's Irish immigrants, it was experiencing a renaissance along with downtown's Canalside historic entertainment district. Condos were popping up along the Buffalo River, overshadowed by the massive grain elevators, some still in use, others long abandoned. The Ward was now a mix of the old and new: a neighborhood fighting to keep its identity while trying to balance an influx of young, hip, urban adventurers. In what had once been a rundown community struggling to survive, property values had skyrocketed, dive bars had become microbreweries, and sagging buildings were torn down and replaced with canoe launches and kayak rental shops.

There were still places to hide in the Old First Ward. The address she had come across the night before in her public records search of Melissa St. John's brother's current properties had jumped right out at her. Listed as commercial, he had owned it for seven years—longer than any of their other holdings. Just past the Old First Ward Community Center, Lauren made a right. She followed along the quiet street, which had once been lined with houses, before time and demolition had spaced them far apart in the twenty-first century. Coming up on an old suspended railroad bridge, she pulled off to the left shoulder. She'd be facing on-coming traffic, such as it was on a Tuesday night in one of the more isolated spots in the First Ward, but she knew from checking Google Maps that she'd have the best vantage point with the least amount of visibility from that spot. Modern satellite technology was wonderful.

Settling back in her heated seat, Lauren removed her binoculars from their case. Standing alone for almost an entire city block, the one-story brick building looked small and boxy surrounded by its eight-foot-high fence. The windows were all glass block, the door steel. Halogen lights lit up the exterior, illuminating the front parking area where two older pickup trucks sat, loaded down with tools and equipment. Parked on the street in front of the gate were two full-sized white vans. She searched for security cameras but didn't spot any. A red Honda Accord sat parked in front of the main door. *A regular little fortress,* she thought as she switched from the binoculars to her camera. *But not very bright to leave their gear in the back of the vehicles. All some kid has to do is jump the fence, grab a tool, and over they both go.*

Using her zoom lens, she zeroed in on the little complex, snapping pictures of the fence, the door, the gate. There was no business name anywhere on the building, just a dented metal sign hanging from the gate warning people that blocking their driveway would get them towed.

While zooming in on one of the license plates, the main door swung open and a man wearing a tan Carhartt jacket came out. He slung a canvas tool belt over his shoulder as he approached the gate. Lauren snapped a couple of shots of him as he opened the padlock and unthreaded the chain that held the separate halves of the gate together. He let the hardware fall to the ground, walked over to an aging Chevy loaded down with construction gear and hopped into the driver seat. After backing out onto the street, he exited the idling truck and carefully relocked the gate. Luckily for her, he drove off in the opposite direction.

She waited a full three minutes before she turned off her SUV and got out. She wanted to get a better look at the setup. She left her big camera behind. Her cell phone would do up close.

Lauren made her way along the side of the road, thankful there were no neighboring houses and only a few street lights, all on the opposite side. Crunching through what was left of the ice and snow, she approached the building from the south. Walking up to the rusty chain link fence, she studied the building. There was a listing wooden shed in the middle of the backyard area, which was not visible from her vantage point under the bridge. Junk cluttered the concrete pad up front, reaching all the way to the fence: white plastic buckets, broken tools, a pulled-apart car engine. A snow shovel was propped up next to the door.

Crouching down, she pulled out her cell phone and pinched the screen to zoom in on the Honda's plate. She hit the button and a bright flash lit up the yard and building. She'd forgotten to turn the flash off.

A flurry of barking came from the far side of the building as two huge Rottweilers charged at the fence. Caught off guard, Lauren fell backwards on her ass and scootched through the gravel and ice as fast as she could manage. The dogs hit the fence with a crash, jumping and snapping at her.

In her shock, Lauren dropped her phone. It lay face up, her screen-saver showing her daughter's pictures, right at the base of the fence.

"Son of a bitch," she whispered as the dogs strained against the wire of the fence to get at her, still in a barking frenzy. Brownish red flecks flew from the rusted chain links and fell on the phone's screen.

Lauren looked around for something to snag the phone away from the fence; a stick, a pole, anything so she wouldn't have to reach her hand in for it.

She spotted a tree branch a few feet away and crawled over to it. It was big and awkward, but it would do the trick. She got herself as close as she dared and thrust the three-foot long piece of wood at her phone, trying to swipe it back to her. The dogs tried to stuff their muzzles through the chain link to get at the stick.

"Wow. This is a surprise."

David Spencer stood by the front bumper of the Accord, his hands stuffed into his jean pockets, a tight black thermal shirt stretched over his muscular chest. A smile spread across his handsome face.

Still on her knees, Lauren snatched her gun from the holster at her back, drawing down on David.

His hands shot in the air. "Hey, Detective! I'm unarmed!"

"Call off your dogs," she said, letting the gun dip lower, but not putting it away.

"Caesar, Rudy, come here." He slapped his thigh and the dogs ran over to him. David reached down and rubbed both dogs between their ears. They sat looking up at him, jaws open and panting. "Better?" David asked her.

She leaned forward and grabbed her phone. "Thanks."

"Stay, boys." He dropped brown bone-shaped dog biscuits at his feet. While the dogs scarfed down their treats, David approached the fence. Lauren saw a rusted, patched-up spot in the wire next to where he stood, held together with white zip ties. "Overreact much?" He laughed. "Pulling a gun on me? Why are you here, Detective?"

Lauren couldn't think of a lie fast enough. "Are you checking up on me?" he asked before she could answer, threading his fingers through the wire, bringing his nose almost to the fence.

David's eyes were still a deep, warm brown, but other than that, the boy that Lauren Riley had met almost two years before was gone. His thin, athletic frame had been replaced with hard muscle from daily workouts. The soft planes of his handsome face were now solid and severe. He'd dyed his brown hair blond. She had seen that the last time they were face to face, but it still threw her. He wore it deliberately and meticulously tousled, a sharp contrast to the bed-headed kid who came to court every day when he was trying to beat a murder charge.

"Are you going to call your lawyer uncle on me?" Lauren got to her feet, letting her gun fall to her side but not holstering it. Her heart was hammering in her chest, her black jeans soaked through the seat and knees. She suppressed the urge to wipe the mud from herself.

"I'm a big boy now. I can handle my own problems. But you still haven't answered my question. Why are you here?" Even his voice was different. Deeper, colder.

"Can't I be curious about what you're doing? We did go through a lot together, didn't we?" The dogs had wandered back over to the fence, one sitting on either side of their master, jaws hanging open in panting smiles that showed off their jagged white teeth.

David's smile dazzled as he shook his head. "What a bunch of bullshit that is. You know what I think?"

"What?"

"That the obsession you said I had for you is actually the other way around. You coming here to spy on me? For no reason? Either you're trying to pin something on me or you've developed some really unhealthy feelings."

"Listen, I'm sorry." Lauren backed up, a fierce blush spreading across her cheeks. "This was a mistake. I can see you're doing fine. Working. Taking care of business. I won't bother you again." David's knuckles were white as he gripped the fence. Lauren could see the tension in his face as he worked his jaw, even with the pleasant persona he was trying to maintain.

He looked down at the patch job on the fence. "I always thought this wasn't very secure. That if the dogs were motivated enough, they could tear right through that hole. Lucky for you I came out when I did. These guys are pretty fierce."

"I've always been lucky." She eyed the weak spot. If he gave the right command, would they bust through the chain links? One of those dogs could tear her to pieces, let alone two. She'd have no chance, gun or not. "You've been lucky too. But I'm embarrassed I got caught checking up on you so—"

"You come to where I work, pull a gun on me, and expect me to accept that you're just checking up on me?" He shook his head. "I don't believe it."

"You startled me. That's why I pulled my gun. It was reflexive."

"That still doesn't explain why you're here. Are you investigating me?"

She didn't answer, just watched the way the muscles flexed in his arms as he gripped the fence.

"And why is the gun still in your hand?"

She took another step back, pretending to stuff her gun back in her holster, but keeping her hands behind her, ready. "Sorry." She couldn't believe she was apologizing to the little murderous fucker. But she had to make him believe this was nothing to go running to his uncle or her bosses about.

He gave the fence a rattle as he pushed off, setting the dogs to barking again. "That's okay," he called over the noise as he walked back toward the door. "You wouldn't have shot me anyway."

"You don't think so?" Lauren asked. The dogs were jumping at the fence, but not as ferociously as before. And not near the weak spot.

"I know you wouldn't shoot me, Detective Riley." A shaft of dull yellow light fell across the stained concrete as David pulled open the steel door.

"Why's that?"

He hung half in and half out of the door. Even with the steel and distance between them, Lauren felt exposed, like David could turn on her in a heartbeat.

"I learned a lot of things during the time I spent in jail. The most important one was recognizing who was a threat and who was a victim." The words dripped from his mouth like ice water running down her spine.

"So I'm not a threat?" she asked. "I'm a victim?"

His mesmerizing smile returned.

"Not yet," he said and let the door fall closed behind him, leaving Lauren standing cold and muddy in the dark.

9

The next day Reese took the morning off and came to the office late in the afternoon, acting as if nothing had happened. Lauren sweated for hours wondering if he was really going to come in or just blow her off until she left for the task force. She exhaled a silent breath of relief when he showed up after lunch, dumped his stuff on his desk, and started catching up on some paperwork. *It's emotional blackmail.* Lauren watched him out of the corner of her eye as he casually pecked away at his computer keyboard. *He knows the silent treatment drives me nuts.*

Still reeling from the incident with David Spencer the night before, Lauren tried to make herself busy with some old files that needed to be reorganized before they were packed away, keeping one eye on her partner. David hadn't called his uncle, Frank Violanti, or made a complaint to Internal Affairs. Not yet. If Reese knew what she'd done, that might be the final straw in their partnership. She decided to keep it to herself.

How she felt about what had happened with David was another matter. She'd been stupid, careless, and he'd caught her. Now he had leverage over her. She had no idea how that was going to play out, but eventually, she knew it would. David was too smart to let an opportunity like this pass.

"Let's go check out this coffee shop," Reese finally said, getting up with his coat, hovering in the doorway.

Lauren knew better than to question. Relieved, she gathered up her things, put her jacket on, and was in the car on the way to Chippewa Street without another word. Reese drove. She watched out the passenger side window and waited for him to say something. His avoidance of arguing drove her nuts. Just once she'd like to have it out with him, have him really tell her off. But he always exited, cooled off, and then acted like nothing was bothering him.

"Reese—"

He held up a hand to silence her. "Unless you're about to say something about Brianna McIntyre's disappearance or the way my new jacket really shows off my physique, I don't want to hear it."

She did her best to make peace. "Your jacket really hides your love handles."

He turned the car onto Chippewa Street, slowing to look for a parking spot. "Something for the ladies to grab on to. As opposed to you, who has more of a greased pole thing going for her. The men just slide right off."

She laughed, relieved that the tension was broken. "Meaning?"

He angled his way in between an old Chevy Malibu and a Buick Regal. "Ain't no man going to try to get to the top if he has to work that hard."

She let that pass. "I'd rather have Watson back. What are the chances I could have him this weekend?" Watson was Reese's West

Highland Terrier who had also come to live with her when she got stabbed. Lauren had tried everything she could to convince Reese to leave him with her, but the best she could get was occasional overnight visits.

"Pretty good, as a matter of fact." He threw their unmarked car into park. Grabbing the OFFICIAL POLICE VEHICLE placard from between the seat and the console, he tossed it on the dash. "The chick I'm seeing is deathly afraid of dogs. It's actually a little weird. But we're supposed to go to Niagara-on-the-Lake on Saturday, and I don't want him to be alone for that long."

"Why in the world would you date a woman who's afraid of dogs?" Lauren asked as she got out. The midday traffic was light, but Chippewa was so narrow she scrambled over the melting snow bank to the sidewalk. They both ignored the parking meter. Cop cars didn't have to pay, but sometimes Lauren dumped a couple of quarters in just for show.

"Did I mention she's a yoga instructor?"

Now Lauren laughed out loud. "Enough said."

"I figured." Reese looked up at the front façade of the coffee shop. What used to be The Snow Belt Bar was now Uncommon Blends Coffee Café. It was actually making more money as a coffee shop than it did selling alcohol. On a street overloaded with more than twenty bars and night clubs, a high-end coffee shop filled a niche that had long been ignored. While the rest of Chippewa slept during the day, Uncommon Blends had a line winding from the bar almost to the door and every seat was taken with business people, hipsters, and students. Reese and Lauren excused themselves past the people waiting in line and stood among the tables.

"You see this?" Lauren pointed to a flyer taped to the inside of the window. It was Brianna McIntyre's missing person poster, probably put there by her mother or one of the volunteers she had recruited to help her when Brianna first disappeared.

Reese nodded, gazing around the room. The telltale brass bar fixtures were still in place. In fact, nothing had changed except bottles of flavored syrup had replaced bottles of liquor on the shelves behind the bar and espresso machines stood where the taps used to be. "I'll get in line. Grab us a couple of coffees, get a feel for the place. If this is what it looks like on a weekday, it's probably bedlam during their Friday night happy hour."

Nodding, Lauren drifted through the customers toward the window seat Brianna McIntyre had been sitting in. Two young women in their twenties sat facing each other, but were shielded by the screens of their open laptops. Angling herself behind the one with the blunt-cut reverse bob, she tried to get a line of sight on what Brianna would have been looking out at.

Cars lining either side of the street. Parking meters. A sign declaring they were in the Chippewa Entertainment District. The fronts of the businesses across the street.

She looked at the corner of Chippewa and Pearl. The side patio of a bar called Slattery's had once been the home of her great-grandparents' corner store. Her grandfather used to tell her stories of working for his dad on Chippewa Street when it was the red-light district, of how he would hold on to the money of the prostitutes who lived in the rooming houses above the store. They'd pull a wad of bills out of their bra and he'd pocket it for them while they worked. They'd come back at the end of the day, collect their earnings, slip him a dollar, and tell him to be a good boy. He was twelve.

Her dad once asked her grandfather why he always gave the street walkers credit and he replied, "Because those working girls always pay their bills." The store had been torn down long before she was born, but that corner always made her think of her Gramps, even now.

Her eyes wandered to the bar directly across the street, next to Slattery's Pub, falling on its plate glass window. The Hot Spot had changed names at least a dozen times since she'd been on the job. It was a problem bar with a rich, out-of-town owner who, every time he lost his liquor license, "sold" it to an associate and reopened under a new name. The other bar owners on Chippewa Street hated the place because it allowed kids in under twenty-one. In the Hot Spot's management's thinking, a wrist band was a magical shield that prevented eighteen-year-olds from acquiring alcohol once they got inside the bar. And drunk eighteen-year-olds wandering around Chippewa Street were a turn-off for mature drinkers who spent more money.

Her gaze was still fixed on the place when Reese came back with their coffee in take-out cups. "Hey, Reese." She took hers and motioned with the cup at the Hot Spot. "Did they ever talk to anyone over there?"

"They did a video canvass. Half the bars have cameras on the front door, but from the inside. There's a city camera there." He pointed out the white globe hanging from the pole at Chippewa and Franklin. "I don't think its line of sight reaches this far. The next city camera is on Chip and Delaware."

"No cameras in here, on this door?"

"No. All the cameras here are positioned for employee theft, not drunken brawls. I looked at the tapes. Nothing that could help us."

"Let's go across the street. I want to check on something."

The Hot Spot was open, but only a few hard-core drinkers were sitting at the bar when they walked in. The place was dim and dank, like a dungeon in a medieval castle, and didn't smell much better, Lauren guessed. The bartender looked up at them, the serpent tattoo that snaked around his neck crept up along his cheek until its open mouth, complete with dripping fangs, gaped under his right eye. He wore his long hair down and scraggly, not in a neat man bun like the baristas across the street. He was on the shorter side, but thick. Lauren could tell he made them for cops the second they walked in.

"Can I help you guys with something?" His deep voice wasn't menacing, merely curious.

Lauren and Reese moved their coat flaps in unison to reveal the badges on their hips. The bartender leaned forward, propping himself up with both tattoo sleeved arms. "Something wrong, officers?"

"No." Reese walked over and shook his hand, which was twice the size of his. "We're following up on a case and just want to have a look around."

Spreading his arms wide, he motioned to the empty space, "I'm experiencing a bit of a lull right now. Go right ahead." A homeless-looking man with four or five dollars in change in front of him put his pint glass down and silently tapped the bar. The burly bartender simultaneously filled his glass with another draft beer and pulled four quarters from the pile. "It's dollar drafts before five," he said by way of explanation. "Can I get you officers anything?"

"I think we're good. But thank you," Reese said.

Lauren was standing in front of the picture window, staring at the coffee shop across the street. Reese sidled up next to her. "What do you see?"

"I have a perfect view of the table Brianna was sitting at." The two women were still there, both typing furiously into their laptops. "Someone could have watched her from this window."

Reese reached out and dragged a finger down the glass. It left a clean streak and the tip of his finger grimy. "We know they don't clean much in this place."

"The big letters on the window would partially cover anyone watching."

"Hey, boss." Reese turned and pulled a picture of Brianna McIntyre out of his back pocket. "You ever see this girl?"

He reached a meaty arm across the bar and took the picture. "A couple of detectives came by, but that was months ago. They showed me this same picture. Is that the girl that's missing?"

"That's Brianna McIntyre." Lauren walked over, leaned against the bar, realized it was sticky, and took a step back. "Did you ever see her in this bar?"

He shook his head and handed the picture back to Reese. "No. But she's not really the type to frequent this kind of place, ya feel me?"

"Have you worked here long?" Lauren asked.

"About a year and a half. Two months ago, I got a battle-field promotion to manager when the last one went to jail." He smiled, showing off strangely even, white teeth that made Lauren wonder if they were fake. Maybe knocked out in a brawl sometime. "It's a shit show in here, but it pays the bills."

Above the cloudy mirror behind him was a giant clock with a beer logo on its face, whose hands ticked the hour and minutes away. Something about the sound of the buzzing second hand brought the story of the hookers hiding their money back into her mind. The bartender noticed her noticing. "I'm a freak about time. I wear a watch, constantly look at my cell phone. My girl says it's OCD. I love that clock. My name's Galen, by the way."

She nodded, thinking. *When you don't want to get caught with something, you hide it. In a place where no one would think to look.*

"Do you have a bathroom here, Galen?"

He pointed down a dark hallway. "Ladies room on the left." Then wrinkled his nose. "The cleaning lady hasn't been in there in a while. You sure you can't hold it?"

"I'm more interested in the men's room."

Galen's face contorted even more. "Right next to the ladies' room. But just to give you an idea of its current condition, I usually piss in the alley out back."

"Good to know. Thank you."

"I'm trying to get the owner to dump some money into this place, but it's falling on deaf ears. He could care less about a clean shitter."

Lauren nodded and headed in the direction of the washrooms.

Reese followed her as she walked down the dim, cramped hall, pausing before the men's room door. "What are you doing?" he asked as she rapped her knuckles against the wood.

"Just a hunch." When no one answered, she pushed the door opened and ventured in with Reese on her heels.

The smell hit her nostrils like a heavyweight MMA fighter's fist. Her gag reflex wasn't what it used to be, but still, the place reeked. A line of four urinals with matching yellowish-brown stains down the front lined the far wall. A single sink ringed in black mold sat dripping under a glass block window.

"Gotta go?" Lauren teased as she scanned the room.

"I think I can hold it," Reese said, dumping his coffee cup into the plastic trash bin next to the sink.

Lauren kicked the door to the single stall open with the toe of her boot. An equally nasty looking commode sat next to a broken toilet paper dispenser. "Grab me some paper towels will you, please?"

He turned and cranked on the handle then ripped off a two-foot long brown piece of paper. Reaching back, she took it from him, tore it in two, and used it to lift the top off the toilet tank. There, sitting half an inch above the water line on the flush mechanism, was a cheap-looking black cell phone. Lauren carefully set the porcelain lid off to the side.

"Son of a bitch." Reese bent forward to get a better look.

"I'm calling Evidence and Photography." She pulled her portable radio out of her jacket pocket.

"How did you know?" he marveled as she was just about to key the mic.

"I didn't. It might not be the burner phone used to call Brianna, but I'm betting it is."

Reese gave a low whistle. "What am I going to tell poor Galen outside?"

"That he just got the night off." She keyed the mic on her portable and said, "Cold Case 1271 to radio?"

10

The techs at the Erie County crime lab confirmed that the phone was indeed the one used to call and lure Brianna McIntyre. While that didn't do much to identify who had abducted Brianna, it did tell Lauren a lot about the methods her abductor was using. He was being cautious, leaving the phone behind before the crime. He had scouted the locations beforehand, making sure he'd have a visual on his victim. And he hadn't bothered to come back and dispose of the burner phone because he was certain it couldn't be traced back to him.

With the task force starting in five days, Lauren wanted to make the most of the time she had left in the Cold Case office with Reese. Sixty days was a long time to be away from the cases they were working on, especially when she wasn't sure what the conditions at the task force were going to be like. Carl Church had convinced the county to lend one of its buildings in the city to use as the temporary task force home. It was downtown on Oak Street, but Lauren had heard parts of it were still under construction. *Still, it's better than being housed at the state attorney general's office or one of the other municipalities involved; a neutral space would be the most conducive for teamwork,* Lauren thought.

Reese had a whole laundry list of things he wanted to take care of before she left. "You don't get a vacation from your real job," he reminded her. "And you're not sticking me with all this crap before you go."

His blunt insults were music to her ears; they told her that their relationship could survive her going to the task force after all.

It was Friday, which meant Reese also had a multitude of weekend plans, so his urgency to get some work done was tripled. There was no way, Lauren knew, he was coming in on a Sunday morning to do busywork he could get done right then.

"I want to find Betty Ray today," he told her as soon as she came in the door. "And I know it rhymes, so keep that comment to yourself."

Lauren snapped her mouth shut and stowed her tote bag in her desk drawer. She had wanted to work on adding cases to the new Murder Book.

Since she had come back to work, she'd been slowly adding to the spreadsheet on her departmental iPad, remembering to save often. It wasn't the old fashioned olive-green three-ring binder she used to use on a daily basis, but unless the thief could erase the Internet cloud, it could never get stolen again.

Reese took off his Buffalo Bisons baseball hat and twirled it on his index finger. "Betty was supposed to come in so I could re-interview her on that deli murder from Jefferson Avenue. She's ducking me."

"She's about eighty years old," Lauren reminded him, mentally putting her Murder Book plans on hold. "Are you sure she wasn't put into a nursing home?"

"That's what I'm afraid of." Reese balled up a piece of paper and shot it into the trash can over by the spare interview room. "I think her grandkids are hiding her because they don't want her to be involved."

"Can you blame them?" Lauren threaded her Glock along her belt to her right hip, then buckled it. "Dante Henderson is a stone-cold killer."

"Yes. Exactly. That's why we need to put him in jail."

Dante Henderson had at least three bodies on him they knew of, none of which they could prove until Reese had found Betty's statement in the file saying she was in the deli when the robbery occurred and said she knew the young man who shot the owner, but only as Henny. At that time, Dante Henderson hadn't yet reached the peak of his criminal career and that nickname meant nothing to the original investigating detectives.

"I want to go over and peek out her son's house on Michigan Avenue. You ready to take a ride?"

She picked up her Tim Hortons cup, checking the contents—three-quarters full. "Let's go."

The drive over to the East Side took them down on Main Street past the new medical corridor, where millions of dollars of construction was going on in multiple projects. Yellow-helmeted construction workers wove in and out of scaffolding along the road. If someone had told Lauren ten years ago this type of investment was going to happen in that section of the city, she would have laughed. Now the joke was on the people who had written off that area. Business was booming.

But beyond that, in the neighborhoods, life went on as if none of that was happening.

Lauren was always happy to let Reese drive. The radio chatter was steady for a Friday morning. It was a holiday weekend and everyone, whether you were of Irish descent or not, took St. Patrick's Day very seriously. Buffalo had not one, but two parades: the downtown parade and the Old First Ward parade. Since the holiday fell on a Sunday this year, everyone had started the party early on Thursday night. As they drove along Main Street, people had on green jackets, shamrock apparel, and leprechaun hats. She wondered how many of them were just coming home from the night before or starting their Friday party early. Lauren was grateful for her gold detective's badge; parade weekend was always a nightmare for patrol officers trying to rein in the fights and drunks.

Reese turned down Northampton Street to cut over to Masten Avenue. "Her son's house is near the corner, next to the Dollar Store." He pulled a picture out from his visor and handed it to Lauren. "I Google Mapped it."

It was nice to be able to see the houses they intended to drop by on before going there. Google Maps gave them the layout of the outside, what structures were on either side, and the general condition of the property. It was so much better than flying in blind the way they used to do it. The house was a wood frame double, flanked on one side by a store and by another double on the opposite side. Lauren wondered when the picture was from. A kid's tricycle was on the porch along with a battered-looking porch swing. It was hard to tell what time of year the picture was taken, other than not the dead of winter. No snow was piled up, no shovels against the porch, no cars in the driveway covered in ice.

It was almost ten o'clock in the morning and the streets were just starting to wake up in the neighborhood. They parked along the curb across the street to watch the house for a few minutes. Lauren's old lieutenant, Charlie Daley, had taught her to always sit on a house, no matter how routine the matter, so that you knew exactly what you were walking into. She had passed that habit down to Reese when they started working together because his first instinct was to jump out of the car and rush right in.

Betty's son was a mail carrier and probably at work, so there were no cars parked in the driveway. The swing and the tricycle were both gone from the porch, but someone had painted the shutters a nice cheery blue since the Google Maps picture was taken.

"Think she's in there?" Reese asked, staring at the front picture window.

There was no movement, no sign of life coming from the house at all. "Hard to say. Let's give it a minute and we'll go check it."

The car radio crackled to life. "Any car in C-District, I'm getting a call of a robbery in progress at the Dollar Store at 890 Masten Avenue. Caller says a man with a knife is demanding cash from the register."

Reese and Lauren exchanged a quick glance.

"Son of a bitch," Reese said, slipping his Glock out as he opened his door. Lauren followed suit, gun at her side.

They were just about to cross Masten Avenue when a man with a ski mask came bolting out of the store in a Boston Celtics jersey. He made a quick turn and ran north on Masten. Something silver glinted in his left hand.

"Call it in! Call it in!" Reese yelled back to Lauren, dodging the cars on Masten as they both gave chase.

Lauren yanked the portable radio from her back pocket and keyed the mic as she ran. "Radio, this is 1271. We're chasing that robbery suspect down Masten towards Eaton Street."

Reese was ahead of her, cutting the distance between him and the suspect. The suspect pulled off his ski mask and threw it, looking back as he did, then doubled his efforts, realizing he was being chased. He cut down Eaton Street and immediately ran up a driveway and into the yards.

"The suspect is in the yards on Eaton Street, Radio," Lauren updated, huffing along through the debris-strewn backyards. "Skinny white male, six foot, wearing a green basketball jersey."

For a second, she lost sight of Reese in the back tangle of yards. She stuffed the radio in her pocket and turned around and around, trying to orient herself: a rusty swing set, a snowblower, broken patio furniture.

Panic started to wash over her. She knew you never, ever lose sight of your partner. The sound of her own heartbeat filled her ears.

A dog started barking. Then she heard the sound of wood breaking to her left. Lauren sprinted through a cut in the bushes into the next yard over.

Reese had the man backed against a tall wooden fence. In his left hand he had a knife with a five-inch blade. Reese had drawn down on him with his Glock. There was nowhere left for the skinny junkie to run.

"Drop the knife!" Reese yelled. About six feet separated the two men. Lauren came up next to her partner, the barrel on her own Glock pointed at the man's chest.

"You got nowhere to go. Drop the knife," she yelled. The radio in her back pocket screamed with the chatter of coppers coming to back them up.

The man's eyes darted from side to side, looking for an opening.

"How much did you get, man?" Reese asked, his voice out of breath, but calm. "Twenty bucks? Come on, man. Drop the knife."

The noise of sirens and tires squealing filled the air. Their backup was all over the street behind them but didn't know where they were. They might as well have been a million miles away.

The knife flashed in the morning sun, tip pointed upward. Lauren's breathing evened out as her muscle memory and training kicked in.

Everything seemed to slow down. The details in front of her became sharp and focused, like she was viewing the scene through a telescope. She could see the black hooded sweatshirt he had on underneath the jersey, the beads of sweat dotting his forehead, and his shaggy brown hair sticking to it in spots. Paint-stained baggy jeans hung from his hips and his beat-up white sneakers were caked in brown mud. A scraggy mustache under his nose twitched as the knife bounced slightly in time to his ragged breathing.

She watched him through her gun sight as he shifted his weight from side to side, debating his next move.

"Don't make us shoot you over nothing," Lauren called to him. "Drop it!"

His chest heaved up and down with adrenaline or drugs or both. He was going to make a play.

The man suddenly threw the knife to the side of him, feigned like he was going to slam into Reese, then ran straight at Lauren. A split second before he would have plowed into her Reese tackled him from the side, his gun still in his hand.

Lauren holstered her weapon and jumped on the pair rolling around in the muddy snow patches scattered in the backyard, managing to grab one of the suspect's arms and twist it behind his back. She hooked her leg through one of his, causing them to fall back in a jumbled knot against the fence.

Reese straddled the guy and grabbed his other arm with one hand while the suspect tried to fight them off. The man kicked and spit, screaming, "Get off me! Get off me!"

They were both huffing and exhausted when the first pair of coppers came crashing through the neighbor's bushes.

Rolling off him together as the patrol guys cuffed the suspect, Reese and Lauren looked at each other. Covered in mud and dead leaves, twigs sticking out of Lauren's hair, they caught their breath while a young cop brought the guy to his feet. "You guys okay?" he asked the panting detectives.

They both burst out in tension-laced laughter.

Stifling the laugh, Reese let out a low whistle. "That was close." He brought himself up on one knee, his khaki pants stained and wet.

A heavy-set cop offered her hand and helped Lauren up. "Too close," Lauren said, trying to brush the muck off her own pants without much success. The reality of how near they'd come to shooting that man washed over her and she said a small prayer of thanks. Every cop's worst nightmare is an on-duty shooting, even if it is justified.

"Great job, detectives!" an eager-looking young officer called to them as he helped lead the suspect out of the yards. The man's head was hanging down, greasy hair framing his gaunt face, all the fight suddenly drained out of him.

"I didn't know what to do with my gun," Reese said, finally holstering it. "I'm fighting one-handed and trying to keep my gun away from him with the other, while you're all over him like an octopus."

She had been all over him, even if she was huffing now. *I must be getting myself back together*, she thought. *All those early-morning walks are paying off.*

A lieutenant neither one of them had ever seen before showed up and started organizing the scene: ordering cops to string tape, look for witnesses, and safeguard the evidence. Apparently, a wad of one-dollar bills he'd stolen had leaked out of his pocket and left a trail down Eaton Street into the yards. Lauren hadn't noticed in the heat of the chase.

"I don't think we're going to find Betty today," Lauren told Reese. He reached over and plucked a stick out of her ponytail and dropped it on the ground.

"I just hope no one stole our car," he said, turning around to get his bearings. "I left it running at the curb when we hopped out."

An old-timer with a huge belly walked by and slapped Reese on the shoulder. "Nice pinch," he told them and went to stand over the knife until the crime scene unit showed up to collect it.

"Wouldn't that be just our luck?" Lauren asked.

"Yeah," Reese agreed. He tried to wipe some mud from his forehead with the back of his hand but only succeeded in smearing it around. "It would be."

11

Saturday mornings had been reserved for phone calls to her daughters since Lindsey left for college two and a half years ago, no matter what, even if Lauren's Friday had almost consisted of an on-duty shooting of a robbery suspect with a knife.

When Lauren had been in the hospital, the girls had convinced her to get on Facebook. In these last few months, after the Schultz case broke, they had managed to get her to start FaceTiming with them in a group. Today, especially, Lauren needed to hear the voices of her daughters and see their faces to help bring her down from those few awful seconds when the situation in the yards yesterday could have gone either way. Those were the moments cops replayed in their heads over and over and over, second guessing every move, even if everything had turned out all right in the end.

Now on Saturday mornings not only did she get to talk to her girls, she actually got to see them, for which she was extremely grateful. Her daughters were overjoyed Lauren had finally embraced modern technology. They had pitched it to her as a way for Lauren to keep an eye on them. But somehow, since Lauren had gotten hurt, the tables had turned on who was looking out for whom.

So the Saturday morning ritual continued, with Lauren in her kitchen, but set up with her iPad on the table, rather than plugged into the house phone on a three-way call.

"Mom," Lindsey said, her dormmate snoring in the background, "you need to eat. You look terrible." Lindsey was in her third year at Penn State, Erin in her second at Duke, and both were still on the fence about what they wanted their degrees to actually be in. It was a sore subject for Lauren, who liked to remind them they could have wasted her money closer to home. Lindsey had finally settled on getting a finance degree, after Lauren assured her FBI profiler jobs were extremely hard to come by. Erin was still floating around in the nebulous Art Department, waffling between Art History and Art Education. No matter what the final outcome, both would be heading to grad school soon. Lauren could visualize her 401k evaporating before her eyes.

"And go get your hair done. It needs more layers," Erin agreed, joining in. "Get some highlights put in. It's getting too dark."

Erin had added pink streaks to her own deep brown pixie cut. When she'd first told Lauren she planned to do it, Lauren was sure Erin would look ridiculous. It turned out adorable, so what did she know about fashionable hair? Maybe Erin was right.

"I'm walking three times a week, trying to get back in shape," Lauren defended herself. "Me and Reese had a crazy day yesterday, so I can't be that much of a ruin." She didn't want to go into the details with her daughters; that she was sore from head to toe from wrestling with a man she'd almost shot. Let them think she and Reese just had a lot of paperwork piled up and argued about it the whole day. That was totally believable.

"You're not a ruin, Mom. We just worry about you," Erin said. She was in a park somewhere; a flowering bush served as her backdrop. She attended Duke University and loved everything about it. When she did get home, she was itching to get back within two days. The weather in North Carolina looked like a picture postcard of spring. Sunny blue skies dotted with fluffy white puffs peeked out over the bushes, as opposed to the Buffalo area, which was still wrapped in iron gray storm clouds and melting snow.

"I'm fine. Don't worry."

"How is Shane?" Lindsey liked to use Reese's first name to irk her mother. Reese played into it when he was around, but only to a certain point. He knew there was a line he dare not cross, even in jest, when it came to Lauren's daughters.

"My partner is just fine, thank you," Lauren replied. "I'd like to say he's keeping me out of trouble, but then we have a day like yesterday and I know that's not true." But part of her knew they had worked together perfectly as a team. And it was because of that, that everyone involved had walked away. There was something special about that kind of partnership, she knew. Yesterday reminded her of how lucky she was to have Shane Reese at her side, instead of some trigger-happy cowboy type.

"I'm counting on him to keep you safe," Lindsey said. Behind her, her roommate snorted and rolled over in bed. "And what happened yesterday?"

"I think my safety is not an issue at the moment. And yesterday was nothing. Let's talk about something else, please."

Outside Lauren's kitchen window, a round, fat robin poked at patches of brown grass. It was the first one she'd seen this year, and it stirred hope that spring might finally be on its way.

"Okay," Lindsey agreed. "Are you seeing anyone?"

Lauren brought her hand to her mouth to stifle a laugh at Lindsey's bluntness "No. There has been no change on that front since we all went to your Aunt Jill's house in Seattle for Christmas." That was true enough—not a single date or even a phone number asked for. And she wasn't the least bit disappointed.

"I am," Erin announced. "His name is Marco and he's an Italian exchange student from Rome."

Lindsey's face brimmed with approval. "Nice."

"I don't want to hear this." Lauren pretended to cover her ears. "What about your grades? How are both of your grades?"

"I want to hear about Marco," Lindsey overruled Lauren. "Tell me everything. Is he tall and gorgeous?"

Talking with and seeing her daughters was always the highlight of her week. She wanted to tell them she missed them terribly, but she knew, especially after everything that had happened, they might actually come home if she asked. She didn't want that. She wanted more for her daughters than she had given herself, and college was the road to that. One of Lauren's biggest regrets in life was that she'd never gotten to get a degree. She'd raised her babies, working two waitressing jobs until she finally got the call for the police job. Not that Lauren wasn't grateful for the department, but she knew if you polled a hundred cops, ninety-nine of them would say they didn't want their children to follow in their footsteps.

Sitting in her cozy kitchen, talking with her daughters while a robin fished for worms on her back lawn, seemed like a little slice of heaven to her just then. Maybe everything had worked out the way it was supposed to.

If I could just exorcise the demon of David Spencer from my brain, she thought as she sipped her coffee and listened to Erin mimic Marco's thick accent in adoration, *life would be pretty damn good.*

12

Two days before the official start of the new task force, Reese and Lauren had to head over to County Court for a suppression hearing on a statement they had taken from a witness. In late February they'd made an arrest in the drug-related murder of a heroin dealer. The suspect's girlfriend had told a counselor in her rehab about watching her boyfriend beat his supplier to death in his own apartment six years ago.

The witness said her ex-boyfriend, Justin Adams, had ransacked the place looking for drugs or money, but had come up empty. The only thing he'd stolen was the victim's wallet. When questioned by Reese and Lauren, the girlfriend stated that the boyfriend still had the victim's ID in a drawer in his bedroom. The victim's name, Michael Smith, was so common that the suspect used his ID from time to time since he had numerous warrants out for him under his real name. A search warrant based on her statement produced the ID, but the boyfriend claimed he had found it in a drug house. Now his defense attorney was trying to suppress the statement, and if successful, have the charges against him thrown out due to lack of evidence.

"Can you believe this shit?" Reese asked, as they crossed Church Street to the median, where they waited for a break in traffic. "We have things to follow up on now that we found that phone and we get stuck at a freaking suppression hearing all morning."

Lauren played devil's advocate. "What else does the defense have? Now that Carly is sober, she makes a damn compelling witness."

"Let's just hope she stays sober." Reese craned his neck, decided the coast was clear, motioned for her to follow, and crossed the rest of the way. "She's only twenty-four and has been in and out of rehab three times already."

"That's what the defense is betting on, I think. Her ex-boyfriend wasn't even a suspect until she spilled it to her counselor," Lauren replied as they pushed their way through the revolving door into County Court.

Two long lines had formed on either side of the entry, with people putting their belongings through the metal detectors, stepping through, and getting wanded on the other side. Thankfully, cops got to skip that awful ritual by holding out their badges, to which the deputies, all of whom they were friendly with, would respond in loud voices, "Good morning, Detectives."

Everyone looked hungover, including the deputies. Buffalo's famous annual St. Patrick's Day parade had taken place the day before. Broken bottles, trampled shamrock hats, and garbage still littered the length of Delaware Avenue. The lock-up at City Court was full of people sleeping off a public intoxication or disorderly conduct charge.

"What part are we in?" Reese hit the up button for the elevator.

"Part 18, third floor." She pulled the court subpoena from the back pocket of her black pants and scanned it quickly. "Judge Tierney."

"I like her. She's fair," Reese said as he stepped into the car.

Just as the doors were about to close, an arm shot out. Frank Violanti jumped through the reopening doors. "Wow. This is a surprise. I just got retained to defend Justin Adams and look who's heading up to the courtroom; my two favorite Cold Case detectives."

Lauren eyed Frank up; she'd talked to him by phone but hadn't seen him in person in over a year. He was still going for the little-boy-in-his-daddy's-suit look, with spiked-up gelled hair that didn't make him five foot six. He was clutching the handle of a very expensive-looking black briefcase, stuffed, Lauren was sure, with every piece of paper they'd produced on Justin Adams. Pieces of paper he would twist to his advantage once he got the two of them on the stand.

"It's good to see you, Lauren," he said. "It really is."

"Frank." That was all he was going to get out of her if he was about to cross-examine her.

"It's good to see you, Violanti." Reese clapped him on the back of his pinstripe suitcoat as they got off on the third floor together. "Now I know we'll win this suppression hearing for sure."

Violanti wagged his finger at Reese, grinning. "We'll see. I want you on the stand first, Detective Reese. That might be all I need." He gave a goofy wave and headed for the double doors to Judge Tierney's part.

"That was awkward," Lauren remarked after Violanti had gone inside. Lauren and Reese had to sit on the brown padded benches outside the courtroom and wait to be called. Since they were both potential witnesses, they couldn't be in the courtroom while the other testified. The bailiff would come out and call them in one at a time.

"You took ten grand from him," Reese reminded her. "Did that feel awkward?"

"When I realized his client was a psychopathic murderer, yeah."

Reese wasn't buying it. "Get off your high horse. You didn't give it back and you really thought the kid was innocent when you started on the case."

"In case I haven't informed you before, I didn't renew my private investigator's license this year. As of January first, I am no longer a PI in the state of New York."

"Really?" Reese cocked an eyebrow. "You let all that extra money go?"

"I hadn't been taking on too many cases since the whole David Spencer thing. For what I was taking in, I could have made just as much money coming in on overtime for the department. It just wasn't worth it anymore."

"And no selling your soul to guys like Frank Violanti, either."

She picked a piece of lint off her black suit coat. "Are you my moral compass now?"

The bailiff leaned out of the door. "Detective Reese?"

"Only if you want to start including anonymous one-night stands in your lifestyle." He winked at Lauren, got up, and headed inside the courtroom.

Lauren clasped her notes in front of her and waited. She could have pulled out her phone and played a game, but she needed her mind on the case. When you had to testify, you had to have every detail correct, referring to your notes if you needed to, as many times as you needed to. Especially in a situation like this, where losing the hearing could mean the judge tossing out the entire case.

Fifteen minutes rolled by. She reviewed the transcript of the first interview with the witness, Carly Simcock. A half hour passed. She tested herself by writing the pertinent dates and times by memory on a scrap piece of paper. After forty-five minutes and five more lists, Reese came strolling out.

"The assistant district attorney says she doesn't need you to testify."

Exhaling a sigh of relief as she got up, Lauren glanced back to the courtroom. "How did it go?"

"The judge is allowing the statement in. Against much protest by Violanti. That man is relentless." Reese rubbed his bald head with his right hand as they headed for the elevators. "You can say what you want about your experience with Frank Violanti, but I know one thing for sure."

"What's that?"

"If I ever get myself mixed up in some serious shit, I want him to be my defense attorney."

13

Lauren hadn't been back in her office ten minutes when a text from Violanti flashed across her cell phone screen.

Can we meet somewhere? We need to talk.

Lauren was more than a little surprised and extremely curious. He was representing a client she would have to testify against at some point in an upcoming murder trial. For him to try to arrange a meeting could blow the whole case. If the DA or his client ever found out, it would be a mistrial for sure. Another text came in.

It's about David.

What about him? she texted back, angling her phone away from Reese so he couldn't see the screen. Not that he was paying any attention to her; he was busy at the computer typing up the interdepartmental memo about the suppression hearing that would become part of the permanent file. It took all his concentration to jab out a coherent sentence with just his index fingers.

Meet me. Name the place.

She wondered if David had ratted her out about her little nocturnal visit and Violanti wanted to read her the riot act. Somehow, though, she hadn't gotten the feeling from him in the elevator that he wanted to threaten her for harassing David. He had a nervous energy about him that she had chalked up to pre-hearing jitters. She should have known better.

Waffling about whether to meet him, she waited a full five minutes before texting him back.

How do you feel about cemeteries?

14

Lauren told Reese she was going for a ride to grab some food from this great little Polish restaurant that had just opened in Kaisertown. Since Reese typed using the two-finger hunt-and-peck method, they both knew he was going to be there for a while, so he gladly rattled off an order to his partner.

She was really heading over to Arcadia Cemetery off Walden Avenue. One of the only cemeteries left in the city and eclipsed by the sprawling Forest Lawn, Arcadia had been serving East Side communities since 1891. Lauren knew from meeting informants there that the wrought iron driveway gate would be closed and locked until around Easter, but the sidewalk gate would be open. It was the perfect place, especially when the main gate was secured, to meet with people who wanted to remain invisible.

Lauren parked on the street and looked at the entryway. Reese had a massive phobia of cemeteries in general, but he absolutely refused to go into Arcadia simply because of the looks of the front gate alone.

While the cemetery itself was well maintained by volunteers, time and the weather had taken its toll on the entrance archway that had the name ARCADIA spelled out in rusty wrought iron. It looked like the cover of an eighties horror novel.

She got out and crossed the street, pulling her jacket around her neck to block the cold March wind. Violanti wanting to meet her had caused her anxiety to spike. She wondered if he was about to give her the heads-up that David was filing formal charges against her. That would be the end of her participation on the task force, and maybe a do-not-pass-go ticket to her thirty-day suspension.

The East Side had been predominately Polish for about seventy-five percent of the twentieth century, when it slowly began to morph into an African American community. Now the cemetery was a mix of cultures and ethnicities, like the neighborhood itself. There were even some green carnations left on a small grave close to the sidewalk entryway, catching Lauren's eye.

Violanti had said he'd meet her by the entrance, so she waited there, back to the wind, puzzling over the reason for this clandestine rendezvous.

She only had to wait five minutes before she saw a powder blue Cadillac Escalade pull up behind her car. The behemoth gleamed with shiny chrome fittings. The giant tricked-out truck made Violanti look like a little kid getting off one of the big rides at the fair as he exited.

He gave a wave in recognition and crossed the busy street.

"What in the hell are you driving?" she asked as he walked over to her.

"Oh, that? That's Justin's payment for his murder trial. I accept cash, cash, and liquid assets." He adjusted the wool scarf around his neck, tucking the ends into the collar of his expensive-looking camel-colored coat.

She eyed the obnoxious vehicle again. "How does a junkie afford an SUV like that?"

"His grandma died and left him some money. He bought this and shot the rest up his arm. It's sad, really."

"Yes," Lauren agreed with fake sympathy. "It was also sad when he bashed Michael Smith's head in."

"Allegedly," he reminded her. "But that's not why I asked to meet you here."

"I'm listening."

He was plucking at the fingers of his soft-looking brown gloves, like they were just a tad too small. "It's about David. And you have to promise me you won't tell anyone what I'm about to say because I could get disbarred for violating attorney-client privilege."

"He's not your client anymore. The Katherine Vine case has been over for more than a year."

Violanti ignored that comment and went on. "A little birdie told me the DA's office—in conjunction with the Attorney General's office, State Police, Garden Valley, Buffalo and Chautauqua County Sheriff's Office—are forming a task force to investigate the girl who was found off the thruway. And the deaths of Joe Wheeler and Ricky Schultz. I heard you were going to be on that task force."

"Those little birdies have gigantic beaks."

"Come on, this is Buffalo," he said. "Now promise me this is off the record."

She shook her head slowly from side to side. "You know I can't make that promise."

"Yes, you can. You just don't know whether you'll keep it or not."

Is Violanti the only man in my life who actually knows me? she ruminated to herself. "Okay then. I promise."

Violanti looked around to make sure there was no one about to overhear him. The cemetery itself was devoid of any people. Walden Avenue was a busy thoroughfare, but no one had time to pay attention to a couple of mourners in a graveyard. "I started representing David again when Joe Wheeler got his job back. Wheeler started investigating Amber Anderson's murder hard. I think he was doing his own research while he was suspended, but Wheeler came after David full-force when he got reinstated. He was picking up witnesses, re-interviewing people, coming around to David's job sites and talking to their tenants. David was really pissed."

If Garden Valley PD had known that, they'd kept it to themselves, preferring to look at her and Reese and then the Schultz brothers as suspects, or so they'd made it seem. Unless Joe Wheeler hadn't told his supervisors what he was working on, which would have been typical of him, as he only wanted people to know about a sure thing. *Yes,* Lauren thought. *I could see him investigating David lone-wolf style until he had enough to make a case, especially after David's acquittal.*

"Why are you telling me this now?"

Violanti choose his next words carefully. "I have no proof that David has done anything criminal, ever. And I don't want to see him railroaded if someone else is responsible for those two girls' deaths or the cop murders. But if someone could show me something other than circumstantial evidence, I'd gladly pass him to a colleague for representation and walk away."

"How could you say that about your own godson? The kid you begged me to help you defend? I thought you were convinced he'd been framed."

Violanti's mouth set in a grim line, he thought for a moment, then said, "Because he's changed over the last year. I can't explain it. Especially now that he has Melissa bankrolling him."

What is Violanti playing at? she wondered. *He's busted his ass defending David at every turn, and now he's telling me he'll let him swing in the wind.* "I still don't understand what you're trying to tell me."

"What I'm telling you is, while I have no direct evidence that my client has committed any crime at any time, I highly suspect him to be capable of some of these allegations, and it might be beneficial to us both personally if we keep a line of communication open while you investigate."

"Off the record," Lauren clarified. A line of communication with Violanti, however unethical, would certainly give her an advantage over David. But they were both crossing a very dangerous line.

Violanti nodded. "This conversation never occurred. If I did obtain evidence of his guilt, I would step aside. Right away. It might even look like a signal, of sorts."

"Don't be so dramatic, Violanti. Stop speaking in tongues. Just tell me that if I have to find David Spencer right away, you'll let me know where he is."

"I can do that." He shoved his hands deep into his pockets and turned to leave.

"Frank," Lauren called after Violanti, stopping him in his tracks. "Why are you doing this? Why now?"

Violanti's face sank into a look of such sadness Lauren thought he might actually cry. "Because I have a son of my own now who needs protecting. I promise, I'll help you as much as I can."

15

Lauren Riley stood in front of the Smart Board in the meeting room, which was now acting as a screen for her PowerPoint presentation. The city had lent the task force the future home of a city-run adult learning center on Oak Street. While construction crews banged and bolted and drywalled the rest of the building together, the task force was confined to the management offices that had already been finished. Far from ideal, it was the only space available on such short notice.

Four sets of eyes stared at her from the table. Four investigators chosen from their agencies to be on what the press had dubbed the Cop Killer Task Force.

Officially, the task force had been set up to give local law enforcement extra resources—not just with the two cop murders, but with any recently unsolved homicide. With the exception of the city of Buffalo, no municipality west of Rochester or south of Niagara Falls had their own dedicated homicide squad. For places like Garden

The silence that followed his statement seemed to drag on. No one wanted to interrupt the stare-down between Lauren and Bates. Slivers of light shone through the gaps in the white industrial-grade blinds that covered the windows, slashing Bates's face with too-bright March sunshine, a rarity she couldn't even enjoy now.

A flush rose to her cheeks, but her tone stayed even. "I was cleared of any suspicion within thirty-six hours of his death. Even Erie County District Attorney Carl Church approved me for this task force."

Bates snorted in response. "Because he wants to see you fail. He wants you out in the open and exposed for getting a murderer off, once and for all. He doesn't care if Joe Wheeler's or Ricky Schultz's murders get solved. Tie them all up in one neat package and the public will swallow it. And if we can't tie them to David Spencer, well, he's still out there. Thanks to you."

"Detective Bates—" Kencil calmly tried interrupting, but Cam Bates was on a roll.

"No. No. No." He stood up and spread his arms out, his navy blazer flapping open to reveal his gun and badge on his hip. "Am I in the wrong here? Those two girls in the woods could be this David Spencer kid, but those two cops? No way. And I'm not buying my chief's theory that one of the Schultz brothers killed Joe Wheeler to try to frame Riley and her partner. How does that explain what happened to Ricky Schultz? It's all bullshit. And I know I'm not the only one who thinks so."

Lauren's eyes traveled around the faces before her, looking for an ally. All she saw was the neutral stares of men she didn't know, who didn't know what to believe. She could say that video showed that she had never left her gated community during the time frame when Ricky was murdered, that her computer showed her online, that her cell phone had only pinged off the tower closest to her house, but Bates had made up his mind. She needed to keep him from convincing the rest of the task force.

"I think we should listen to what she has to say before we start making accusations we can't back up."

Everyone's head swiveled around to the Chautauqua County Sheriff who had been assigned to the task force. It was Jack Nolan, the same guy who had handed Brianna's wallet to Lauren at the crime scene. The same guy who'd carefully copied the reports she and Reese had brought to his station. He was plainclothes now, with a black sport coat over a yellow button-down shirt. He had angled his chair out and away from the table to see the Smart Board better. Manny Perez's deep-set, dark eyes locked on him. Lauren could almost see the line being drawn through the middle of the table, with her and the sheriff on one side and Bates and Perez on the other.

"I think you're right, Jack," Kencil swooped in to rescue their first meeting. "Go ahead and finish your presentation. Then I'll go over all the forensic evidence we have for each of these crimes. In your red binders there's a hard copy and a thumb drive containing the slides to both of our presentations and to the case files involved. Lauren, please, go on."

She did, but she was tense and distracted, knowing at least two of the task force members were dismissing everything she had to say. Bates wasn't even looking at her. Holding a clear plastic cup half-filled with spit from the chewing tobacco he had stuffed in his lower lip, he gazed out the single window of the room and occasionally hawked another glob into his spittoon.

Lauren clicked to a slide of the Hot Spot's bathroom. "We recovered the burner cell phone used to contact Brianna McIntyre. It was found hidden in the toilet tank in the bathroom of the bar directly across the street from the coffee shop. It had been wiped clean: no prints, no DNA was found. It contained text message conversations between the victim and the person she was supposed to meet. The phone was bought and activated at a corner store on Grant Street near Ferry, on the West Side of Buffalo. Video from the store has long since been taped over. The purchaser made no calls to any other number—"

"Joe Wheeler was my friend," Bates said loudly, to no one in particular. "I'm on the Cop Killer Task Force. That's what I'm investigating."

Is every detective in Garden Valley an asshole? Lauren thought as she went to her next slide. It was unfair, she knew. Cam Bates had always been decent to her when they'd come across each other before Joe's murder. Cocky, but decent. As much as she had hated Joe, he'd had a life and friends and his work. The Joe Wheeler who Cam Bates knew was not the Joe Wheeler Lauren had known. Cam blamed her for Joe's death. All she could do was hope the evidence the task force uncovered pointed him to the right vehicle for his anger: David Spencer.

She finished her presentation and let Kencil take her place in front of the Smart Board. She sat in the unoccupied chair next to Nolan, grateful not to have to take the empty seat over by Cam Bates. Kencil methodically went through the evidence from Joe Wheeler's and Richard Schultz's murder scenes while the four cops followed along in their binders, making notes.

Manny Perez kept his comments short and sweet. Fiddling with the button on his brown sport coat, he gave a quick summary: Amber Anderson had been a frequent runaway. Her body was too decomposed to give a cause of death. There were no hard suspects. Thanking everyone, he waited a moment for questions. There were none. He sank back into his seat.

Both Nolan and Bates declined to present. "I think Lauren and Manny covered everything I have." Nolan flipped through the papers stacked in front of him. "No need to rehash the details."

Kencil stood again, palms flat on the table, leaning forward so everyone could hear. "What I'd like to do is split our task force into two separate investigations, since that's what I'm hearing anyway. I think Nolan and Riley should investigate the deaths of Amber Anderson and Brianna McIntyre, and Bates and Perez should dive into the Wheeler and Schultz investigations. I'll be the point man. Everybody brings me their reports at the end of the day. I'll go over them, look for connections, brief the higher ups, and we'll have a morning meeting, just like this one, every day so we're all on the same page." Gazing around the table, he was looking for objections. When there were none, he continued: "Either there are connections between the victims or there aren't. We're just as likely to find out there are four murderers out there as one. We have to approach these cases with open minds. If you can't do that, then go back to your department right now. Tunnel vision doesn't get homicides solved."

Lauren twisted in her chair. Tunnel vision for David Spencer was all she had. And Cam Bates's tunnel vision was aimed directly at her. Kencil was right to split the team in half the way he had. At least the opposing sides had a fair and impartial referee.

"And remember, the departments from which these cases originated are still doing their own investigations. We're supposed to be assisting them. Sharing information with them. Don't hold back leads from me because you don't want to pass them on to a certain department. If I find out any of you are doing that, you're off the task force."

Bates muttered something under his breath.

"What was that, Detective Bates?" Kencil prompted, looking Bates squarely in the eye.

"I was just wondering if those detectives will be as forthcoming with us." He was talking about Reese, Lauren knew. And herself.

"I'll make sure they are. We have sixty days and the clock is running, people. Are there any other questions?"

When no one answered, Kencil dismissed them to their cubicles lining the center room. Lauren had tried to set up her space quickly that morning. She had been running late and hadn't wanted to be the last one in the conference room. From an oversized tote she had stashed under her generic metal desk, she pulled her laptop and wireless mouse. Running her hand over the surface of the desk, she realized it was too smooth and she'd have to bring one of her old mouse pads from home. There wasn't even a desk calendar. She surveyed her space. Except for the desk and two matching chairs, it was absolutely empty. The temporary walls only went up about six and a half feet, so the sound of Cam Bates talking to his wife on the phone about their baby teething carried over the space quite clearly.

She had gotten lucky, though; her cubicle was the last one and sided against the conference room wall, so she only had one neighbor instead of two. That the neighbor had to be Cam was unfortunate, but she could work around that. She had to.

"The computers for your desks, the fax and copy machines, and the coffeemaker are all being installed tonight. Since we're in the city, everyone will be issued a Buffalo Police radio. This will be for emergencies only. Copies of everyone's cell phone numbers are posted on the bulletin board out here on the wall," Kencil yelled from the middle of the hallway. Even with her cubicle door closed she could hear him perfectly clear. "We'll be connected to the Buffalo Police Department's computer hub. Remember that everything you pull up, look at, or print out is documented."

"No porn here, Perez," Bates called over the cubicle wall.

"I'll stop by your office for that." He laughed, along with the chuckles of the other task force members.

Lauren had a ceramic coffee mug with green shamrocks painted on it in her bag. Instead of putting it in her drawer, she put it next to her laptop and filled it with pens and pencils. *Maybe it'll bring me some luck,* she thought, and moved it to the other side of the laptop before moving it back again. She needed to go to an office supply store and buy a clock to hang on her wall. And some colored file folders. And a hole punch to add paperwork to her binder.

Glancing at her phone, she saw it was only ten fifteen in the morning. She slid her tote back under the desk and walked out her cubicle door. It had a lock, but why bother? Bates could literally stand on his desk and jump down into her office if he wanted to.

Nolan's cubicle was the last one on the other end of the hall, right across from the small kitchen area that would soon hold their coffee-maker. His door was open a crack and she could see him bent down, unpacking his things from an old army-green duffel bag. She walked over and rapped on the thin door. He looked up at her. "Hey." He smiled.

"Do you want to take a ride?"

Nolan dropped a notebook back into his bag. "Where to?"

Crossing her arms, she leaned against the door frame. "Headquarters. I want to steal a couple of filing cabinets."

16

If Nolan thought she was joking, he was only half right. Behind police headquarters, on the Franklin Street side, were piles of used office furniture the department was throwing away in preparation for the move. Chairs, broken desks, bookshelves, and filing cabinets were stacked and strewn haphazardly around the side door all the way to the sidewalk so the garbage men could come around and scoop it up. Eventually. The bulk of it had been sitting there for over a week.

Lauren had instructed Nolan to keep his Explorer running in the no-parking zone beside the refuse pile. Picking her way through the garbage, she spotted a small, taupe-colored three-drawer filing cabinet pinned beneath a three-legged table. "If it's not locked, I think this one will do." She maneuvered herself over and grabbed onto the back of the table. Underneath her the pile of garbage shifted and she compensated, keeping her balance.

"Wait, I got this." Nolan stepped over a mound of melting brown snow and grabbed the other end, helping her lift it off and over. As they flipped the table, he asked, "You okay, Riley?"

Surprised at the concern in his voice, she looked up, catching his hazel eyes on her. "Why wouldn't I be?" she asked, hoping to end his anxiety for her well-being right there.

"What's the deal with you and Cam Bates? Why does he have such a hard on for you?"

She stopped what she was doing and stood straight up. "Do you know any of the history about me and Joe Wheeler and David Spencer?"

He shrugged. "I know a little. What I saw on the news, what I've heard from other cops."

"I'll give it to you in a nutshell then." She wiped her sleeve across her forehead. She was actually working up a sweat picking through garbage, or maybe now it was the memories of garbage from her past. "I was married young. I had two daughters and my husband ran out on me. I met Joe Wheeler when we were in the police academy and we got engaged. But not before he turned me into his own personal punching bag for a couple of years. I dumped him, married someone else, and got dumped myself. Flash forward to a year and a half ago, and a woman named Katherine Vine gets murdered in the suburb of Garden Valley, and Detective Joe Wheeler arrests a kid named David Spencer for it. I got hired by his defense attorney godfather to help in his murder trial."

She shook her head, trying to clear it. "I helped David Spencer get acquitted for a murder he most surely committed. The body of his ex-girlfriend Amber Anderson was recovered while the jury was deliberating." She laughed bitterly. "Deliberating. And then they came back with a not-guilty verdict. Flash forward a year, and Joe Wheeler gets murdered in his own driveway. After he gets his job back from being suspended for stalking and assaulting me. Cam Bates and Joe Wheeler were friends. He thinks I had something to do with Joe's murder. End of long, sad story."

She waited there, on top of the pile of debris, for Nolan's reaction.

"Good to know," was all he said, and yanked a broken chair leg out of the way.

She appreciated his concern and hoped that explanation helped clarify some things and put other things to bed. While it was sweet of him, the last thing she needed was to be treated like some sort of fragile doll that would break if Bates played with her too hard.

Still, she felt she had to add, "I'm a big girl, though. I can handle guys like Bates."

A car door slammed, cutting off any reply Nolan might have had forthcoming.

"What are you doing, Riley?" Ben Lema called out as he headed from the unmarked car he just parked near the back door. "Redecorating your house?"

"Something like that," she laughed, pulling on the file cabinet's drawers. They opened just fine. "Any chance there's fresh coffee upstairs?"

"If not, there'll be a pot on by the time you get done garbage picking." Ben gestured to Nolan. "Bring your friend."

Nolan gave a wave, grabbed the cabinet, and pulled it from the pile. "Thanks," he told Lema. "Sounds good."

"We'll see you in a few minutes then," Lauren called, trying to extract herself from the tangle of office refuse.

"Don't hurt yourselves." Lema swiped his way into the side door and disappeared.

The file cabinet was small and empty, so Nolan didn't have any trouble getting it into the back of his Explorer. It was a recent addition

101

to the pile; there was no mud or snow in the drawers or smeared on the sides. Nolan heaved it in, then wiped his hands on his pants. "Is that it?"

"Unless you see something you want," she replied, surveying the junk left on the corner. It was still warm out, a little over forty degrees, and water dripped from foot-long icicles hanging from the second-story gutter, making the sidewalk slick. "I think that one will be enough for me."

"I think I'm good." He smiled. "Especially if you let me keep some of my files in your cabinet."

"It's a deal." Nodding towards the side door she asked him, "Ready for some coffee?"

"Where can I park?" Police headquarters was notorious for its lack of parking. That was one of the reasons used to justify the move.

Scanning the street, Lauren saw another fellow Homicide detective, Vatasha Anthony, getting into her unmarked car. "See if you can squeeze in there when she pulls out." Lauren pointed. "And make sure you lock the doors; I don't want my sweet new filing cabinet to get stolen. Now I have to go grab some folders from the third floor to fill it with."

Getting more of her things was on the agenda, as well as coffee, but the number-one reason to stop at headquarters was to see Reese. They hadn't argued about her going to the task force; that wasn't the way their relationship worked. He would let her go do her own thing while he did his for sixty days, and they wouldn't speak of it. But it still bothered her. Even when they had lived together for a short time after she had gotten stabbed, never once did they have what would have amounted to a deep and serious personal conversation. She and Reese had done really well working together during the week it had taken for Church to set up the task force. They had followed up on leads, worked some loose ends on a couple other homicides, and made a great armed robbery arrest. But they had not talked about her being on the task force and his not being on it. That was just how their relationship went.

Still, Lauren worried about lasting damage she was causing.

Ben had told the truth about the fresh pot of coffee. Lauren's nostrils filled with the familiar scent of newly brewed java as soon as she swiped into the Homicide wing. Nolan looked around at the stacked boxes, the peeling paint, and the sagging light fixtures. "I will never complain about my working conditions again," he said, accepting a Styrofoam cup from Lauren.

"I would tell you it's not that bad, that it's just because of the move, but that would be a lie." Lauren poured her own coffee and gestured towards the doorway. "My office is down here."

She spotted Ben Lema talking with Marilyn, the Homicide report technician, in the front office. It didn't seem like anyone else was around. Sometimes the Homicide office buzzed with activity, sometimes it barely hummed.

Lauren almost stopped and knocked on the door frame when they got to her office, but she shook that off as being stupid. It was still her office. Hadn't Kencil said they needed to work with the investigating officers? And weren't she and Reese the investigating officers for Brianna McIntyre's murder?

Reese was hunched over the keyboard of his computer, pecking something out. He looked up when they entered the room. Despite her misgivings, Reese cracked a smile as soon as she and Nolan came in. "Hey, Nolan," he said, standing and stretching out his arm to shake. "Good to see you again."

"You too." Nolan gave Reese's hand a pump.

"They put you on the task force?" Reese asked, taking in Nolan's sport coat and dark slacks.

"Me, Manny Perez from the State Police, Cam Bates." Nolan shrugged. "I'm the lead investigator on both Brianna McIntyre and Amber Anderson for Chautauqua County. Amber went missing from Garden Valley, so I assume Cam Bates is the lead on that end."

"I guess that's why you're here. Brianna's my missing person's case."

"*Our* missing person's case," Lauren corrected.

His green eyes flashed at her as he gave his lopsided grin. "Our missing person's case. This is great. We're one big happy family. I see Riley got you some coffee. Why don't you grab a seat?"

"Cam Bates does not want anything to do with either of us." Lauren settled into her chair after Nolan parked himself in one of the extras next to Reese's desk.

"Can you blame him?" He ran his fingers over the smooth shape of his head, pausing just for a second at his new scar. Lauren had noticed him doing it since he'd had his head shaved and decided it was now one of his tells. "He thinks you and I had something to do with his friend being murdered."

"It's ridiculous."

Reese leaned over his desk towards Nolan and told him, "That's why I love working with Riley. Every day is an adventure. Remember that video where she stuck a fork in the guy's face?"

Nolan couldn't suppress his grin, irking Lauren. The last thing she needed was the two of them ganging up on her. She cut to the chase. "Do you want to work with us on Brianna's murder or not?"

He reared back, hand on his heart in mock surprise. "Are you asking me to join the party? Because I wasn't invited, you know."

She reached over to swat at his arm, but he jerked away before she could connect. "Cut it out. I think we should drive by the coffee shop, show Nolan where Brianna went missing from. Maybe take a ride past David Spencer's house."

Reese shook his head. "Pulling Nolan to the bottom of your downward spiral right away, I see."

"I volunteered," Nolan countered. "I asked my chief to be on the task force."

"Lucky for you," Reese said, putting his hat on, "that there was an opening."

Lauren narrowed her eyes but bit her tongue as Reese stood, sending a shower of crumbs from his pants onto the floor. "Sorry. I had some of that fantastic rum cake Marilyn makes. She brought it in this morning." He grabbed his coat off the back of his chair and pulled it on.

"Aren't you going to clean that up?" Lauren asked, eyeing the pile of brown crumbs sitting on the carpet near the leg of his chair.

"Naw. The roaches will get it all." Reese winked at Lauren as he headed for the door. "Hit the light. You know they like it better when it's dark."

Outside on the street, Reese hopped in the back passenger seat of the Explorer, leaving Lauren acutely aware of his presence by jamming his knees into the back of her seat. "I know you got some long-ass legs, but could you move the seat forward, please?"

Fumbling around for the lever, she inched the seat up to give him room. If Nolan thought anything was strange about Reese and Lauren's relationship, he kept it to himself as he drove the three of them over to the Chippewa Street coffee shop.

"I knew you'd come crawling back to me," Reese said from the backseat. "I just didn't think it'd be so soon, partner."

"Is this the part where you say, 'I told you so'?" she asked, looking at him in the rearview mirror.

"Oh no." Reese waved her off, smiling. "That part comes much later."

17

The members of the task force spent the next day putting their office cubicles together and dragging in various equipment and gear from their home departments, including the discarded filing cabinet that Lauren and Nolan wedged in her cubicle's corner. In the corridor Lauren could hear technicians installing a fax/copier/printer combo that was ten years younger than the newest model at Buffalo Police headquarters.

Their expedition back to the coffee shop turned up nothing except three cups of fresh coffee and a discarded *Buffalo News* off one of the empty chairs. The Hot Spot across the street was closed, a handwritten sign on the door telling customers it would reopen at five. They'd gone back to headquarters, dropped Reese off, and called it a day.

Now Nolan was sitting across from her, a take-out cup of coffee in hand, ready to dive into the two cases that had been literally dumped into his jurisdiction. As Lauren turned on her departmental iPad, her cell phone buzzed on her desk. She picked it up and looked at the number on the screen.

It was her neighbor Dayla.

"I have to take this," she told Nolan, hitting the accept button. "Hello?"

Nolan flipped back and forth between Amber Anderson's crime scene photos and Brianna McIntyre's. Engrossed in the obvious similarities of the two dump jobs, he didn't notice the color rising in Lauren's cheeks.

"Thanks for calling. No—don't be upset." Lauren's voice had taken a hard, flat tone that had Nolan raising his head. "It's nothing. I'll handle it."

Getting up from her desk without a word to Nolan, Lauren stormed into the hall. She paused for just a second to determine where the sound of male bantering was coming from and threw the door to the conference room open on Perez, Bates, and Kencil sitting at the long table drinking coffee. Or in Cam Bates's case, dipping chewing tobacco and drinking coffee simultaneously.

"You interrogated my friends?"

"Whoa." Bates put his hands up in an effort to either calm her or protect himself. "We *questioned* a few of your neighbors. Except for that Dana lady, you don't seem to have any real friends."

"Dayla," she corrected, the anger in her voice spiking. "How is this acceptable? That these two are harassing people I know," she demanded of Kencil, "and insinuating that I'm a murder suspect?"

"I'm not insinuating anything," Bates replied, spitting a wad of chew into his plastic cup. "I said flat out you *are* a suspect."

"Bates and Perez told me what they were doing. I figured if they got it out of their systems right off the bat, they could move on to more viable suspects," Kencil said, as if that was the most logical explanation in the world. Sitting up straighter, he smoothed his yellow tie over his pot belly, a ceramic mug of coffee steaming on the table in front of him. Lauren realized if she had been looking for Kencil to really rein those two birds in, she was going to be left sorely disappointed.

Nolan came up behind Lauren, but she made no notice of it. She was focusing her anger on Perez and Bates. "I'm telling you both right now. Stop harassing people I know. Stop questioning them, stop contacting them, stop looking for them."

"And if we don't?" Perez asked. Not waiting for an answer, he turned to Bates. "Because I still have a lot of questions."

"Me too. Lincoln Lewis told us she'd flip out, but it's all good now," Bates said to Perez. "None of the people we talked to knew much anyway."

"Oh, you're getting information from Lincoln Lewis now?" Her hands balled into fists at her side.

"Lewis would love to have us figure out what your deal is," Bates retorted. He tipped his chair back and threaded his hands behind his head with a smarmy grin on his face. He had a brown piece of chewing tobacco stuck on his bottom lip that Lauren wanted to slap off his face.

"You're about to find out what my deal is, Bates—"

"That's enough," Kencil warned, stopping her in mid-threat. "It's over. Lauren, they won't be bothering any of your people again."

"How can a task force function when two of the officers involved are investigating one of the others?" she asked him, palms down on the table, leaning in toward Kencil. "It's the most ridiculous thing I've ever heard of."

"I'll make sure they've moved on to other leads now that this line of inquiry has yielded nothing. Isn't that right, gentlemen? You've wasted enough time chasing her ghosts."

Bates gave an exaggerated shrug. "Sure, boss. Whatever." Perez just nodded along, sipping his coffee.

Turning on her heel, Lauren brushed past Nolan and exited the room. Nolan followed her out into the hall. "Lauren," he called, stopping her before she hit the door to the outside.

"Yeah?" It came out sharper than she meant.

"Wait for me." He crossed the hall and began to follow her into the parking lot.

Lauren turned and walked to her SUV. She got in and drove away without looking back.

18

"I'm glad you agreed to meet me, especially after that scene I caused yesterday at the task force office," Lauren said loudly, to be heard over the traffic. She had parked the beat-up Chevy she'd checked out from the department's motor pool behind Nolan's shiny new Explorer on the shoulder of the thruway. Cars flew by, whipping her hair around her face with every pass.

"You didn't cause that scene. Bates and Perez need to focus on the actual investigation and not you."

"Thanks for sticking with me on that and for this," she said, motioning around the desolate stretch of road. She stood on the matted brown grass along the side of the 90 West, facing Nolan.

"It was nice not to have to get up an hour early," he admitted as he walked toward her, meeting her near the rough patch that passed for a path into the tree line. The cars racing by ruffled his short brown hair as well, leaving it tousled and mussed. He didn't try to fix it. "And

I have to say, the atmosphere in that office is stifling to a guy like me. I need the woods and the water and the country air."

Lauren looked down one end of the thruway and back up the other, getting her bearings. She herself had traveled the 90 West dozens, if not hundreds, of times. That particular section, just past the Barcelona lighthouse, really didn't take you into a populated area until you crossed the border into Pennsylvania and got close to Erie, about thirty miles south. It was also just far enough away from Lake Erie to avoid any of the beach communities that lined the shore.

"I wanted to try to travel the route from the coffee shop to here, see what I passed. What the killer passed." She kicked a stone down the slight incline from the road into some scraggy bushes. "I don't believe he brought Brianna right here from the coffee house. I think he took her to another location first, killed her, and then drove her body out here and dumped it."

"It'd be hard," Nolan said, gazing off down the path as if trying to picture the logistics of it, "to get a body, even a woman the size of Brianna, out of a car and all the way through the woods to the dump site alone."

"Unless he came prepared." Lauren stepped down off the shoulder onto the path, following Nolan's lead. "If he waited until he had everything he needed. A dolly, maybe? I don't know, a fucking little red wagon would do the trick. If he had a secondary location after the coffee shop, he had all the time in the world to get rid of the evidence." She hated referring to Brianna's body as evidence. It seemed so cold and clinical.

"We're looking at three scenes then, right? The coffee shop, this unknown place, and here."

Lauren stepped carefully along the rocky path. Her city-issue boots, which served her so well in her normal urban environment, were clunky and heavy out here. She looked at Nolan's footwear as he made his way deeper into the woods: well-worn black hikers.

"It would make sense. Take her to the other location. Do whatever it was he did, then wait for the right moment to bring here out to the clearing. This is a busy road right now, but at three in the morning on a weeknight, all you'd have is a few passing truckers who wouldn't be bothered if they saw a car parked off on the shoulder."

They picked their way through the trees, following the red flags taped to the trees left behind by the state police to mark the way to the crime scene. "You think he was that careful with the first girl? Amber Anderson?"

Lauren stepped over a large rock covered in brownish-gray moss. "No. I think he panicked and got lucky. And he thought, if it worked the first time, why wouldn't it work again?"

Nolan held back a thin branch so Lauren could pass. Letting it snap back in place roused two birds that launched themselves from the highest of the boughs. "We installed motion-sensitive deer cameras all around here, in case whoever dumped Brianna decided to come back and relive the moment."

Smart, Lauren thought. *That's what I would do.* "We're on camera now?"

Nolan pointed to a tree ahead of them. "Can you see that? On the trunk? It's painted in camouflage. Very hard to see at night. We have the flashes set to black infrared, so there's no flash when it takes a picture. It only produces black-and-white photos at night, but the quality is good."

"Have you caught anything on camera yet?"

"See these?" He pointed to some deep, vertical furrows in the bark of a tree. "These are rut marks. The male deer make them with their antlers during the rut season in the fall. We must have captured a hundred pictures of deer since we set up the cameras, but only one person."

"He wasn't our suspect?" Lauren stepped out into the clearing where Brianna's body was found. Once again, the nearby trickle of water filled her ears, but she couldn't see a source.

"No. It was a seventy-two-year-old man walking his dog. Turns out he lives about a mile and a half from here. He and his dog were just curious. This area is pretty quiet. There's not much out here. All those police cars must have piqued his interest."

Lauren looked around the clearing. Now that it was devoid of cops, crime scene techs, photographers, and investigators, the desolation of the place sank in: the bare trees, only a few with spring buds on them, the patches of leftover, dirty snow, the stark, cloudless spring sky. No one would come this way again for a long, long while. There was no reason to.

"The killer picked a good spot," she said, more to herself than to Nolan.

Nolan hooked his thumbs into his front pants pockets as he surveyed the scene. The clearing had a solemn vibe to it. Both Nolan and Lauren could feel the heaviness of the place engulfing them. The incredible sadness of two young lives thrown away there hung in the air like an invisible fog.

Lauren exhaled a deep breath. "Okay. I guess there's nothing else to see here."

"What were you expecting?"

She shrugged. "I don't know. Something we missed the first time, like in all the mystery movies. Where I say 'Ah-ha!' And we find that last piece of evidence that ties everything together."

"Didn't you have one of those moments in the bathroom of the Hot Spot?"

"Finding the burner phone didn't solve anything. It just confirmed what we already knew." She had hoped it would yield something, but it had been exposed to hundreds of flushings, effectively washing away any trace of evidence.

Nolan gave her a wistful smile and started back on the path toward their cars. Lauren dutifully brought up the rear.

"Seems a waste for you to just turn around and head back to Buffalo. And it's already"—he checked his watch—"almost noon. Do you want to grab something to eat?"

"Do you know a place?"

A wide smile spread across his face. "Ever been to Lily Dale?"

19

Lily Dale or the Lily Dale Assembly, as it officially calls itself, claims to be the world's largest center for Spiritualism. An hour south of the city of Buffalo and about twenty-five minutes from where Lauren and Nolan had met, it was world famous for its community of mediums. In the summers, when Lauren was a teenager, her friends would all pile into one of their junky cars and they'd drive down to Lily Dale, making a day of it. As Lauren sat behind Nolan's truck, watching him talk animatedly with the lady at the gate, the old memories came flooding back. Which she supposed was the purpose of the place.

Lily Dale is a tiny community, with beautiful Victorian homes squashed next to each other along the narrow streets. Even in the muddy spring, the houses looked inviting and bright. As they inched their way toward their destination, Lauren took note of the little wooden signs on the front walks. Either an AVAILABLE or UNAVAIL-ABLE swung from eye hooks. She knew from past visits that they usually gave you a map at the gate with all the mediums' house numbers listed. But it had been her and her high school friends' strategy to just walk around until they "got a feeling" and knocked on the door to get a reading. Except for the very last time they had come.

That last time, she'd been seventeen and her best friend Marie had convinced her to see a medium her aunt had gone to. The aunt had sworn up and down there was no way the woman could have known all the things she did and that she hadn't given her any type of clues. Marie was in love with the captain of the basketball team and desperate to know if they'd end up together. She'd also sucked their other friend Nichole into going, so the three of them made reservations ahead of time and nervously debated about what this woman was going to tell them the entire ride to Lily Dale.

"I know Luke and I are going to get married," Nichole had said from her perch in the backseat of Marie's beat-up Toyota. "We just had our eight-month anniversary and he said wherever I apply to college, he's going to apply there too."

Lauren was surprised Nichole had even come with them, she was so wrapped up in herself and Luke. "What do you think she's going to tell you?" Marie asked Lauren, who was riding shotgun.

"I don't know," she admitted. "This stuff kind of scares me. What if she tells me I'm going to die in a fiery car crash on the way home?"

"They never tell you things like that," Marie said. "My aunt said they'll just say to be careful when you drive or pay attention to the road. They never tell you really bad stuff."

They paid their gate admission and pulled over to check the map the lady had given them, looking for the woman's street. "Here it is." Marie's finger tapped the page. "Susan Stubnicki. She's supposed to be one of the best."

"For seventy-five dollars a half hour," Lauren said, "she better be." That was her entire babysitting haul for the month.

They cruised down the street and made the left onto an even narrower road. Marie pulled alongside a purple and pink Victorian two-story gingerbread cottage. The sign was turned to UNAVAILABLE. Marie parked on the road and they stepped out into the gorgeous summer twilight. A symphony of crickets were already chirping as they made their way up the stone path to the woman's door. All along the street people were strolling, enjoying the evening, nodding to them knowingly as they waited on the front porch for the medium to open the door.

"Come in, ladies! Come in." A middle-aged woman with flaming red hair and about a hundred jangling bangle bracelets on each arm held the screen door open for them. "I'm Susan Stubnicki. You can call me Sue."

"I'm Marie, this is Lauren, and that's Nichole." Marie pointed them all out in turn as they stood shoulder to shoulder awkwardly in the medium's hallway.

Lauren was the tallest of the three of them by far, all legs and freckles and blond hair. She immediately attracted the attention of the medium. "I want to do you last," she told her. "There's something very special about your aura."

"What about my aura?" Marie pressed as Sue led them into her home, which was much more normal than any of the other houses they had visited when they had come before. No dream catchers, no hanging crystals, no tie-dyed wall hanging. Just an ordinary living room with a long couch and a matching chair that faced a television set. On the floor, under the coffee table was a huge brown dog, fast asleep on a braided rug.

The woman regarded Marie for a moment and then said, "You're surrounded by positive energy. Which means you attract positive energy. But you have to be careful not to let toxic people into your life."

Marie was ecstatic. "I am a positive person! Ask my friends!"

"Why don't I take you first?" she suggested, slipping her arm around her back and guiding her towards a hallway off the living room.

"Okay. Bye guys." Marie was practically bubbling over with excitement.

"You ladies have a seat on the sofa. We'll be out in a jiff," Susan called over her shoulder as they disappeared into the house.

"So what do we do while we're waiting?" Nichole whispered as she and Lauren planted themselves on the couch.

Lauren picked up a battered copy of *Better Homes and Gardens* off the table and rifled through it. Underneath the table the dog snorted and rolled over. "I don't know. Try to feel the spirit vibes."

"Funny. You're just being bitchy because you don't believe in this stuff."

"It's not that I don't believe." Lauren threw the magazine back down. "It's just I want some proof. The last time we came, the guy was so vague, he could have been talking to anybody."

"Just be open to the experience." Nichole reached down to pet the dog. "Don't take all the fun out of it."

Lauren put on a smiley face and waited for Marie to come out. When she emerged from the hallway, Nichole almost pounced on her. "What'd she say? What'd she say?"

"That you're next," Marie jerked a thumb back toward where she came from. "Go on, she's waiting."

Nichole scurried off.

"So what *did* she say?" Lauren asked.

Marie shrugged. "Nothing earth-shattering. That I'm going to go to college. I'm going to get married and have at least two kids. She sees me walking and walking in the near future, that maybe I'll get a waitressing job soon. It was okay. I just thought she'd tell me more."

"Married? Kids? Isn't that a lot?"

"I guess I just thought she'd tell me something more exciting."

Nichole came out after less than fifteen minutes, tears running down her face. "She's wrong," she huffed, Kleenex stuffed under her nose. "There's no way me and Luke are breaking up. I want to go home. Now."

"We can't go," Marie told her. "Lauren didn't get a reading yet."

"That's okay. I'm good." Lauren started to gather her things, relieved that she was keeping her babysitting money.

"But we made an appointment," Marie said. "She'll be pissed."

"No, it's all right." Sue was in the door of the hallway. "Take your friend home. She needs to think about some things."

"What about Lauren?" Marie asked.

Sue didn't answer for a second, then gave a small smile. "Lauren's going to be just fine. Just fine. You girls go ahead. Spend Lauren's money on some comfort ice cream."

Just as she was about to walk out the front door, Sue called, "Lauren?" She half turned.

"Believe in yourself. Even when you feel like no one else does."

Believe in yourself. What a bunch of bullshit, Lauren had thought at the time. Susan Stubnicki might as well have handed her a poster with a kitten dangling from a branch that said *Hang in there!*

And that was the last time she'd ever been to Lily Dale.

Now almost twenty-three years later, a lady was waving them both through the main gate. Lauren knew there was a gate fee in the summertime when the "season" was in full swing. She didn't know if it was free in the off season or if the lady knew Nolan and just let them in.

They both rounded a corner and parked in front of a large ginger-bread trimmed house, with an upper and lower porch, painted white with bright green and pink trim. A sign on the door proclaimed it the LAKE HOUSE RESTAURANT AND INN in gold letters. Behind the Inn, Cassadaga Lake sparkled, even with the gloomy weather.

Nolan walked up the front steps and waited for her on the porch. "I love this place. It just opened last year. The owners decided to put a year-round restaurant in their inn. Henry makes the best coffee in Chautauqua County and their desserts are amazing."

A line of multicolored rockers tipped back and forth in the breeze as Lauren mounted the steps to meet up with him. "It's beautiful," she commented, taking a second to look around at the quirky details. The overhang of the roof was decorated with intricate scroll-sawn woodwork. A gold cherub sat on the corner of an oversized, empty cement flower pot in the corner, head resting on his fist, staring out over the lake. *Still too early in the year to plant flowers*, she thought. *One morning frost and they'd be dead.*

"You come here a lot?" she asked, as he held the door open for her. Stepping through, her shoulder brushed his hand.

"Tim Hortons and McDonald's every day can wreak havoc on your stomach. You must know some funky little spots to eat in the city."

"Not as funky as this," she said, marveling at the leaded glass angels inset in the upper panes of the windows that lined the dining area immediately behind the reception desk where you first walked in.

A man in his late sixties with wispy white hair greeted them at the desk. "Jack! Good to see you." He reached out and clasped Nolan's hand between his. "Your favorite table just happens to be open."

All the tables were open. "Looks like we just beat the rush," Nolan joked.

"You should have been here yesterday at noon. We had a bus trip from Pittsburgh stop by. Twenty-two people: all tired, hot, and hungry at once. I tell you, when it rains, it pours."

Grabbing two menus from a stack on the desk, Henry led them over to the farthest table, sitting against the wall under one of the impressive windows with a spectacular view of the lake. Due to its almost-corner position, it was one of the only two-seat tables in the dining room. "I didn't get your name, miss," he said, pulling her wooden chair out for her.

"I'm Lauren. It's nice to meet you. I'm working with Nolan—I mean, Jack," she corrected at the last second.

"Good, good. It's wonderful to make your acquaintance. Jack doesn't come in as much in the off season. The wind off the lake can be treacherous."

"Lauren lives in Buffalo," Jack offered, opening his menu. "She knows a thing or two about wind off a lake."

"Then you absolutely understand what I'm talking about." Henry gazed out over the water, squinting at the ominous clouds. "The forecasters are calling for snow in the next two weeks. Just once I'd like for that fat little groundhog to predict an early spring and be right. Anyway, Beth will be over to take your orders shortly. And I'll start you off with your usual coffee. And you, miss?"

"I'd love a coffee too, please. Black."

"Coming right up." He tapped the back of Nolan's chair and disappeared behind two double doors Lauren assumed led into the kitchen.

"Beth is Henry's wife. She's also one of the registered mediums in the community."

All the mediums that gave readings in Lily Dale had to be registered. From what Lauren knew, it was a lengthy and difficult vetting process to ensure that scam artists and quacks didn't take up residence in the community. That being said, not once did any of the mediums she had visited as a teenager tell her she'd be married with two kids by the time she was twenty. She really could have used a heads-up on that one.

Beth entered the dining room from the same double doors, carrying two glasses of water. "Jack, it's so good to see you." She put a glass in front of each of them. Like Henry, she was in her late sixties, but her hair was frosted a beautiful honey color and twisted into a knot at the back of her head. She wore a loose-fitting pink dress made of some gauzy, flowy material. Around her neck she wore a large silver cross and a huge amethyst crystal on the same black cord. The purple stone glinted, even in the dim light.

"Hey, Beth. I want you to meet my friend, Lauren. Lauren, this is Beth."

Lauren accepted a warm, soft handshake from Beth, who smiled at her knowingly. "Do I detect a skeptic in my midst?" she asked, not unkindly.

"I guess you would know that, wouldn't you?" Lauren questioned, meaning it as joke, then realized how nasty it sounded.

She laughed out loud. "No, honey. It doesn't work that way. I can't read minds, see the future, or give you the lotto numbers any more than you can. But I can tell when someone shakes my hand like they don't want me to touch them too much."

Lauren's face flushed. "I'm sorry. I didn't mean to insult you."

Beth waved her off. "You'd have to try a lot harder than that to insult me. It's part of the job, a lot like being a female cop, I'd imagine. Always trying to get over the initial skepticism."

Lauren wanted to ask if Henry had told her she was working with Nolan, or if she had heard them talking, or if she could see the bulge of her gun under her jacket, but she clamped her mouth shut and smiled back at her.

"Lauren's had a rough year," Nolan offered. "I don't think I'd want my fortune read either."

Beth gave Nolan a playful side eye. "Here comes your coffee." She stepped aside so Henry could put the metal tray on their table and unload the cups, creamer, sugar, and spoons. Lauren took a tan earthenware mug and held it between her hands to warm them up. She hadn't realized they were so cold until she touched Beth's.

"You want to try the special?" Nolan asked Lauren, looking at her over the top of the menu. "The ham and swiss on their pretzel bread is amazing."

"Sure." Lauren managed a smile, a real smile, as she passed her menu back to Beth.

"Thanks, dolly." She gathered Nolan's menu as well, then leaned in and whispered in Lauren's ear, "The man you've been waiting for feels exactly the same way you do. Don't blow it."

"What?" Nolan asked at the dumbfounded look on Lauren's face as Beth walked away. "What did she tell you?"

Lauren took a sip of her coffee. It was a little too hot and burned her tongue. "Actually, it was nothing I didn't already suspect."

20

Lauren and her neighbor Dayla sat at her kitchen table the next afternoon, where Lauren first apologized about the intrusion from her fellow task force members, then told her the story of her and Nolan's lunch at Lily Dale. Dayla listened with rapt attention, sipping green tea and nodding along. Cam Bates had been right when he said her neighbor was her only friend. Non-police friend, anyway. Lauren had lost most of her friends when she got pregnant and married right out of high school. She had been changing diapers while everyone else was going to frat parties and sorority mixers. She wouldn't trade her daughters for anything in the world, but she had paid the price in the friend department. However, having the dynamic force that was Dayla as a friend seemed to fill any immediate voids in Lauren's life.

Today, Dayla's dark-brown hair was twisted in crazy curls, framing her striking ebony face. Tomorrow it'd look totally different. Dayla wasn't one to stick with anything too long, except maybe her plastic surgeon husband. She was in a tea-sipping frenzy over the news of Jack Nolan. "Do you like him?" she asked.

"He's a good guy. Never been married. He has one sixteen-year-old son with an ex-girlfriend who lives in Colorado. He spends a month out there with him every summer." She thought about it for a second, then added, "He's a very good investigator."

"Yeah, that's all great. But do you *like* him?" Dayla wasn't about to be thrown off her love trail by Lauren's Jedi mind tricks.

"He's handsome. And nice. Maybe too nice for me." Lauren's eyes wandered out the back window, over her muddy yard. "I don't know," she hedged, then added, "I mean, look at me. I'm not exactly super-model material right now."

"You have let yourself go," Dayla agreed. She didn't leave the house until she was fully made up and completely accessorized, even to get the morning newspaper. "But it's not like you got stabbed and almost died a couple months ago." She snapped her fingers. "Oh yeah, that's right, you did."

Lauren appreciated Dayla's encouragement but had to confess, "I never worried about attracting a man before, as narcissistic as that sounds. Now I can't believe any guy would even take a second look at me, let alone want to date me."

"It's a well-known truism that bitchy women always attract men." Dayla added skim milk to her tea, stirring it with one of Lauren's good silver spoons. "Sure, guys say they like the sweet types, but it's always the raging harpies that get the best-looking men."

Lauren added some sugar from the bowl on her table into her coffee. She usually took it black, but she had a craving for something sweet. "So now I'm a bitchy, hideous beast. Thank you."

"Don't get your panties all in a bunch." Dayla wrapped a stray curl around her finger before letting it spring back into place. "All I'm saying is that attraction is more about attitude than looks. Before I met my husband, I beat out a lot of better-looking women because I knew I was someone worth knowing."

"Somehow, I don't think that's a hard and fast rule."

"Hard and fast is another way to play it entirely," she laughed, snorting on her green tea. "What does Reese think of this guy?"

"He likes him, I think. It's not like I sat him down and asked him for a critique."

Dayla's brown eyes sparkled over the top of her teacup. "Maybe you should."

"We're going on a class field trip, children," Kencil said, standing in front of the Smart Board at the Monday morning task force meeting. "Dr. Inez at the morgue has the preliminary results on the body and wants to go over them with us."

"Oh good," Bates said. "We'll get to walk around all day smelling like a corpse."

"That's an improvement for some of us," Perez joked.

Kencil ignored the banter. "The good doctor wants us there at noon. I suggest eating lunch after the meeting. Apparently, Buffalo's Underwater Recovery Team pulled a particularly bloated body from the lake last night and the smell is a little overwhelming."

"Going to autopsies always makes me hungry," Bates said. Lauren tried to imagine how many autopsies Bates had actually attended, working for a town with a virtually nonexistent murder rate. When Bates noticed the strange looks on his co-workers faces he defended himself. "What? I don't know why. Perez, don't look at me like that."

The office of the county morgue was housed on the grounds of the Erie County Medical Center, in a nondescript building far from the hustle and bustle of the emergency room or surgical theaters. Most people who visited or were treated at the hospital weren't even aware that autopsies took place there on a daily basis. Some days it was multiple autopsies.

Dr. Inez had been the medical examiner for the last year, meaning Lauren had had only limited contact with him. Most of her cases were far older, so she was constantly calling the former medical examiner, who was now retired and living in Arizona, to go over his autopsy reports with her.

"You been to a lot of these?" Nolan asked in the Explorer on the way over. Lauren had offered to drive in the Buffalo unmarked car, but Nolan declined. "I'm sorry, but all your cars smell like lemon cleaner mixed with rancid Cheetos," he'd apologized. She couldn't fault him for speaking the truth, so she hopped in his ride, which was immaculately clean.

"Enough." She produced a small tin of Vicks VapoRub from her pocket and held it up. "Old-timers used to smoke cigars, but that's been outlawed. I'm no hero; I shove a little of this in each nostril. Your eyes will water at first, but it's well worth it."

"I'm glad to see you're always prepared, like a Boy Scout."

"Girl Scout," she corrected. "Besides, I'm sure they don't have our body back from the anthropologists yet. This is just to bring us up to speed with what they've figured out so far."

"Good to know," he said, easing them onto the 33 Expressway heading away from downtown.

"The whole place will still smell like dead bodies, though."

He broke into a smile. "Also good to know."

"We'll probably be in Dr. Inez's conference room, not where they perform the actual autopsies. But it still smells like dead bodies."

He got off on the Grider Street exit. "You're killing me," he laughed. Lauren liked how the edges of his mouth crinkled and the way his smile reached his eyes. And when he laughed, Nolan's shoulders shook slightly, like he laughed with his whole body.

They pulled into the morgue's lot right behind Perez and Bates, parking a few spaces away from them. Everyone waited inside their vehicles for Kencil to be done with a phone call, then emerged all at once.

We're finally a team when we're heading into the place where they slice and dice the bodies, Lauren thought. She wound her scarf around her head one more time, wrapping the bottom of her face with the soft fleece material against the wind.

Lauren and Nolan got to the outer door first, and Nolan held it for her. He let it fall shut on Perez and Bates.

The outer reception area looked like any other doctor's office, with framed prints of sunsets and mountains with motivational quotes on the bottom: *Winners never quit, and quitters never win! Reach for the stars! Hard work pays off in easy living!*

A curly-haired secretary smiled at them when they walked in. "You must be Dr. Inez's noon appointment," she said pleasantly, pushing a clipboard toward Nolan. "Please sign in, everyone. The doctor will be right with you."

They passed the clipboard around to each other, then stood awkwardly in the center of the room. There was no one else in the reception area, but none of the five of them would sit down.

"You smell that?" Lauren whispered to Nolan, then palmed him the little metal jar. "Right into your nostrils."

"How does *she* not smell that?" he asked, nodding to the reception-ist as he swiped his index finger into the Vick's.

"She's used to it."

Lauren watched Nolan surreptitiously turn his back on the rest of the task force and stick his finger up each nostril. He immediately sneezed twice in a row. "Bless you," Kencil said absently. Bates was already looking a little green around the gills. Central police services made all the recruits attend an autopsy in the police academy, but they warned each class it wasn't what they'd see that would make them sick but what they'd smell. Three guys in Lauren's class threw up. Knowing the routine, the morgue personnel had placed extra garbage cans strategically around the room. Lauren wondered how Bates had done during that first autopsy, and if he'd attended one since. She was guessing from the looks of him, his cavalier attitude from earlier was all for show.

Hungry now? Lauren wanted to ask Bates as he fidgeted by the door.

Dr. Inez appeared from a door behind the reception counter. A dark-skinned man in his mid-fifties, he was into physical fitness, to the point of obsession. Other Homicide detectives said he was always showing off pictures of himself at Iron Man competitions, marathons, and other extreme athletic events Lauren wouldn't drag herself to even if someone were paying her. Her own physical therapist had de-manded a minimal amount of physical movement from her or she wouldn't approve Lauren's return to the police department. It was all she could manage to walk briskly three times a week and she hated every second of it.

Looking jacked even under his black shirt and white lab coat, Dr. Inez walked around the front of the counter and gave them each a crushing handshake. "Welcome, welcome," he said, then motioned to another door off the reception area. "Let's head in here and go over the findings we have so far."

Lauren wondered as she followed the doctor into the conference room if he kept his dark hair slicked back because it was more aerodynamic that way.

The room itself was pretty standard, with a long rectangular table in the center and a big flat-screen TV mounted on the wall at the far end. There were no motivational pictures hung on the industrial blue walls. It was all business in here. The doctor had a laptop set up at the head of the table and packets of paperwork stacked next to it. *Nothing if not organized,* Lauren thought as she took a padded office seat, so unlike the hand-me-downs they had on loan in the task force office. Nolan grabbed the chair next to her.

When everyone had settled in, Dr. Inez took his place at the head of the table, feeling around on the laptop's touchpad, causing the screen behind him to light up with the seal of Erie County.

"I put together a PowerPoint, along with some handouts you can take with you." Inez handed the stack of papers to Kencil, who was sitting closest, and he passed them along.

"We're going to go over the crime scene photos first, which will explain some of the findings." He hit the touch pad and the words BRIANNA MCINTYRE *Case number 19-657,* popped up in black letters.

"First off, the forensic anthropologists we work with at the university employed their forensic odontologist, and we do have confirmation on her identity through her dental records. On pages six and seven of your handouts, you'll see the comparison information." The sound of flipping pages filled the room. Lauren looked at both teeth charts, with their handwritten notes trailing down the margins, pointing out various teeth and their unique characteristics. There was no doubt; that body belonged to Brianna.

"I'd like to have us all look at this first crime scene photo, so I can point a few things out." The screen changed to the body in the clearing and Inez stepped right up to it. "Here we can already see signs of animal activity"—he circled his index finger over the pelvis area, still encased in the pleather skirt—"causing the body to be pulled into two parts, as well as some scattering of the smaller bones in the left hand and forearm. There are gnaw marks on some of the bones, consistent with small carnivore activity." He tapped the pad and brought up a closeup of one of the phalanx, a pale yellowish finger bone, that showed telltale bite marks etched into it as it lay on top of a small clump of dirty snow. In the city, Lauren was used to rats getting at bodies found in abandoned houses. She had no idea what animal had done this. Squirrels? Raccoons? This was a perfect example of her urban experience coming up short at a rural crime scene.

Inez hit the pad and the next picture came up. It depicted the skeletal remains pieced together on a metal morgue table, what was left of Brianna's clothing still on her body. "Here we have the body reconstructed. Not every bone was recovered, once again, probably due to animal activity. However, we do have some interesting findings, even at first glance."

The body looked so sterile and impersonal pieced together. Like a dollar store Halloween decoration left out in the November rain.

He tapped again and a closeup of the neck and spine area appeared. "This right here"—he leaned in and pointed to what almost looked like a small broken horseshoe—"is the hyoid bone. For those of you not familiar with human anatomy, this little bone usually sits at the anterior midline of the neck. It is not attached to any other bone; it's held in place by muscles and its main function is to aid swallowing. However, it is quite common in a strangulation death for the hyoid bone to be fractured, as this one clearly is. It shows no signs of animal interference, either."

"So she was strangled to death?" Bates asked.

"Possibly." Inez flipped to the next photo, where the clothing had been removed. Brianna's rib cage was now fully exposed, as well as her pelvis. "If you'll turn to page eight, you'll see the full body diagram."

Everyone dutifully turned to page eight. "Our victim has evidence of possible circum-mortem blunt force trauma here"—he pointed to the base of the skull—"and here. At the sixth and seventh ribs."

"Circum-mortem?" Bates asked.

Mister tough guy hasn't done his homework, Lauren mused to herself. *He should know these terms inside and out if he wants to work murders.*

"It's Latin for 'around the time of death'," Inez explained patiently. "She has evidence of a skull fracture and broken ribs."

Kencil leaned forward, elbows on the table. "Best guess, doctor? What's the cause of death?"

"Impossible to say for sure due to the decomposition, but given the fracture of the hyoid bone, skull, and ribs, I'm definitely listing the manner of death as homicide. If I had to give an educated guess—and granted, a defense attorney would have a field day with this—I'd say she was struck with a blunt object, at some point she was struck again, breaking her ribs, and then strangled."

"Can you say for sure those fractures weren't caused after death?" Bates asked. Refusing to use *post-mortem*, Lauren noted.

"Detective, we can never say definitively what caused what damage, unless you have the death on video." A note of annoyance had crept into Dr. Inez's voice. "What I can give you is my educated, expert opinion, having done hundreds of autopsies, if not thousands at this point in my career."

"Can we get a better idea of the time of death, doctor?" Perez asked, trying to smooth things over. "I'm talking about months, not hours or days."

He shook his head. "If she went missing in May of last year, I'd say the condition of the body was consistent with exposure to the elements during that time period: a hot summer, then a winter freeze and thaw. But other than that, the best marker is her last known whereabouts. Time of death is notoriously hard to pin down. Unfortunately, it's not like the TV shows where the coroner pulls a magical maggot out of a torso and says, 'May the thirtieth at three o'clock.'"

The doctor clicked through some more slides, but the information they needed was already on the table. It was, in fact, Brianna, and she was murdered.

"We won't get the trace evidence reports, hair findings, or DNA evidence for some time. The university has to send those out to specialty labs. A couple of weeks, maybe."

"How much will they really be able to tell us, given the condition of the body?" Kencil asked.

Inez shrugged. "Investigators have gotten lucky in the past, but I wouldn't hold up your investigation waiting for those items."

"Thoughts?" Kencil asked the group once Inez had gone through the last slide and shut the PowerPoint off.

"Brianna was strangled and dumped in the same spot as Amber Anderson. That's a direct connection," Lauren said.

"The hyoid bone wasn't broken in the Katherine Vine case," Bates pointed out.

"But Amber Anderson's skeleton was so incomplete, her hyoid bone was never recovered," Lauren countered. "The significance is in the strangulation, not the bones themselves."

"Exactly," Bates said. "We don't know how Amber died. I mean, I believe she was the victim of a homicide, but that won't get us far proving a case against a suspect."

Lauren turned to the page that showed two sketches of a skull, front and back. Along the back a black line was traced, showing the fracture. She held it up. "If Brianna was ambushed, the suspect could be using a ligature like in Katherine Vine's case, a silk scarf, to exert control of the victim over an extended period of time. Slowly cutting off the airway and bringing them in and out of consciousness would not necessarily fracture the hyoid bone."

"I think the important thing here is that Amber and Brianna were both brought to this remote location because it worked for the killer. Neither body was discovered for an extended period of time," Perez joined in. "Katherine Vine's death was totally different. The suspect in that case, who was arrested within hours of the murder, didn't try to hide her body at all. I just don't see her connection to Amber and Brianna."

"And for all we know, Amber met the same guy online, or maybe in person somewhere and not on a dating site, who knows? Her being acquainted with David Spencer may just be a coincidence," Bates threw in. He reached inside his shirt pocket for his can of chew. Kencil narrowed his eyes, gave him a sharp head shake, and Bates let it fall back down.

"I don't think it's a coincidence," Nolan said. "I think he killed Amber Anderson, dumped her body, got away with it, then killed Katherine Vine. He left Vine in the car because there *was* no personal connection to him. I really don't think David Spencer thought they'd connect Katherine Vine to him the way they did."

"Except Joe Wheeler was a good detective and figured it out right away." Bates was looking directly at Lauren, who met his gaze unblinking. She wasn't about to back down to him. Especially not over Joe Wheeler.

"Thank you, doctor." Kecil stood and stuck out his hand, signaling the meeting was over.

I guess he doesn't want the kids to bicker in front of company, Lauren thought as she accepted another crushing shake from the doctor. She gathered up the information the doctor had handed out and headed for the door. They passed back through the reception area, nodding to the secretary, and walked out into the parking lot without talking to each other.

So much for cooperation, Lauren thought as she climbed into Nolan's truck. *And so much for coincidences.*

In Lauren's mind there was no such thing as coincidence. But there were definitely connections.

22

Lauren never went to the gym, ever. Her lack of fat had always been her number one problem, not an abundance of it. However, her physical therapist, whom she still saw once a week after work, recommended she walk to help build her strength after her stabbing. Actually, he had done more than recommend; he'd threatened to pull her clearance to go back to work if she didn't do *something* physical, and walking seemed the least intrusive activity.

Three mornings a week at six a.m. Lauren dutifully packed a water bottle, grabbed her iPhone and ear buds, put on the ratty old sweatpants Lindsey had left behind when she went to college, and drove over to Carmichael Park to walk exactly three miles. Then she came home to get ready for work. She could have walked around her gated community, but the convenience of that would have made it too easy for her to blow it off and stay in bed. She felt stupid enough marching around the park. The least she could do was spare herself the humiliation of having to wave to her nosy neighbors as they drove by on their way to work.

It was still dark at six a.m. in March. The dawn seemed to want to bow down to the winter nights as long as possible.

The forecaster on the news radio station was predicting bad weather in the coming week. Buffalonians were notoriously addicted to news about the weather: talking about it, reading about it, complaining about it. The forecaster opened the phone lines for calls and was inundated with complaints about plows, salting, and a lack of snow shovels left in the stores this time of year. *You'd think they'd carry them year-round,* Lauren mused, listening to her fellow citizens complain. The park was only a couple of minutes' drive from her neighborhood. It was so convenient, she forgot it was there most of the time, only rediscovering its usefulness when Reese started bringing Watson over for visits. She'd walk him through the park, let him sniff at the other dogs and pee on everything. It was like Disneyland for him.

She had to remind Reese to try to bring Watson over that weekend.

Lauren pulled on a pair of fleece-lined gloves as she climbed out of her Ford in the parking lot. The air was so cold she could see her breath in white puffs. *Stupid knife wound to the lung,* she thought as she crossed the lot to the paths. *If Vince Schultz hadn't stabbed me, I'd still be in bed right now.*

She hated the main jogging path, which seemed clogged with people most of the time. You spent more time dodging out of the way of runners than actually walking. Lauren's usual routine consisted of cutting down one of the lesser traveled paths, popping in her earbuds, and trying to get her three miles in as fast as she could manage.

As she started to pick up steam, she checked the pedometer on her iPhone. She had point eight miles under her belt. She wanted to turn around and get back in her car, but she knew she needed the exercise, and as much as she hated to admit it, she was getting stronger. Perhaps even stronger than she'd been before the stabbing, despite the weight loss and how she looked. Working cold cases didn't usually put much physical strain on detectives. She'd certainly let herself slack off in the fitness arena since her days in a uniform.

Lauren picked up her pace, exhaling clouds of steam as she pumped her arms in the brisk morning air.

She first became aware of someone behind her through her sixth sense, that feeling that she wasn't alone. She stopped on the asphalt, pulled an earbud out, and turned around in a full circle, scanning the trees that lined the path. Peeling off her gloves, she stuffed them into her jacket pocket. Now that she'd been walking, she was warmed up. *Maybe that's why I'm on high alert,* she thought. *My heart rate is above flatline.*

She waited almost a full minute before plugging the earbud back in and starting mile two.

She walked another two hundred yards but could not shake the feeling that someone was behind her. She stopped again, took both earbuds out, and draped them over her shoulders. "Hello?" she called, walking backwards, facing the way she'd just come. "Is someone there?"

She hadn't expected an answer. The path was clear and empty as far back as she could see. She turned around, leaving the earbuds out, and started to walk.

The attack came ambush-style from the side.

Someone slammed her face forward into the grass onto the side of the jogging path. She tried to thrust her hands out to break her fall, but her arms were pinned to her sides.

She hit the ground full force, knocking the wind out of her. The arms around her middle released her and she felt something slip over her head, around her neck, then jerked tight.

Lauren grabbed at it with both hands, barely managing to get the first two fingers of her left hand under the line as she gasped for air.

A body was crushing her down, pinning her, as the rope pulled tighter.

Lauren bucked with her legs, throwing her attacker off center just enough to get her whole left hand under the rope. She pulled it forward, fibers cutting into her palm.

"I—am—not—" she managed to huff out between her clenched teeth, as she yanked on the rope with all her strength, "—the one—to fuck with!"

"Hey!" a far away voice yelled.

She twisted her whole body, the way they'd taught her in the police academy, and kicked up and out. She felt her legs connect with another person, even as stars swam in front of her eyes.

As quick as the attacker had struck, he was gone.

Lauren coughed into the matted brown grass, trying to catch her breath. She rolled over onto her back, panting and blinking at the breaking sunlight through the trees.

"Are you okay, lady?" A young Hispanic kid stood over her, camouflaged backpack slung over one shoulder, a cell phone in his hand. "I called 911 already."

She tried to sit up slowly, her right hand gingerly touching her throat. It hurt to swallow. Her left palm had an ugly red line burned across it. "Did you see him?" she asked. "Do you know what he looks like?"

The kid shook his head. "I was way down there." He pointed farther along the path. "Cutting through on my way to work. That guy was choking the shit out of you." He knelt down next to her. Her eyes focused on him. He was maybe eighteen or nineteen and smaller than she was. "I yelled at him, and then you did that twisty thing."

"Thank you," she managed, still rubbing her neck.

He reached over her, then stuck a piece of white nylon rope under her nose. "He was choking you with this."

So much for an uncontaminated scene, she thought, then asked, "Was he wearing gloves like you?"

He looked down at the green and black knitted gloves he had on. "I think so. And a hat. And glasses. I think."

She put her hand on his shoulder and he took ahold of her elbow, helping her to her feet. In the distance, the faint sound of a siren began creeping up from the south. "Thanks again," Lauren told him, trying to steady herself. Her iPhone was lying with her knotted earbuds in a pile in the grass. He bent down and picked them up for her.

"You didn't get a good look at him then," she stated more than asked.

"It's still kinda dark," he said with a slightly lilting accent. "All I know is he was wearing all black and he was taller than you. And you're pretty tall, for a lady."

23

Lauren had the first officers on the scene keep it quiet that it was a cop who was the victim. The first thing she did was have them call their supervisor, Lieutenant Duluth, to the scene and cancel the ambulance. "Are you sure you don't want to get checked out?" Duluth asked as she sat next to him in his patrol car.

She gingerly touched her neck with the tips of her fingers. "I'm all right. It's my hand that hurts most, but what are they going to do? Put a bandage on it? I can do that back at the district house."

Duluth was young for a supervisor. Lauren figured him to be in his late twenties. He was one of those quiet guys who never went to parties and took everything very seriously. "You want to use your maiden name for the report. That's what my guys told me."

She nodded. "The press has access to our incident reports. With all the attention on the task force, I don't want them focusing on me."

"I'll have them do that, but you still have to come to the district and give Grace Harvey a statement. If we have some crazy guy attacking women in the park, we have to get it out there, whether you're the victim or not. And I called the commissioner's office and left a message for her. I'm sure she's going to want to know about this."

She'd deal with Commissioner Bennett later. She just wanted to get the district stuff out of the way. Grace Harvey, or Harvey as she liked to be called, was one of the older Delta District detectives. She and Lauren were well acquainted, and she'd know how to handle the situation once Lauren explained things to her.

All around them, joggers and moms with strollers stood just outside the crime scene tape, trying to figure out what was going on. The sun had come up, but the overcast sky filtered out anything resembling sunshine. Three police cars blocking one of the jogging paths was going to attract attention, even if it was one of the lesser-used paths.

She opened and closed her hand, wincing at the sting. *That's going to leave a mark,* she thought, looking down at the crimson rope burn across her palm.

Lauren sat in the lieutenant's car and waited for Evidence and Photography to come out. She watched them take the rope and bag it, after Andy Knowles took pictures of it.

She'd always thought being the police photographer was the best job in the department. You came in, snapped some pictures, and left. You didn't have to touch anything, didn't have to figure anything out. Andy Knowles had been on the job for years, so he knew exactly what to photograph as soon as someone explained the scene to him. Lauren watched as he bent down, giant camera to his eye, zooming in to get a better look at something on the ground. He took some photos of boot prints that were most likely the attacker's.

Other than that, there wasn't much in the way of physical evidence for the techs to collect. The lab would try to get something off the rope, but Lauren was doubtful. If David had used gloves, the only DNA the lab was going to get was Lauren's and possibly some from the guy who helped her after he picked it up and dropped it back onto the ground.

The poor kid had to go down to the district station house to give a statement too. Thankfully, Harvey took her first. She recounted everything she could remember, and Harvey took it down, asking clarifying questions at the end, exactly the way Lauren used to do in her victim interviews. Working Cold Case homicides, she never did those anymore, just witness and suspect statements. She'd forgotten how exacting a victim's statement could be. And, if you got stuck with a shitty detective, how painful it could be as well.

When she got to the part about the suspect, Lauren held back, describing the attacker as best she could and not like David Spencer specifically. Though she didn't believe it for a second, there was always the outside chance that it was a random attack. Still, the height and weight and build were a match to David.

Cops stuck their heads in the detective office with bullshit questions for Harvey. Lauren knew they'd already heard about what happened through the departmental grapevine and just wanted to see what had happened to the infamous Detective Riley now. She could hear the chatter in the breakroom: *She got strangled this time; what else is going to happen to that broad?* Cops could be brutal to each other.

Lauren went to the bathroom to try to clean up after her interview was done. Her hair, which had mostly come loose from its ponytail, hung limply around her face. She used her fingers to comb it back and twisted the black band into place at the base of her neck. She had a deep scratch on her left cheek she hadn't noticed when she checked herself out in Lieutenant Duluth's rear-view mirror.

The red line around her throat was faint but visible. Andy had taken pictures of both her neck and her hand at the scene. Her hand hurt like hell, but Harvey had managed to find a first-aid kit and put some antibiotic cream on it. "Leave it open," Harvey had told her. "Don't bandage it up, and keep it clean. It'll heal faster."

Lauren definitely had doubts about her medical advice, but she went along with it because she just wanted to get back to the task force office as soon as possible.

The kid who had helped her was sitting on a bench in the hallway when she came out of the bathroom. When she stopped to thank him again, he told her that Harvey had to give him a note to take to work stating he'd been late due to official police business. He was convinced he was going to get fired. "I've been late twice this week," he told Lauren. "That's why I was cutting through the park in the first place."

Lauren fished her business card out of her pocket with her good hand and gave it to him. "If he gives you any problems, have him call me."

The kid tucked the card away and smiled at her. "Thanks, lady."

Harvey had arranged for one of the patrol officers to take her back to her car. As she was being driven back over to the park, she thought about what just happened to her.

David Spencer hadn't meant to kill her; this she knew. Just like she had gone to a place he felt safe and in control, so had he. Leaving the white rope was a message. Katherine Vine had been strangled with a white silk scarf. He was warning her to back off.

Which meant she was getting close.

24

"**Y**ou expect us to believe that you just happened to get jumped in the park by some mystery assailant?" Cam Bates asked, his voice full of contempt and disbelief.

Lauren's jaw clenched. "Are you saying I made this up?" She held her palm out, an inch from Bates's nose so he could take a good look. "Did I make this up too? What about this?" She pointed to the faint ring around her neck.

She had called Kencil from the district house to let him know what was going on and he had delayed the morning briefing until she got back to the office. Now they were all clustered in the conference room, where Bates and Perez were dissecting her story, looking for gaps.

"Isn't it more likely you were the victim of a random mugging?" Perez asked. "You said yourself you've been walking that out-of-the-way path for three months now."

Three hours after being ambushed, Lauren thought, *I'm standing in the task force office, trying to convince my so-called co-workers something significant actually happened to me. Un-fucking-believable.*

"Which is further proof that David Spencer is tracking my movements."

Bates snorted aloud while shaking his head. "I can't work with this woman. She's delusional."

Lauren lunged forward and grabbed the front of Bates's green polo shirt across the table with both hands. The fabric of the shirt bunched up in her fists. She pulled herself so close she could see his crooked lower teeth, pushed back in a jumbled mess from years of chewing tobacco. "You smart ass motherfu—"

Nolan and Perez jumped in and pulled them apart while Kencil hollered from the head of the table, "Both of you are way out of line!"

Nolan had Lauren around the waist as he dragged her toward the white board. Perez was practically sitting on Bates to keep him down.

"You want to put your hands on me, I'm warning you—I hit back," Bates spat out, thrashing against Perez.

"Good," Lauren snarled as she wrestled to get out from under Nolan's grasp. "At least then it's almost a fair fight."

"Enough!" Kencil thundered, silencing everyone in the room. "We're all supposed to be professionals here. Lauren, there is no doubt you were attacked. And Cam, it doesn't matter who she thinks did it. We can't deny it could be related to the cases we're working on." He waved his index finger between the two of them. "Keep your hands and your opinions of each other to yourselves. This is beyond unacceptable."

Lauren relaxed, and Nolan loosened his grip.

"I'm cool. I'm all right," Bates told Perez. Perez let him go and Bates immediately straightened out his shirt while mumbling under his breath.

"Are we good, kids?" Kencil looked around at his detectives, eyebrow arched. "I hope you both got that shit out of your systems because we all have work to do."

"You want to get out of here?" Nolan asked, nodding towards the exit. Bates was still fuming across the room, Perez standing by his side like a sentinel.

"Yeah," she said, glaring at the Garden Valley detective. She half wished Bates would come at her. She might get the worst of it, but she'd get a few good shots in. He was definitely not an all-talk guy. Unless she really did want to brawl for the second time that day, she was done at the task force office for now.

Her phone buzzed in her pocket. She slipped it out and glanced at the screen. It was a text message from Reese. It read: WHAT THE HELL HAPPENED TO YOU???

She should have known getting jumped would get back to Reese sooner rather than later. Not bothering to answer his all-caps question, she tucked her phone away. This was not the time to explain what happened.

"It's nice to see she found another admirer. Always running after her, aren't you, Nolan?" Bates called as Lauren and Nolan were walking out the door. "I guess there's no accounting for taste in some guys."

Nolan stopped dead in front of Lauren, causing her to almost run into him, his hand on the door knob. "Careful," he warned Bates in a low voice without turning around. "I hit back too. Hard."

He held the door for her and they left the office together, crossed the hallway, and went out into the parking lot.

Safe from the scrutiny of Cam Bates and Manny Perez, Lauren let herself fall against the building and covered her face with her hands. All the fear and rage and panic of the day melted into a tired kind of despair. The adrenaline rush had faded into a crash. *I will not cry*, she told herself. *I will not cry.*

Nolan kept his distance for a minute, watching as she tried to control her breathing, attempting to calm herself down. She appreciated that. "You don't have to chase after me," she told him, dropping her hands to her thighs and tipping her head back, eyes closed. Her throat burned when she swallowed.

"I know." He must have stepped closer, because he sounded like he was right next to her. "But isn't that what partners are supposed to do? Have each other's backs?"

I already have a partner, she almost said, but she bit back the words. She could feel him close to her, sense him without opening her eyes. She thought maybe if she did open them, he'd be right in front of her, faces just inches away. And then what would happen?

She drew in a deep stuttering breath but kept her eyes closed tight. "I'm glad you have my back."

For Lauren, it felt like the truth.

25

Lauren ignored Reese's phone calls until the next morning. It was a shitty thing to do, but she knew exactly what he was going to say to her: that it was a mistake to be on the task force, that she was obsessed with David Spencer, that she was in no condition to work without him by her side to keep her out of trouble.

He was right, of course, but she still didn't want to hear it until her throat felt better and she could grip a bottle of shampoo in her hand. So she put her cell phone down on her bathroom sink and tried to scrub herself raw.

She finally answered his call as she was toweling off her hair.

"Are you kidding me?" He didn't wait for her to say hello. "I hear my partner got attacked and she won't even pick up the phone and return my texts?" he demanded.

"I'm sorry. Look, can you meet me for coffee? It's a long story and I'm in serious need of caffeine."

He paused for a moment, like he was thinking it over. "What about the task force office?"

"They can wait."

"What about Nolan?"

"He can wait too."

Reese agreed to meet her at a little breakfast place on Niagara Street called the Rooster. It was after nine in the morning on a weekday, so most of the breakfast crowd had already come and gone. The few stragglers sat at the long counter, sipping coffee and talking neighborhood gossip. No one even looked up when Lauren walked in, setting off the jingling of bells tied to the door. Behind the counter the Asian waitress and her father, the cook, argued over something on the menu. The whole family worked together in the restaurant and they were notoriously good to police officers.

Reese waved her over to a booth in the back where he already had two coffees laid out in front of him.

"Reese, let me explain—"

"Shhhhhh, stop," he shushed, silencing her. "No. First off, are you okay?" He grabbed her hand and examined her palm before she pulled it away. She tucked it under her thigh like a little kid who didn't want her mommy to see she'd been into the nail polish again.

"I'm fine. He got scared off by a kid walking through the park." She shook out a packet of sugar with her free hand before tearing it open and dumping the contents in her cup. Today, she needed the sugar boost.

"And secondly, why the hell didn't you return my phone calls, texts, emails, and Goddamn smoke signals? After what happened to you in November, I earned that, don't you think?" His green eyes were blazing, eyebrows drawn down.

"I'm sorry. I just wanted to go home—"

"And be selfish," he finished for her. "You are just about the most self-centered person I have ever met in my life."

"I deserve that. I know I deserve that." She had to look down into her coffee. Anywhere but at him.

"Sometimes I feel like I'm working alone, you know? You're gone, over at the task force, off again on another adventure without me, but then we have a day like that day on Masten, and I know how well we work together. When we do work together."

She managed to pull her eyes up to his. "I just need to nail David Spencer. I can't help myself, Reese. I know I'm borderline obsessed. It's consuming me." Once the words had finally passed through her lips, she realized how true they were.

"I got news for you: you crossed that border a long time ago." His handsome face had softened into a look of true concern. He reached over and brushed his fingertips across the line on her neck. "How far are you willing to take that?" he asked.

She shivered and sat back in her seat, out of his reach. She didn't deserve his forgiveness. "I need to see this through."

"And if it's not David Spencer who killed those girls and came after you yesterday?"

"Then I'm just about the worst partner there ever was, aren't I?"

A smile stretched across his face as he bent to sip his coffee. "I'm glad you said it."

She laughed, and in spite of herself, tried to enjoy the moment with Reese, like they used to do before she had gotten caught up in all of David Spencer's craziness. The insults, the laughs, the inside jokes; those were the things she needed from Reese to know everything was good.

"Seriously, are you okay?"

She shrugged. "A little banged up, but I've been worse."

He looked her up and down and seemed to consider that last remark. "Actually, except for the strangle marks, you look pretty good. You got some color in those pasty-ass cheeks of yours. The bags under your eyes are minimal, and you're having a very good hair day today—for you, that is."

"I'd say the same to you, but all you've got is some stubbly bumps."

He rubbed his head. "And my nice scar. It makes me look tough, though."

"It makes you look like Frankenstein."

"That's cool too," he said. "He was a badass. I wonder how he did with the villager ladies? Because I'm batting a thousand. I got a number from the lady who supplies the Homicide office with coffee yesterday, and you know how long I've been working on that. I love a woman who plays hard to get. You want some eggs? Because I need some scrambled eggs." He waved to the waitress behind the counter. She smiled and held up her index finger in the universal signal for *just a minute*, then tried to stack a plate on her arm. "Oh, damn. She's cute too. Maybe I'll ask for hers before we leave."

And right then, Lauren knew all was right in the world between her and Reese.

25

The sound of Reese's ringtone shook Lauren out of a sound sleep. She felt around her nightstand, grabbed the phone, and brought it to her ear, still half asleep. "Reese?" she asked. Her throat was dry and scratchy. She looked briefly at the time displayed on her cell. "It's three in the morning."

"Another girl has gone missing."

She sat straight up in bed without bothering to push back the hair hanging in her face. "What? Where?"

"From Chippewa Street. Twenty-five-year-old who works at a hair salon. She told her roommate she was going to meet a guy she met online at a bar for happy hour after work. The Hot Spot. The same bar across the street from where Brianna went missing. That was at six. The roommate couldn't get ahold of her, so she drove downtown and found her car parked in a lot off Franklin Street, but her friend is nowhere to be found."

"She's just reporting it now?"

"My buddy Matt Tamaka, from the B District stationhouse, just called me. The roommate is there right now trying to file a missing person's report."

"I'm getting dressed." Lauren swung her legs over the side of the bed. "I'll meet you there."

"I'm already in my car," he replied, then hung up.

Lauren waited until she was clothed and in her own car before she called Nolan. He was an hour's drive away, so there was no use trying to get him into the city quickly, before they even knew what they had. He answered on the second ring, sounding as groggy as Lauren had felt.

"There's another missing girl."

"Is it related?" She could hear him shuffling around, probably turning on the light on his nightstand or putting his slippers on.

"Too soon to tell. Reese and I are both on our way to the B District stationhouse. Do you know where that is?"

"Yeah. Main and Goodell, right across from the old Studio Arena theater."

"We're heading there now. I'll text you if our location changes."

"I'm on the way."

Lauren clicked off her phone. She stopped at the guard's shack at the mouth of her gated community and gave him a wave as he lifted the wooden barrier. Her mind was awhirl. Another girl. Same bar. For her it was a straight shot, south on Delaware Avenue from her neighborhood near Delaware Park to the Theater District. She didn't care that her hair was yanked back in a messy pony tail, or that she was wearing the same clothes as yesterday or that she had black smudges under her eyes because she was too lazy to take her mascara off before she went to bed. A victim just didn't disappear in a puff of smoke. Lauren needed to find a crime scene as soon as possible. That was the best bet in bringing the girl home safe.

Reese was coming from farther away, so she got to the stationhouse first. She parked her car in the back lot and practically sprinted to the rear doors, waving her swipe card over the lock. A couple of the midnight guys eyed her as she passed them. She knew they would think a girl not coming home at a decent hour from Chippewa Street meant a hook up, not a law enforcement crisis. She ignored them as she pushed through the double doors that led to the detectives' offices.

The precinct detectives would be long gone. They worked a steady day shift. Whoever the midnight lieutenant was might have called one of them in. Matt Tamaka was on Reese's fantasy football league and she knew those guys got together at least once a month, whether it was football season or not. Reese must have told him about Brianna McIntyre. Tamaka was a patrol officer who'd worked midnights at the B District since she met him, when she first got on the job. She found Tamaka sitting at a precinct detective's desk, phone to his ear, holding up an index finger at Lauren to signal her to hold on.

She sat on the edge of one of the other desks and waited. Tamaka's straight black hair kept falling into his eyes as he talked. He was constantly running his hand through his hair so he could see. When he finally put the head set to the landline down, he apologized: "Sorry about that. I called Chief Burke and let him know what was going on. He wants Evidence and Photography at the bar as soon as possible. My lieutenant already has a patrol car with a plate reader on the way to circle the block. He wants you to contact the news stations."

"I'll call Gerry Simmons at home; he's the media liaison," Lauren replied. Gerry could deal with the press. "You have the bar on lockdown?"

"The bartender is there. Maybe six customers who are pissed they can't leave, and I got guys sitting on her car. Thankfully, it's a Wednesday into Thursday and not a weekend. It'd be a zoo on Chippewa

Street." The bars in the city of Buffalo stay open until four in the morning, seven days a week. The closing time was a holdover from the days when the steel plants were king and shift work meant thousands of guys hitting the tavern at two a.m., because they either just finished work or were just about to start. The late-night bar scene was a collective pain in the police department's ass. Ask any old timer and they'd tell you—nothing good happens after two a.m.

"Please tell me she had her GPS switched on in her phone?"

Tamaka folded his arms across his uniform shirt. "A couple patrol guys found her cell phone in the same lot as her car. It was smashed underneath a nearby truck. We didn't tell her friend that."

A lump rose in Lauren's throat. "Where's the friend who reported her missing?"

"She walked out front to try to get in touch with the girl's parents. She's a mess. The missing girl's name is—" He pulled a notepad from the pocket sewn on the front of his bullet proof vest. "Isabella Colon. Age twenty-five. She's a hairdresser at a salon on Elmwood."

Pinching the bridge of her nose with her fingers, Lauren mentally went through the checklist of everything that needed to be done right away. The plate reader was good. It was a patrol car that had a sensor that read and recorded every plate it passed. If a car was stolen or had an expired registration or was from Utah and it was parked on that block, she'd know. "I'm going to head over to the bar. I'll call Gerry on the way."

"I'll finish the missing person's report and meet you over there."

"No. Make sure you get the roommate over to the Homicide office to give a statement. Bring a copy of the missing person's report. I'll meet you there after I check out the bar."

"I wouldn't have thought much of the roommate trying to report her friend missing. She's young and she used one of those hook-up apps to meet with this guy," Tamaka said. "Except Reese told me at our last fantasy football meeting about you two finding that cell phone in that same bar. It can't be a coincidence, right?"

Lauren was already halfway out the door. "I don't believe in coincidences," she called over her shoulder. Then she headed to the Hot Spot.

26

Lauren texted Reese and Nolan her new location. It was just shy of four in the morning and most of the bars had already had their last call. The Hot Spot was lit up like a Christmas tree with three patrol cars lining the street in front of it. Lauren parked her personal car in front of the coffee shop and walked across the street. The temperature had dropped again, but thankfully the snow had held off. The ice was crunchy and brittle under her boots as she stepped onto the sidewalk, like little shards of glass.

A copper was standing next to the front door smoking a cigarette. "Hey Detective, good luck with the bartender in there," he said as she walked up. He was a younger kid, someone she'd seen around but didn't know. "You're in for a real treat with this guy." He twisted his butt against the brick of the building, leaving a nice black burn mark, then dropped it on the ground.

"You want to be a suspect?" she asked. "This is a crime scene. Evidence and Photography are on the way here. Pick that up."

"Oh, man." He bent down and scooped up the spent cigarette. "I'm sorry. I wasn't thinking." He deposited it in his jacket pocket.

Lauren didn't have time to admonish him on crime scene contamination, smoking in uniform, or littering. She opened the door to the Hot Spot and walked in.

Galen wasn't behind the bar. This time it was a thin guy, with multiple face piercings, sporting a severe buzz cut that showed off the sides of his tattooed head. A few people sat scattered around, most still nursing a beer or a mixed drink, just happy to still be hydrated. The bartender stood on the other side of the counter, hands on his hips, clearly agitated with what was going on. "I already told you everything. I have to close up now." He was bitching at a black cop she did know, a woman named Rose Patton, and Lauren could tell he was getting on her last nerve.

"The detective is here now," Patton said as she gestured towards Lauren. "You need to calm down and tell her what happened." Turning to Lauren, she ripped a page with the bartender's information out of her notebook and handed it to her. Moe Lynch, age twenty-nine, lived over on Ashland Avenue off of Elmwood and was pissed at the inconvenience of a woman having the audacity to go missing during his shift.

"Nothing happened! That's the problem," he barked, tucking his vintage Nirvana tee back into the waistband of his skinny jeans. "That girl came in, sat at the bar for like, an hour. She was texting the whole time. Had one drink. Then she got up and left in a huff. Didn't even leave a tip. And now the whole frigging police department is up in my shit. Whatever happened to her, it didn't happen in here."

"Did you talk to her? Did she say why she was here?" Lauren asked as Patton moved away and she moved in.

"I asked her what she wanted to drink, gave it to her, and asked her if she wanted another. End of conversation. Her nose was in her phone the whole time." The cell phone he had clutched in his hand buzzed. He looked at the screen. "My manager is here now, parking his car."

Lauren nodded and asked, "Has she ever been in this bar before?"

He threw his hands in the air. "I don't know. It's a bar. We get random people in here every day. I don't pay attention."

"Do you have the credit card receipts for everyone who came in today?"

Half turning, he pointed to a sign behind the bar that read: NO CREDIT CARDS-NO TABS. "The hard-core drinking crowd and the homeless population tend to leave their American Express cards at home. You wanna pay with credit, you better take your ass across the street to one of the college bars."

"Did anyone talk to her? Approach her?"

"Listen, Nancy Fucking Drew." He ripped a Reward for Information poster of Brianna McIntyre down off the wall next to him and shoved it in her face. "This bitch's mother comes in here once a week to post these things. I keep tearing them down and she keeps coming back. I told her and I'm telling you, get the fuck out, don't come back, and stop trying to tie my bar up with this bullshit."

When the paper hit her nose, Lauren reacted without thinking. She thrust him away from her with both hands, hard. Stumbling back, he wound up with his right fist, but before he could make contact, a tattooed arm shot out and clamped around his throat, dragging him away. Galen was yanking him across the bar, while Patton scrambled to put cuffs on him.

"This ain't your bar, Moe," Galen huffed in his ear, holding him while Patton finished. "I shoulda known it was you tearing those posters down. You're fired, you piece of garbage."

"This is all bullshit! What are you arresting me for? I didn't do nothing!"

"You just tried to assault a cop in front of another cop, your boss, and how many witnesses." Galen released him to Patton with a hard shove.

"You always were an asshole, Moe." An ancient Hispanic man sitting at the bar tipped the last of his beer back with an audible slurp and then told him, "Fuck you."

Lauren rubbed her nose. The missing poster was crumpled at her feet. She looked at the cop holding onto Moe's cuffed hands while he swore at Galen. "Take him to booking, Rose. Maybe his lawyer will convince him to be more cooperative after he spends the night in jail."

The young cop with the cigarette butt came into the bar. "Evidence and Photography just pulled up," he announced.

"Great." Patton marched her prisoner past him. "Connor, you're about as useful as two tits on a brass boar."

He looked around confused, then followed her out. "What?"

"You okay?" Galen asked, reaching out but stopping short of touching her shoulder.

"Thanks for that," Lauren replied. "I don't have time to roll around on the floor with a bartender right now."

Reese burst through the door. "What just happened?"

"Easy." She waved him off. "Uncooperative witness. It's handled."

He came over and examined her face, his forehead creased. "You sure you're okay?"

"Yeah. I'm okay." But the adrenaline from catching another missing person's case mixed with the altercation was enough to make her hands shake. She hooked both thumbs into the belt loops at her hips and curled her fingers into her palms. She'd had enough of fighting with men that week.

"I would have shot him," Galen said. "Could you have shot him if he hit you?"

She gave him an appreciative smile. "No. I was going to knee him in the balls."

Reese and Galen both visibly cringed. She had a lot of boney knee. "Can you get to the parking lot off Delaware from in here?" Lauren asked. Her adrenaline might have been pumping, but they needed to get back to business.

"Yeah, there's a back door through the old kitchen." Galen gestured to a door to the right of the bar. "Only staff uses it now, though."

"I just talked to Tamaka. The roommate says no one has had any contact with Isabella Colon since six fifty-five. That was the last text she got from Isabella. Said that she was done waiting and was going home."

"She said she was pissed," the older Hispanic man chimed in again. "Said she was done. She gave me the rest of her drink. Pretty girl. Real pretty and nice." He shook his head. "It's a shame."

Lauren glanced at the piece of paper Patton had given her. "Mr. Benitez?"

He nodded.

"Mr. Benitez, did she say anything else to you?"

"Just that she was leaving. What happened to that girl? Do you know?" Deeply etched with worry lines, his face was mottled with dark spots from too many days in the sun.

"Not yet. Just sit tight," Lauren said. "Someone will come to take your statement soon." He seemed all right with that, munching on some nuts from the bowl next to him.

"I need you two to arrange to get these witnesses downtown," Lauren told the uniform officers. "But make sure you hold the scene for Evidence and Photo as well. Send them out back when they're done in here."

Galen started to lead her and Reese through the door to the kitchen.

"You call Nolan?" Reese asked.

"We can't wait for Nolan," she said. "We need to check out our missing girl's car parked out back."

The kitchen hadn't been used to make food in years. It was full of empty booze crates, cases of beer bottles, and bags of garbage. The heavy metal door set in the far wall next to an ancient dripping sink had a crash bar to open it. "This door is the only thing up to code in this whole damn building," Galen said, hitting the metal bar with his hip. "Technically, it's a fire exit."

The door opened to a mostly empty parking lot behind the brick building. Lauren could see the entrance on Franklin Street. A metal sign affixed to the side of the next building down declared that the lot was for Hot Spot customers only, all others would be towed. The lot was small, with space for only fifteen cars, if everyone parked correctly and didn't hog two spots. Lauren could tell it'd be a tight squeeze no matter what. Not a lot of room to angle around, the exact type of parking lot she hated.

A lone patrol car was parked, blocking the entrance, engine idling. When they came out, the cop exited his vehicle and met them in the middle, where the only two vehicles left in the lot sat, about ten yards apart from each other. One was a newer model red Acura and the other was a dark green GMC Sierra.

The cop walked forward, an older guy with a full head of white hair that was neatly combed to the side, shook all three of their hands and explained what they had. "The Acura is registered to Isabella Colon, Hispanic female, age twenty-five. Her driver's license lists her height as four foot eleven. If she was grabbed in this lot, she never made it to her car. It's still locked. And"—he pointed to a small black object by the trucks front driver's side tire—"that's a cell phone. It's smashed to pieces. I mean it. If you look close, it's literally in three pieces."

Reese and Riley both squatted down to get a better look.

"The truck?" Reese asked, shining the flashlight app from his city phone at the cracked screen, then sweeping it back and forth in the space between the two cars.

"The truck is registered to a Max Dargavel, a bartender down at Host. He parked it here before his shift started at six. He got a ride home when I told him we're going to have to hold onto it."

"I want that whole side of the truck dusted for prints and swabbed for DNA," Lauren said, straightening back up. "If there was a struggle, our suspect might have touched it."

"No witnesses?" Reese asked. "No one heard a woman screaming or saw a fight in the lot?"

The cop motioned back to the lot entrance. "Brick buildings. That alley runs in between them, but it's a tight squeeze, so no car could get through there. Most of the bars around here blast their music. No cameras in this lot and the city camera on the corner got busted during the St. Patrick's Day parade and the city hasn't fixed it yet."

"How the hell did the city camera get busted during the parade?" Lauren asked in disbelief.

"Some drunk kid climbed up there and hung from it, snapped it right off. You can see the freaking wires hanging out of the pole."

"Unbelievable," Lauren muttered, carefully making her way over to the red Acura. She didn't want to disturb any potential evidence.

Anyone driving down Franklin Street would have known that light was out. *He could have watched her pull in and then waited for her to get mad for getting stood up.* Lauren's eyes traveled over to the broken pieces of glass and plastic scattered by the truck. *Four foot eleven is tiny. She probably had her phone in her hand when he grabbed her. Smashed it. Got her into whatever vehicle he was using and took off. She never had a chance.*

"We need to let Evidence do their thing," Reese said. "We better head to the Homicide office and get these witness statements done."

"Thanks," Lauren called to the cop, who retreated back to his vehicle. She followed Galen back through the door, which he had held propped with his foot the entire time, Reese bringing up the rear.

They thanked Galen and instructed Photography to just get some interior shots of the bar and to head out back to the parking lot. Lauren wanted every single inch of that back lot photographed and combed for trace evidence.

Once they were back out front on Chippewa Street, Lauren turned to Reese. He held up a hand to cut her off at the pass. "I know what you're about to ask, before you even ask it."

"Will you do it? Will you go check out David Spencer's house?"

Reese kicked a chunk of dirty brown snow off the curb into the street, where it fractured into bits. "Are you sure you want me to do that?"

"I can't go. He'd spot me a mile away." She'd let Reese assume that was because of their history. The unlawful surveillance she had done on Spencer was still her dirty little secret.

He hedged. "You shouldn't be the one to interview him, either. You know that, right?"

"Your case, your interview." She fished her car keys out of her jacket pocket. "But we need to start with him."

He let out a frosted breath into the early morning air. It was almost April, but the nights felt like winter. "I'll go sit on his house. See what vehicles are there. Who comes and goes. But only because we don't have another good suspect."

"Thanks, Reese."

"And if it's not him? If you're all wrong about this?"

"Then that's on me, I guess."

"Have you noticed lately that the things that should be falling on you are actually falling on other people?" Before she could respond he turned and walked towards his personal car parked in front of a fire hydrant two doors down from the Hot Spot.

27

Still wearing the clothes she had thrown on in her rush to get to last night's scene, Lauren addressed the members of the task force less than four hours later, wisps of her blond hair straggling into her eyes, hanging loose from her rough pony tail. After she'd finished all the witness interviews and had spoken to the missing girl's parents, she had called Kencil and had the whole task force come in early. "I think it's time to bring David Spencer in for an interview."

"On what grounds?" Bates was in his self-assigned seat at the conference room table, shirt unbuttoned at the collar, red tie hanging limply on either side, like he couldn't be bothered to knot it so early in the morning.

"On his connection to Amber Anderson and where her body was dumped. Which is the same place Brianna McIntyre was dumped. Now Isabella Colon has gone missing from the same bar where the burner phone used to set up Brianna's bogus date was recovered."

"It's a stretch," Manny Perez agreed.

Lauren spread her hands out in front of her. "It's just an interview. You want to talk about a stretch? You two went and talked to my neighbor and two of the guards who work the gate where I live."

"Nothing personal." Bates spit a thick brown wad into his plastic cup.

She suppressed the urge to get up and slap his spittoon across the room. "Asking him to come in for an interview isn't out of line. What's the worst that can happen? He can convince you even more he's not a suspect?"

"I agree with Lauren," Nolan said. "I want to at least talk to this guy."

"It's a dead end. Her paranoid fantasy. It's a total snipe hunt." Bates's voice raised an octave as he slammed his cup down, brown goop sloshing over the side, dribbling down onto the table.

Kencil stood. "Enough, Bates. At the very least we should talk to Spencer about Amber Anderson. Lauren, set it up."

"Sir—"

Kencil cut him off. "You can choose to watch the interview, if he even agrees to it, or sit out. I don't care which. But I would think you'd want to explore every investigative avenue and not dig your heels in just to spite your fellow detective here." He picked his leather folio off the table. "And clean that mess up," he told Bates as he headed for the door.

"Shane Reese is the primary detective on Isabella's disappearance. We'll set up the interview at the Buffalo Homicide office, unless either of you object to that?" Lauren was met by stony silence. "Good. I'll go make some calls."

Nolan followed her out of the room and into her cubicle. "That went well."

The dark circles under his eyes told Lauren he was just as exhausted as she was. Nolan had finally caught up to her at headquarters while she was finishing the harassment paperwork on Moe, the would-be assaulter. "Isabella might still be alive. This has to happen now." She pulled her cell phone out of her back pocket and dialed Reese.

"His girlfriend left the house at seven in the BMW. I haven't seen any sign of David." Reese didn't even bother with a greeting when he picked up. Lauren knew she owed him big time for sitting in his personal car surveilling Spencer's house for hours by himself. But like Reese had said back at the bar, they had no other suspects.

"No other movements?"

"There's a Lexus and a truck still parked in the driveway. I had to grab a coffee and take a piss about an hour ago, right after the girl-friend left. There's a Tim Hortons five minutes from here." *There's a Tim Hortons five minutes from everywhere in Buffalo,* Lauren thought as Reese continued. "But nothing changed while I was gone. His ride is still here, and I saw some activity in one of the upstairs windows. Someone is still inside."

"Kencil says to bring him in for an interview."

"That's good because I was just about to go knock on his door anyway. My patience is spent. And my coffee is gone."

"Don't come here to the task force office. I got this. Take him right to Homicide. See you back at headquarters."

Reese clicked off without a goodbye. Lauren looked up into Nolan's eyes. "You ready to meet David Spencer?"

28

Lauren got the interview room in the Homicide office ready for Reese and David. She gathered up some random papers scattered on the desk, picked a paperclip off the floor and positioned the chairs. Then she took the metal ashtray out, dumping it into the garbage can on the way to grab a fresh one from the storage closet. David didn't smoke, as far as she knew, but then again, she really didn't know a whole hell of a lot about him anyway. Not really. Just what he wanted people to see.

Perez and Bates had decided to come along and were now sitting with Nolan in the monitor room drinking coffee. She joined them once she was satisfied everything was in place, sipping her own coffee in silence. Reese had texted her he had David in his police vehicle and was on the way down to headquarters.

How long is David Spencer going to dominate my life? Lauren did the math in her head. It'd been almost two years now. *A year and nine months,* she thought, *more or less, but who's counting?*

She glanced at the time on her cell phone. 11:58. Isabella Colon had been officially missing now for almost seventeen hours. David would have had about an eight-hour window from the time of her disappearance to the time she was reported missing. A lot could happen in eight hours.

"Isabella is Puerto Rican," Perez said. "Doesn't that go against his profile?"

Lauren swirled her black coffee around with the brown hollow stir stick she used as a straw when her coffee was too hot. "Just because all the victims so far have been white doesn't mean anything. We have hundreds of missing person's reports we need to go over. Especially if we've only been looking at white victims."

"It seems like he's using these Internet dating sites to fish for the best possible victims," Nolan added. "It makes sense that race wouldn't be so much an issue as availability."

"I think that's right," Lauren agreed. "I would say the common factors would be roughly age and attractiveness."

Her phone buzzed in her pocket. She pulled it out, glanced at the screen, and announced, "Reese just pulled in. He's bringing David Spencer up."

"He doesn't see you," Bates told her. "I don't want some love fest going down between you two."

"I'll watch from the other side of the mirror. He won't even know I'm here." She reached over, hitting the RECORD switch for interview room one. "The camera's already rolling, so don't say anything you don't want on tape."

It was agreed that Nolan would go in with Reese first, with Bates and Perez watching from the video monitor room, ready to tag in if needed. Lauren and Nolan walked out into the main office, splitting up. He sat at Reggie Major's empty desk while Lauren slid into the closet-sized observation room on the other side of interview room one's giant two-way mirror.

The setup was a relic from before video cameras, when one or two detectives would interview a suspect and another would take notes on the other side of the mirror. It was a tight squeeze, with room for more than one person only if you stood shoulder to shoulder. It had to be kept dark or else the suspect could see you through the mirror. They were still using 1980s technology in the twenty-first century.

Lauren planted herself in front of the two-way mirror, notebook and pen in hand. Nolan slipped inside, closed the door, and stood next to her in the dark. "This is a throwback, huh?"

"Whatever works," she replied, staring forward at the familiar setup of the interview room. A desk, two chairs, two windows with blinds covering the reinforced glass. It was everything the experts said you shouldn't do with an interview room, yet it had been getting confessions for decades.

Nolan's shoulder brushed against hers as he tried to improve his position. He smelled like Ivory soap and peppermint. "Shouldn't you be out there waiting for Reese?" she asked, suddenly feeling self-conscious.

"I think it's good to know how you're going to look from this side of the glass, don't you?" Nolan asked. Lauren was acutely aware of how close he was, how good he smelled, and how inappropriate the timing was to suddenly find herself attracted to him.

"You should get out there." She half turned toward him, finding him looking down at her.

For a split second she thought he might lean in and kiss her. The craziness of the thought ran through her like electricity. He grasped her arm instead and gave it a squeeze. "Wish me luck," was all he said and walked back out of the room.

When the door clicked shut and she knew she was alone, Lauren let her head fall forward until it touched the glass. This was not the time, not the place, not the scenario to fall for someone she worked with. A missing girl's life was on the line. She needed to push those animal instincts to the back, way back, of her mind, and concentrate on what was happening right now.

She watched the interview room door. There was no clock in the room, no marker for the passage of time. Her stomach twisted in knots as the handle turned. Watching Nolan hold the door open for David, she noted what he was wearing: paint-stained jeans, a blue button-down, and tan work boots. David must have been getting ready to go work on one of Melissa's houses. His blond hair was gelled up in the front; he liked to look good even at work.

His expression was neutral. He could have been being seated at a restaurant as he took the chair directly across from the two-way mirror. He put a black cell-phone face down on the table next to him and looked to Nolan. "Is this okay?"

"Turn off the ringer." Nolan waited for Reese to come in and shut the door behind him before continuing with, "I'm easily distracted."

David picked up his phone, fiddled with it, and put it back down.

"You have any idea why you're here today?" Nolan asked. Reese had faded to the far wall, sitting down, trying to blend into the background for the moment.

David shook his head. "No clue."

"Detective Reese read you your rights in the car, correct?" Without waiting for him to answer, Nolan pulled a rights card from his breast pocket. "I'm going to do it again. Just to make sure you got it."

Nolan read the Miranda warnings, then asked the follow-up questions printed on the back, sliding the card over to David for him to initial each one after it was asked and answered. When that ritual was over, Nolan tucked the card away and got to it. "Can you tell me where you were yesterday?"

"Why don't you tell me why you're asking first?" David's voice was even, but there was a slight edge to it. Not quite a challenge, but enough for Nolan to know right away this interview could go south real quick.

"A girl went missing. We're trying to locate her."

"Why would you think I know anything about that?"

He's fishing, Lauren pressed both her hands on the frame of the two-way mirror. *He wants to know how much we know.*

"I'll get to that," Nolan said, trying to steer him back on course. "Why don't you tell me exactly what you did yesterday from noon on."

As if reciting a grocery list, David went through his entire day, point by point. Worked on a couple houses, went home and took a shower. Melissa was looking at a property, so he ate dinner by himself. Went to the office in the Ward, didn't get back home until after ten. Went to bed. All very cut and dry. All very convenient.

"What time did you leave for the office?" Nolan asked.

He shrugged. "Maybe five o'clock."

"You have an E-ZPass on your car?"

"Nope." He picked at a thread in the seam of his jeans.

"All the driving you must do and no E-ZPass?"

"I'm lazy. Never bothered to get one." He brushed his leg now with his hand, as if he could rub the thread away. "Me and Melissa don't have them on any of our vehicles. You can check, if you haven't already."

We have checked, Lauren made a note on her pad. *But you knew we would.*

"The office in the First Ward neighborhood." Nolan pulled his metal office chair a little closer to David. "Who was there with you?"

176

David draped his hand over his cell phone absently. "No one. Melissa's brothers were gone for the day. It was just me and the dogs."

"What did you do there?"

"Paperwork." He slid the phone back and forth across the desk in a lazy arc. "And some bookwork. We deal with cash a lot, so that means paper receipts. They have to be organized, same as work orders and invoices. Those get dropped off every couple days to the woman who does our accounting for us. If you don't stay on top of it, it piles up."

"You didn't log onto your computer at all?" Lauren knew the answer to Nolan's question before David opened his mouth.

"I sat there for hours trying to make sense of about forty pieces of paper and hundreds in cash that came in. I organize it; the accountant puts it all into the computer."

He knows every computer keystroke can be tracked. Lauren took in David's composed demeanor, his confident posture. Gone was the picking and fidgeting. *David hadn't known what to expect, at first. He's enjoying these questions now.*

"That's a long day at work," Nolan observed.

"Yeah," he agreed, "almost like being a cop. You going to tell me why I'm here now?"

"Did anyone see you between five and ten?"

"I was alone, except for our two dogs. No one but me and the brothers use that office. It's pretty isolated. But you'd know that, right? If you talked to Detective Riley."

"What's that mean?" Reese asked from his back perch.

"It means I caught her spying on me there not too long ago." He studied Reese's face for a second, sizing up his reaction. His knitted eyebrows told David that Reese had no clue about her late-night visit. "I guess she didn't tell you that," he laughed.

Lauren's face burned as Reese folded his arms across his chest. "You make any phone calls? Shoot anyone any texts or emails while you were at the office?" he pressed.

David flipped over his phone and swiped it open. He thumbed the screen, scrolling through his messages until he found what he was looking for. "I texted Melissa at eight fifty-nine saying I was going to be late." He held the screen face out so both detectives could see the message.

He could have left his phone at the office in the Ward, stalked and grabbed Isabella, and been back there in time to send that text. The cell phone tower records would surely back up his story, or he wouldn't have said it.

"Can we see your phone?" Nolan asked.

"You can see it, check my messages, and call your mom. I don't know what you're looking for." He tossed the cell to Reese, who caught it with one hand. "But you're not going to find anything in there."

"You own any white nylon rope?" Reese asked. "Maybe there's some in one of your work vans."

A slight smile curled at the edges of David's lips. "I'm sure we do. Just like every other contractor in the country. It'd be hard to match a single piece unless you had the other end it was cut from though, wouldn't it? And rope gets used and destroyed all the time on jobs."

He's putting on a show now. Lauren's nose almost touched the two-way glass. *He's enjoying this.*

Trying to change the direction of the conversation, Nolan leaned in, narrowing the space between them even more. "Do you know a girl named Isabella Colon?"

David pretended to think about it for a second or two. "Is she a tenant of ours? We had some Colons in a house over on Pennsylvania Street, but they moved out a couple of months ago."

Nolan slipped a blown-up copy of Isabella's driver's license out of a folder on the desk and slid it to him. David picked it up, looked at it, then shook his head. "I don't know her. If she lived with someone in one of our apartments, I might have never met her. I usually only deal with the person on the lease."

Reese stood now but didn't advance. "She went missing from a bar on Chippewa Street last night. A bar across the street from the coffee shop a girl named Brianna McIntyre disappeared from in May. Brianna was found in almost the exact same location as the body of your ex-girlfriend, Amber Anderson."

David sat back in his chair with a smile. "Now I get it. Wow. Okay. You and your partner Detective Riley have another missing woman and you want to try to pin it on me. Nice."

"You don't think those are strange coincidences?" Reese countered.

"I think your partner has a thing for me," David said. "I believe it's getting ridiculous. You know she came to my house a couple months ago, after she got stabbed, right? Then I catch her creeping around my work just two weeks ago." He snapped his fingers as if a light bulb had just gone off in his head. "Did you ever think she might be the one involved in some crazy stuff? I mean, her ex-boyfriend and that other cop involved in her stabbing both ended up murdered. Why am I sitting here and she's out there somewhere?"

"We're not here to talk about Detective Riley," Nolan said. "We're here to talk about you."

"Why? Except for Amber, you got nothing that ties me to anything. And the only thing that tied me to Amber was that I was one of the many guys she banged in our high school."

"Is this the only phone you have?" Reese held up the sleek black cell.

"Aren't you done with this yet?" David asked, zeroing in on Reese. "I remember you sitting next to Lauren at my trial in your cheap suit. Supporting your partner through thick and thin, right?"

Reese's chest heaved slightly as his temper rose. David's smile widened. "I know she probably was a great piece of ass before she got all damaged. A year ago I would have thrown one in her too, but now"—he gave a fake shudder—"not so much. But tell me, Detective Reese, don't you ever get tired of being her sidekick?"

Reese crossed the room in two strides, slamming his palms against the wall on either side of David's head, pinning him in. "You smug little prick," he hissed.

Nolan jumped out of his seat and tried to pry Reese away as David grinned at him. "Can I have my phone back?"

Reese tossed the phone, where it landed roughly on the table. "Your mommy issues are going to get you in trouble someday."

David's face hardened at the mention of his mother.

"What?" Reese taunted. "You don't like that? Me talking about what goes down between you and your mom?"

"Shut your mouth." David's hand clenched into a fist at his side.

"Make me." Reese saw the reaction and pounced, pushing past Nolan, knocking over a chair and crowding into David's personal space until they were almost nose to nose. "You're good at bullying women. It gets you off. How about you bring that shit to a man and see what happens?"

David's chest pumped as his rage built, cheeks red, eyes locked with Reese's.

"Nothing to say now, little boy?"

The door flew open.

"Don't you say another word." Frank Violanti barged into the interview room. A full head shorter than any of the three men in the

180

room, he pushed his way into the already tight space, positioning himself between David, Nolan, and Reese. "This interview is over. Any contact with my client from here on out will go through me."

"Who let you into this room?" Reese demanded.

"I did. I can't stand by and let you kick my client's ass."

"I never laid a finger on him," Reese ground out between clenched teeth. "It was a freaking chair that fell over."

"Can you believe it, Uncle Frank?" David's fury evaporated immediately. As he took a step back from Reese, his voice took on its mocking tone again. "They're trying to accuse me of kidnapping some girl yesterday. I guess Detective Riley and the district attorney must have fallen back in love after she got stabbed because he sees all of these, right?" He motioned to the camera mounted in the corner. "He must know what she's up to."

"Not another word." Frank yanked David up and pushed him towards the door.

David made one last declaration before Frank managed to get him out of the room: "I'm being harassed and falsely accused." He looked directly into the two-way mirror, as if he knew Lauren was standing just on the other side, cocked his head and smiled. "Again."

The door slammed shut behind them.

29

"That went over like a fart in church," Bates said as Lauren came out of the viewing room. She'd dug her fingernails into her palms watching the interview, leaving bloody little crescents. That last remark had made her want to punch through the glass to smash David's smirking face in, wipe it clean for good.

Now that Violanti and David were gone, everyone had converged in the main Homicide office, and Lauren had to tamp down her fury.

"I tried to slow him down, but Linda from the front desk let him in the building, and he must have slipped into the Homicide wing when someone opened the door to leave. One minute, Linda called and said he was in the lobby, the next he's here in the office and we all heard that crash in the room—" Marilyn apologized from her desk.

"I knocked a chair over," Reese said. "I didn't assault the little prick."

"Once the attorney makes contact, it's over. Not your fault," Kencil assured Marilyn.

"The question is: How did Violanti get here so fast? How did he even know to come?" Reese was pacing back and forth, trying to burn off some of his anger.

"Because David Spencer was expecting us," Lauren said.

"That's bullshit," Bates said he as flopped down at Vatasha Anthony's desk. "More of your paranoid delusions."

"Did he make a call after you knocked on his door?" she asked Reese. "Did he ask to call anyone before he got into your car? Did he talk to anyone on the way down?"

Reese swept past her. "No. But he did take a while to open up."

Lauren controlled her urge to kick the trash can next to Marilyn's desk. "He knew when you knocked on his door what was about to happen and called Violanti before he even left the house."

"It's pretty convenient how you fit your theory around the evidence," Perez said, backing Bates up. "But it's not supposed to work that way."

"David didn't ask for an attorney because he knew Violanti was on the way. He wanted to be on video. He wanted to piss one of us off," Lauren countered.

"Bullshit," Bates repeated, eyes locked on Lauren.

"Enough," Kencil said, trying to take back control of the room. "We still have a missing girl out there. We need surveillance on Spencer; I want someone watching the place down in the old First Ward, and I want every camera checked between the two locations. Now." Kencil pointed. "Perez, you take the Ward, and Bates, you follow Spencer. I don't want Nolan or Riley near him."

"And me?" Lauren asked.

"You and Nolan hit every conceivable place between his house, the office in the First Ward, and the Hot Spot for cameras. But concentrate around the bar. We might get lucky."

"I'll follow up with her family and friends," Reese threw in, circling Garcia's desk for the third time. "Maybe they know something we don't. Crazy ex-boyfriend. Drug problems. Maybe a history of taking off for a few days."

"Good. Good," Kencil told him. "The Peace Bridge has already been notified if anyone suspicious tries to cross the border. It's less than twenty-four hours since she disappeared. She could still be alive."

"She could be doing the walk of shame right now from some guy's apartment and all this was for nothing." Bates pinched a wad of chew from its container and wedged it between his lower lip and gum.

"If it was your daughter, would you want us to take that chance?" Kencil asked. Bates replied by spitting a brown lump into a plastic cup he'd found on Vatasha's desk. Kencil ignored Bates's disgusting habit and stayed on track. "No. We're going to run this into the ground until she's located. If she comes home safe on her own, we still did our job. Now let's go." He clapped his hands together, putting any further argument to rest.

Manny Perez and Cam Bates left immediately, with Kencil on their heels. Reese was still amped up from the interview, walking around the Homicide office, clenching and unclenching his fists.

"You need to calm down," Lauren told him. "You can't let him get to you."

"Like he's gotten to you?" Reese shot back. "When were you going to tell me about going to his office by yourself?"

"That was stupid of me. I should have told you about it."

Reese stopped next to Marilyn's desk. "Yeah. You should have. You put me with a suspect in the interview room who had one up on me. That's a setup for failure right there. What the hell is going on with you, Riley?"

"Listen, kids," Marilyn interrupted. "I hate to break up your little domestic, but don't you both have things to do? Like, now?"

Reese spun around, grabbed his jacket from the coat rack, and left.

Awkward silence filled the room. If Nolan hadn't been there, Marilyn probably would have lit into Lauren, but she held her tongue in mixed company. Instead of berating Lauren, she put her head down and started doing the weekly payroll. "Don't you have somewhere to be?" she finally asked, not looking up.

"We have a lot of ground to cover," Nolan said, moving towards the door Reese just exited from. Lauren grabbed her jacket from the back of Vatasha's chair. The rest of the squad was out on a shooting from Oxford Street. Grateful they weren't around to witness her latest fiasco, she followed Nolan to the elevator.

"You want to talk about it?" he asked, once the doors closed shut.

She shrugged her shoulders. "I did some surveillance on my own. David caught me. I figured what Reese didn't know wouldn't hurt him."

She expected a snarky remark back, or a put down, at the very least a lecture, but Nolan said nothing as the elevator car deposited them on the first floor. Which made her feel even worse.

There was no hoping for a next-day forgiveness for this one. *I think I finally crossed the line I've been drawing since we became partners.* She followed Nolan out to his truck, leaving hers in the street out in front of headquarters. *I might just have lost Reese forever.*

30

"It's almost midnight." Nolan pulled away from a convenience store in the Ward towards the Thruway. They had started in Clarence and made their way back to Chippewa Street, then into the Ward. The backseat of Nolan's Explorer now held two old-fashioned videotapes, six burned CDs, and four large empty Tim Hortons coffee cups. By the time they had gotten to Chippewa, a lot of businesses were closed for the day. Some places had their surveillance footage stored offsite, meaning Lauren and Nolan would have to have subpoenas sent to the security companies as soon as possible. Just wading through the footage they already had would take up most of the next day. They had passed Perez sitting on Spencer's office as they made their way through the old First Ward, and Bates had called in a half hour before, sitting on Spencer's house. No movement from any of the cars.

And still there was no sign of Isabella Colon.

"Drop me at headquarters and I'll grab my car," Lauren said.

"Why don't you tell me where you live and I'll drop you off? You look like you're ready to pass out."

"You have a lot longer ride home than I do," Lauren pointed out. The Chautauqua County Sheriff's Office was an hour's drive from the city. She had no idea if he lived even farther south.

"I'm used to it. You can Uber to headquarters in the morning and grab your car."

She gave in, staring out the passenger side window at the passing street scenes that gave way to a thruway eye's view of the city as they made their way north. She let the silence fill the car, relishing the lack of conversation. She was hyperaware of his closeness, the smell of soap and the peppermint gum he was chewing, the way he tapped his right thumb on the steering wheel in time to the music playing faintly on the radio.

"I've never been to your neighborhood," he remarked as they turned off at her exit. "I didn't know there were gated communities in Buffalo."

"A couple," she said, stealing a glance at his profile. She liked the way his dark brown hair fell neatly to the side. She wanted to reach over and thread her fingers through it, to see if it was as soft as it looked. "I'm just too lazy to downsize."

She inwardly berated herself for having those kinds of thoughts when she should be focused on Isabella Colon. But in the confines of the truck, just the two of them, she could hear every breath he took, and her attraction to him seemed suddenly overwhelming. Like he was finally something good at the end of a truly horrific day. That was magical thinking, she knew. A Band-Aid for everything that had gone down and gone wrong in the last twenty-four hours, but still, the pull was undeniable.

They stopped at the gate where the guard waved them through once he spotted Lauren, taking down the plate as they pulled in. Nolan wound his way through the narrow streets until they found themselves in front of Lauren's house. It sat totally dark, not even the porch light on, looking almost vacant in the moonlight.

"I'll walk you to your door," Nolan said. It wasn't an offer and Lauren didn't try to stop him as he got out and followed her up her driveway to her front walk. His jacket was open, flapping in the cold night breeze.

She fumbled her keys out of her coat pocket and slipped her key in the lock, twisting the knob. Pushing the door open a crack, she paused and turned back to Nolan. "Do you want to come in for a drink?"

He shook his head. "I drank so much coffee in the last twenty-four hours I'll probably have to stop four times on my way home."

She lingered, hand still on the knob, and looked up into his hazel eyes. "No, I mean, do you want to come in?"

Her face flushed as she stood half in and half out of her doorway, ashamed at clumsily asking a man to come to bed with her. She lowered her gaze to the buttons of his shirt, embarrassment swallowing what was left of her confidence.

"Hey." He tipped her chin up with his hand, their eyes meeting again. "Not tonight. But maybe we could go to dinner in a couple days when all this craziness dies down. On a date. Me and you."

His hand slid along her left arm, stopping to catch her fingers in his for a second before taking a step down, away from her. "Okay?"

"Okay," she replied, still feeling the warmth of his fingertips against hers, watching him back up to his car, shoving his hands deep in his pockets. He stopped by the driver's side, waiting for her to go into her house.

"Goodnight, Nolan," she said, slipping the rest of the way through her front door.

From behind, she heard him call, "Goodnight, Lauren."

31

Lauren picked up her SUV and drove to the task force office the next morning with a stomach full of knots and a head full of regrets. She'd gotten caught lying to one partner, hit on another and got shot down, and, worst of all, hadn't found Isabella Colon.

She'd laid in bed half the night replaying the different scenes from the day before over and over in her head in an endless loop: What could she have done differently? There was no guarantee that things would have turned out differently in David's interview had Reese known about her trip to the office down in the First Ward. David would have tried to get under Reese's skin no matter what. What David hadn't expected was for Reese to hit below the belt, so to speak. It had shaken his calm, cool façade and exposed the real David, if only for a moment.

But in the end, it didn't matter. Isabella was still gone, and they were no closer to finding her.

Pulling into the side lot, she spotted Nolan's vehicle. Another round of regret bubbled up in her as she parked as far away from it as she could. *He must think I'm a real piece of work*, she thought as she gathered her things that were spread out on the passenger seat. *A class act. Trying to get a guy in bed in the middle of a missing person's case.*

She didn't want the sex, not really. What she had desired most was just to be close to him. To feel something other than numb or mad or frustrated. She had failed miserably in her attempt. She wasn't the hotshot twenty-something detective anymore. She was a middle-aged woman with bags under her eyes and saggy pants, who should have been focusing on her victim and not on herself.

Kencil was standing at the copier in the hallway when she came in, watching paper get sucked in the top and copies spit out into the tray on the side. She paused when he looked over at her. "No morning meeting today," he said. "Everyone still has their tasks. Just make sure to check in with me. If nothing breaks, we'll have a full sit-down tomorrow and go over what we do have." He picked up a stack of papers and tapped them into conformity on the top of the machine. "Nolan told me you two picked up some videos. He's in the back fast-forwarding through the tapes and the disks. Nothing so far."

"Bates and Perez?" she asked.

"They have nothing. Spencer went to work this morning. Bates is sitting on his office as we speak. I spoke to Reese a few minutes ago. He talked to as many people close to her as he could. He's got a couple more names to track down today if you want to hook up with him at some point."

"Anything on the physical evidence? Any prints on the truck?"

"I think the truck is a dead end. The techs lifted a couple of partials near the handles, but only one that wasn't too smudged to be put into IAFIS." IAFIS was the national fingerprint database. "There was one good full print right on the driver-side handle of her car, so it's most likely hers. Your evidence techs are going to process the inside of her vehicle today. Maybe something will pop."

She knew the DNA would take longer. "Do we have a sample of Isabella's DNA to compare any samples with?"

"I don't know if Reese grabbed her toothbrush or hairbrush from the roommate. Double check on that and let me know as soon as it's confirmed, please."

"I'm on it," she replied, heading into her cubicle. Perez and Bates were nowhere to be seen. Maybe she could shut the door on the rest of the task force for a minute and put together some kind of work plan: figure out how to avoid Nolan, and find a way to talk to Reese alone.

Setting her laptop on her desk, she logged into the WiFi. Lauren wanted to map out all the businesses that had been closed so she could try for more videos. She'd also had one of the report technicians in headquarters email her the list of city cameras and their locations. She pulled it up. A red asterisk after the intersection name meant that the camera was malfunctioning, damaged, or obstructed.

There were a hell of a lot of red asterisks.

She hit the print button and sent it to the fancy copier Kencil had just been playing with. There had to be one working camera near David's office in the Ward.

"You busy?" Nolan stuck his head in the door, didn't wait for a reply, and came in.

She cringed inwardly as he came in, trying to control the blush rising to her cheeks. "I'm just trying to piece together the rest of the video canvass."

He looked rested and ready to tackle the day; his tan work pants were unwrinkled, and his sport coat covered a crisp white shirt. *I bet he's the type that gets by on four hours of sleep every night,* she thought, *then gets up and walks his golden retriever, works out, and chops wood before coming in to work. While I'm sitting here in a blouse I picked off the floor and the same black pants I had on yesterday.*

"I'm ready to go whenever you are," he said. Reaching over to pluck out one of the pens she had stuck in the coffee mug on her desk, he twirled it between his fingers. "I got here about an hour ago. Fast-forwarded through the most likely videos, but we got nothing. I figure we'll try to grab the rest today and then I'll go over them, starting from the bar, working our way to the Ward."

She nodded. "Sounds good. I'll print the rest of these addresses and we can take off."

"I want to stop and talk to Reese, see what the family had to say."

Reese was the first and last person she wanted to see. He hadn't called, texted, or emailed since the interview. She had to come clean, apologize, and hope he'd forgive her. Again. "Okay," she told Nolan. "Give me five minutes."

"It's all over the news, by the way. The media has already decided Isabella's disappearance is connected to Brianna's. So be careful of cameras and reporters lurking around." He turned to leave, taking her pen with him.

"Got it." She breathed a sigh of relief as soon as he shut the door. She could handle it if he just pretended their last conversation never happened. Hell, she'd had to do it for numerous guys she'd worked with over the years who had a few drinks in them and decided it would be a good time to hit on her. But she hadn't been drinking with Nolan. They'd been neck deep in a case and that made it so much more wrong.

Gathering the things she needed—her folio, portable radio, and copies of Isabella's picture—she made her way back into the hallway to the copier to grab her paperwork. The sounds of something being sawed buzzed through the space as construction continued on the other side of the building.

She walked past the conference room at the end of the hall to a much smaller media center they'd set up. It had a television on one of those old-fashioned black plastic carts that teachers in her elementary school had used to wheel around equipment when they wanted to show the kids a documentary on PBS. The bottom shelves on this cart held a VCR, a DVD player, a Blu-ray player, and on the lowest shelf, a knotted mass of cables to connect any kind of portable recording device to the TV itself.

Nolan was depositing one of the DVDs back into its clear plastic evidence bag. "Ready?"

"Where was that one from?"

"The convenience store on Pearl Street, close to Allen. Lots of cars going by, but the angle is bad. Can't read the plates, can't make out faces. You can tell the make and model if you play it in slow motion, but the top half of anything higher than a sedan is cut off." He threw it in the canvas bag he had propped on a chair next to him. "That one is pretty much useless."

She waited for him to collect his things, then followed him out to his car without a word. She didn't know why they always seemed to take his car rather than hers, other than the smells. Partnerships often evolved in ways that neither party intended, and once the routine was set, that was the script they became inclined to follow.

"About last night—"

As soon as those infamous words come pouring out of his mouth, Lauren shut him down. "That was a mistake, okay? I apologize. I was exhausted and frustrated and pissed off. Can we please forget I said anything? Act like it never happened?"

Turning his key in the ignition, the truck rumbled to life. "Okay," he said, looking both ways before turning right onto Oak Street. "On one condition."

"What's that?"

"You come out to dinner with me tonight."

"Tonight?"

"Yeah." He was heading for police headquarters, so he made a left. "No matter what time we get done. Anywhere. Tonight."

They cruised down Swan Street, stopped at the stop sign, and turned right on Franklin before Lauren could think of an answer. "I think I'd like that."

"Good." He spotted a parking space in front of headquarters and skillfully pulled in. "Then let's get to work."

32

Marilyn informed them that Reese had already come and gone and suggested that Lauren call him on the radio to see if he needed help. As the official den mother of the Homicide detectives, she always tried to smooth over the various domestic squabbles long-time partners were bound to have, but even Marilyn knew this one was more serious than a few harsh words thrown at each other.

"We'll see," Lauren told her as she downloaded the latest reports on Isabella's case to her iPad. Marilyn sat watching her with a frown, but she didn't push it.

Lauren checked her messages, grabbed a few things off her desk, and she and Nolan were back in the Explorer ready to tackle the video canvass again.

Lauren turned the talk radio channel on, listening to the host and callers discuss whether a serial killer was loose in the area. She hated that term: serial killer. It seemed to brand those people as some sort of celebrity instead of what they were: monsters and cowards. Arnold

Archer, the big-mouth host, was spouting off on the possibility that Isabella Colon had been snatched by some Internet creeper. Someone close to the investigation must have talked to the press and disclosed her online date. Archer was warning his female listeners to take down their web profiles. *Finally, he gets something right.* Lauren hit a button on the console, changing the station to classic rock.

"You going to try to talk to Reese? I'd really love to hear what he got out of the family yesterday."

She waved her hand over her iPad case. "It's all in the reports he sent."

"Not everything. Not his gut feelings. If you don't call him, I will."

Lauren and Nolan did not have the type of partnership she and Reese had, where she would have felt free to go tell him to piss off and let her handle it. And Nolan knew it. He was trying to force her hand to talk to Reese.

"I'll shoot him a text," she said, digging her cell out of her back pocket.

"Good. Let me know what he says." The first stop on their list was just ahead on their right, a run-down liquor store with a sign in the front window that announced: WE CASH CHECKS! Nolan pulled into the side lot and threw the Explorer into park. "You get on that. I'll handle this." Jumping out before she could protest, Lauren was left sitting, holding her phone.

She stared at it for a few seconds, trying to muster up the words of apology Reese deserved. A couple of guys, maybe twenty-one years old, walked by and looked at her through the truck window before heading into the store. She took a deep breath, let it out slowly, then hit Reese's contact number and thumbed the screen, composing her text.

Hey, Nolan and I want to meet up with you and talk. What time is good for you?

She had chickened out; played like everything was fine. Who was the coward now?

Her cell began to vibrate. The screen showed a picture of a baseball hat with the Buffalo Bills logo on it. She hit the accept button and brought the phone to her ear.

"I was just about to call you." His familiar voice sounded normal, like nothing had happened. That didn't bode well. She knew Reese. He was picking his moment. "I've got to drive way out to Silver Creek to talk to Isabella's grandmother right now. She'd been living with her until three months ago. Then I have a couple more interviews in the city. I won't be around until late. I'll text you, and if you and Nolan are still around, we can meet up."

"Reese, I just want to say I'm sorry—"

"Nope." He cut her off. She'd given him the opportunity he'd been looking for. "You don't get to say that anymore. I thought about you a lot last night. A lot. I came to the conclusion that I can either find someone else to work with or accept the fact that you're going to go off on your own and maybe get yourself killed. Those are my options."

"And?"

"Honestly? I don't know yet. But right now, we have a job to do. Let's do our jobs, find Isabella, arrest David Spencer, and then we can decide whether to divorce or not. Because our definitions of being partners are not the same."

His use of the word *divorce* was like a punch in the gut to her. With two failed marriages under her belt, at just under four years together, her partnership with Reese was officially the longest-lasting relationship she'd ever sustained with a man. He'd hung up, but she sat staring at the picture of the baseball hat that was still on her screen.

He'd stood by her during David's trial, never left her side after she had been stabbed, and now she was on the verge of losing the one good man who had ever touched her life.

"You get ahold of Reese?" Nolan slid back into the driver's seat, empty-handed.

She avoided the subject. "No video?"

"It's a digital system that goes to the security company." He held out a business card. "We have to have the DA's office send a subpoena. Where to next?"

She pulled her map out and studied it. "We should knock on the doors of these houses," she pointed to the ramshackle doubles across the street. "You never know, right?"

"Right. And Reese?"

Lauren stashed her map away in her folio. "He said to text him later about meeting up."

"See? That wasn't so bad, was it?" Nolan shot across the street, parking against traffic at the curb.

No, it wasn't, she thought as she climbed out. *That's what makes it worse.*

33

Hours later Reese called Lauren and told her he was going to be caught up until at least seven in the evening, but to swing by his house after that to talk. "I have to let Watson out of his crate. The woman next door comes over around noon, but this is too long for him to be cooped up."

"I'll text you when I'm on the way home."

Lauren and Nolan completed their video canvass, requested printouts from all four of the fixed plate readers in the city from the day before, searching specifically for any of the vehicles registered to David, Melissa, or her company, and checked in with Kencil. By seven o'clock they were exhausted, hungry, and driving up and down every street in the Old First Ward, looking for any business, home, or vacant lot with a camera they might have missed.

There was still no sign of Isabella.

"What if we *are* on the wrong track?" Lauren rubbed her eyes with the heels of her hands. They felt itchy and raw from squinting at grainy videos all day. "What if it's not David?"

"Any doubt I had was erased during that interview yesterday," Nolan replied, turning right onto Ohio Street. "I was expecting some young kid, some scared rabbit, not that guy."

Lauren settled back into the seat. The sky was turning orange and yellow and red as the sun sank down over the lake in the west. That was how Lauren had been taught direction by her dad growing up; the sun sank into Lake Erie. That was west. In the twilight, the city looked quiet, almost abandoned in this part of town as they turned onto Tifft Street. Rush hour was over, most of the residents were home by now, enjoying dinner on a chilly March night. The weather still hadn't broken, and it was practically April. Whoever said that March comes in like a lion and out like a lamb had never been to Buffalo, where the lamb didn't show up until almost June sometimes.

Lauren's phone vibrated. It was a text from Reese.

I'm on my way now. Meet me on Beyer Place.

"Turn left up here." Lauren guided Nolan through the South Buffalo streets. Reese had inherited his great aunt's house on Beyer Place about a year before. It was tiny, almost more of a cottage, with no backyard and neighbors on each side so close you could touch their walls if you stuck your arm out of his window. It had its upside too, though. It faced Cazenovia Park, with its trees and baseball diamonds and basketball courts. There was even a nine-hole golf course on the other side.

She wasn't in the mood to reminisce about her old stomping grounds. She called out directions until they were cruising across Cazenovia Park, out onto Seneca Street. They took a right. Adjacent to the park were several residential side streets. Reese's place was nestled in this little area.

Pulling onto Beyer Place, Lauren pointed to a small blue house sandwiched between two doubles. "Right there. But I don't see his car or one of our unmarked units."

The squat, boxy house was probably built at the turn of the twentieth century for a newly arrived family member by the owners of one of the neighboring houses. It had no garage and no driveway, just a narrow sidewalk to the front steps. Nolan parked in the street and turned the truck off.

"He'll probably be here any second," Lauren said, gazing over Nolan's shoulder into the thick trees that ringed Cazenovia Park. It was dark now; the March sunset had given way to a starless, cloudy sky.

Nolan kept his right hand curled over the gearshift, his other still gripping the wheel. "Lauren," he said, turning in his seat to face her, "what I said earlier, about dinner, it's because I want this to happen." He motioned between the two of them, his hazel eyes searching hers. "I want you to know—"

"That's Reese's car." Lauren cut him off as the unmarked Chevy turned the corner. Flashing his headlights in recognition, he pulled past them into a neighbor's driveway, turned around, and parked behind them.

Nolan and Lauren exited the Explorer at the same time, his words still hanging in the air between them, and waited for Reese to walk up.

"Thanks for coming out here so late. I know you have a long drive home, Nolan." The two men shook hands, then the trio started to make their way toward Reese's house.

"It's not a problem," Nolan replied just as they were about to turn onto Reese's walkway. "I just—"

CRACK

As the sharp sound pierced the quiet evening, Reese's head snapped to the left, like he had just gotten stung by the world's biggest bee. His forward momentum caused him to stumble and trip on his own foot in the shock of it. He pitched face down onto the concrete sidewalk with a sickening *thunk*. A pool of bright red blood immediately spread out like a sick halo around his head.

It took both Nolan and Lauren half a second to process what just happened. Lauren threw herself down next to Reese, while Nolan took cover by the wheel well of a parked car. Lauren knew she was out in the open, a literal sitting duck, but she tried to shield Reese. "Did you see where the shot came from?" she called to Nolan, while wrestling her portable out of her pocket, fumbling to get a grip on the black plastic.

Nolan drew his sidearm and peeked around the front of the car. "I think from that cluster of trees over there." He nodded his head in the direction of a thick knot of leafless Sycamores.

There was so much blood. Reese wasn't moving. Lauren couldn't even tell if he was breathing until she put her hand on his back. "Help me get him into your truck," Lauren yelled, desperation rising in her voice.

Nolan popped his head up for a second and dropped back down. "No. Get on the radio and get an ambulance here. We can't move him."

Lauren had to suppress her instinct to throw Reese in the Explorer and take off. The rational part of her brain knew they had to stabilize him, but the street cop in her wanted to get him to the hospital as fast as possible.

"Radio, we have shots fired. Shots fired on Beyer Place." She barely managed to keep her voice steady as she looked at the house numbers, trying to figure out exactly where they were. "510 Beyer Place. Officer down. I repeat, officer down."

Nolan ran for the cover of a tree, just on the other side of the road, flattening himself against it, waiting for another shot to ring out.

Lauren yanked off her jacket, pressing it against the right side of Reese's head where blood streamed from a deep gash.

Nolan snaked his way from tree to tree, towards where the shot had been fired.

"No. No. No," Lauren repeated as the blood soaked through her coat. "Stay with me, Reese," she pleaded. "Reese?"

Nolan was gone, off trying to grab whoever had done this, but Lauren could only focus on her partner.

He was alive, but she didn't dare try to turn him over. His face was tilted to the left, his eye closed. The scar from the staples he got in his head in December was visible; she could see it peeking out from under the drenched fabric of her jacket.

Her portable radio was going crazy with officers responding to her call. In the distance, the sounds of multiple sirens cut through the night. She didn't look up, not even when the first police car came screeching to a halt only a couple feet from them.

Other police officers surrounded her, kneeling down next to her, trying to talk to her, trying to talk to Reese, trying to figure out what happened. All she could do was repeat, "The shot came from the park," again and again and again.

The paramedics had to pry her away from him, still holding her bloody coat, so they could turn Reese over and work on him. Four firefighters helped get him on a backboard after the paramedics put a collar on his neck, all while keeping pressure on the wound.

An A District lieutenant tried to question her, but even as she answered, her eyes were glued to her partner, refusing to move from his side as she was jostled by the firefighters and the ambulance crew that was working on him.

She wanted to scream, *What are you waiting for? Get his ass to the hospital!* But the words were caught in her throat.

His chest was rising and falling, that much she could tell. He was still alive.

For now.

Every light in every house on the street was on; people filled every porch and lawn, watching as they hustled Reese into an ambulance and the cops taped off the crime scene.

Reese looked unreal to Lauren—his face bloody, his neck in a plastic collar, strapped onto a gurney. A huge abraded lump had manifested on his forehead where he had hit the sidewalk.

A firefighter helped Lauren into the ambulance but made her sit by the back door. It seemed like she was miles from Reese as she watched one paramedic, barely in her twenties, start an IV, while her partner kept pressure applied to the wound.

"Can you hear me, Detective?" the woman kept asking him as she affixed more medical devices to him. "Can you open your eyes?"

Reese just lay there. If he could hear, he didn't or couldn't respond.

Lauren didn't know where Nolan was. She couldn't bring herself to shift focus off Reese enough to care. He had gotten shot in front of his own house by someone who had lain in wait. There was only one person who was angry enough with Reese to do that.

Reese was wrong when he said staying partners might mean watching me get myself killed, she thought as she held onto the bloody jacket like a life preserver. *It meant he would get himself killed.*

34

The ambulance rushed Reese to the Erie County Medical Center, even though Mercy Hospital was much closer. The emergency room trauma doctors there saw gunshot wounds almost daily and were prepped and ready when the ambulance came rumbling up the ramp to the big double doors.

The ambulance doors swung open to blinding white light and the silhouettes of doctors and nurses, who swarmed around the back of the vehicle and shouted orders at the paramedics as they rushed Reese into the hospital.

Lauren wanted to stay with Reese in the ER. "You have to wait while we work on him," a female doctor told her, blocking her from the entrance.

"I'm staying with my partner," Lauren protested loudly and violently, jerking away from an older male nurse with short gray hair who tried to take her arm to guide her toward the lobby. "That's my partner in there!"

When Lauren tried to charge ahead, the nurse yelled to two young cops who had just walked in, "Help me get her into one of our comfort rooms." The cops each grabbed an arm and forced her down the hall and through a door with bright blue flowers painted on it. Inside, the windowless room was painted a cheery yellow and furnished with an overstuffed couch and chair.

"What the hell are you doing?" she demanded as they hustled her inside. The cops roughly sat her on a lumpy green sofa, holding her there for a few seconds in an effort to calm her.

"You need to stay here and not wander while the surgeons work on him," she heard the nurse call from behind. "If you leave, we won't be able to find and update you."

She tried twisting out of the officers' grips. "Get off me!"

"Detective Riley," the shorter of the two cops said, trying to sound comforting. "It's okay. He's going into surgery. Your partner's going to be okay."

"Stay here," the nurse insisted. He had on blue scrubs without any cute decorations on them. "You can't do him any good right now. I'll be back as soon as I can to tell you what's going on.

"Watch her," the nurse told the two cops standing by the door. "Don't let her leave here."

"I'm calling my supervisor," the taller cop said as Lauren got up and strode across the room.

The nurse shut the door in her face.

She could hear the cops, the firefighters, the nurses, and the staff bustling around in the corridor. She wondered if that fucking nurse had locked her in.

Does it matter? They won't let me see him anyway. Standing in the middle of the yellow-walled room, she pressed her fists into her cheeks and closed her eyes, biting back a scream.

What just happened? What just happened? What just happened? Lauren's mind raced.

Outside the door, someone dropped something metallic in the hallway, snapping her to reality. She looked down at her hands, black with crusted-over blood, clutching her wadded-up coat. It looked like someone had taken a brush and painted a dark crimson streak down the front of her light blue button-down shirt. She was thankful the room had no mirrors; she might have lost it at the sight of herself with Reese's blood literally on her hands.

Okay, she told herself, *Reese is alive and they're treating him. They work miracles here every day. I need to keep it together. I need to be with him.*

I need him to survive.

35

Lauren lost track of time. People came and went out of the comfort room. She'd tried to leave several times, only to be told she had been ordered to stay there by the commissioner. Barbara Bennett had come in herself to talk to Lauren, telling her that Nolan was still out with the detectives and car crews sweeping the park and the surrounding neighborhoods.

"A .22 rifle has been found dumped fifty yards away from where Reese had fallen over." Bennett was wearing a sweater and jeans. It would have struck Lauren as odd, like seeing her grade school teacher outside of school, if the situation wasn't so desperate. Bennett could have been wearing a tuxedo for all Lauren cared. "The shooter could have had a car waiting on the narrow street that runs behind where the gun was found or escaped on foot into the more densely treed and remote part of the park."

Lauren listened to her explanations, barely keeping her focus, before demanding to see Reese. "They've kept me in here long enough," she told Bennett.

"Trust me, Detective Riley," she assured Lauren, "as soon as it's possible, I'll make sure you're with him."

Bennett left to go oversee the search. Lauren couldn't give two shits. She needed to be with her partner.

Other cops and detectives came in to talk to her, to see if she was okay, if there was anything they could do. It sounded like the entire department was on the other side of the door. Reese was very well liked, much better liked than she was. He was on the police department's baseball team, played in a big fantasy football league, went to all the retirement and promotional parties she'd stopped going to long ago. If Bennett had already made it to the hospital, Carl Church was likely to follow. Lauren definitely did not want to see him. He'd called her bait, and she hadn't comprehended the ramifications of that. Now Reese was trying to survive them. After Bennett left, she asked one of the cops standing guard outside her door to only let Homicide people in. She wasn't interested in making small talk. Her single purpose was to get to Reese, no matter what.

Even when Ben Lema and Joy Walsh from the Homicide squad showed up, their words were just background noise. Joy's wild black hair was sticking up everywhere at odd angles. Ben's face was pulled into a mournful frown.

"How are you holding together? You need anything?" he asked.

Rewind the last five hours of my life, she wanted to say. *And one minute alone with David Spencer. Oh, and I want my partner to survive.* But she held her tongue. Joy and Ben were just doing what she would have done if the roles were reversed.

"We had a patrol car go and get Reese's parents. They're on the way now," Joy said, giving Lauren's shoulder a supportive squeeze. "I made sure to tell the cops to bring them directly to you, here."

"We're going to head back out," Ben told her. "Try and see if we can track down this prick."

Prick. Reese had called David a little prick in the interview room. Lauren had seen Reese pushing David hard and hadn't intervened. *Why didn't I stop him? I saw things getting out of hand in there and I let it go.*

She tried to push those thoughts away, to concentrate on Reese's parents coming to the hospital as the two detectives left her to go back out on the street.

Reese's parents. Both retired, his mom was an African-American school teacher and his dad an Irish fire captain from the Old First Ward. They lived out in Orchard Park now, by the Buffalo Bills football stadium. She could picture Reese's mom, tiny, more darkly complected than Reese but with the same flawless skin. Maybe if his parents got there the doctors would let her in to see Reese.

She paced the length of the room, back and forth, back and forth, silently praying. *Please, please, please …*

An unknown amount of time later—Lauren had lost any sense of time, there was only then and now—Reese's dad pushed open the door, holding it so his wife could enter. Lauren could see a knot of police congregated in the hall, stepping back in deference to the couple. Lauren turned to the ugly green couch and quickly tried to stuff her coat between the cushions, but it was too big. Thankfully, she'd been able to use the small attached bathroom to clean herself up, including turning her shirt inside out, but the coat was a horror show.

Reese's mom stumbled into Lauren's arms, wrapping herself around her son's partner. "What happened?" Tears were flowing freely, her whole body wracking with sobs.

Reese's dad put his hands on his wife's shoulders and gently eased her onto the couch, sitting next to her. He was tender with his wife, wrapping a protective arm around her shoulders, but rage clouded his face.

"I don't know." Lauren sat in the wing chair across from the couch. "We met at his house to go over some things we were working on and there was a shot." She took a deep breath to steel herself. The time for going to pieces was over. "It happened so fast."

"Did you see who did it?" Reese's dad's voice was cold as ice. He was angry. Angry that his only son was in the hospital, condition unknown, and his wife was barely keeping it together.

Lauren shook her head. "No. Whoever it was shot from the trees inside the park."

"Do you think they were shooting at you?" he asked point blank.

"I—" That thought hadn't even occurred to her. "I don't know. It was one shot. I only heard one shot."

"The police who brought us here wouldn't tell us anything." Reese's mom—Sandra, her name was Sandra, Lauren remembered—said, "But on the police radio, officers were saying he was shot in the head."

"Was he shot in the head?" Reese's dad, Peter, asked. He was the same height and build as Reese, but his face was rounder, meatier with age. "They herded us in here. We haven't seen a doctor yet. I don't know what the hell is going on."

Sandra was practically sitting on Lauren's coat. If she looked down and to her right, she'd see her son's blood soaked into the fabric of Lauren's jacket.

"I haven't talked to a doctor yet, either." She couldn't bring herself to tell them what she knew, so she deflected. "And they won't let me see him."

Peter stood up, his face flushing red, his jaw line so much like Reese's. "This is bullshit. I want some answers." He marched over to the door and stuck his head out. "Who's in charge here?" he demanded. "Hello? I want to speak to someone right now!"

He was met by several cops who used the same tactics on him that they'd been using on Lauren since she'd been stuck in the room: swarm, placate, push back inside, and shut the door. "What kind of horse shit is this?" he asked no one in particular, turning around in a full circle with his arms out. "My son is shot, and I'm being held hostage in a fucking reception room!"

"Peter," Sandra called softly, patting the couch next to her. "Sit with me. Please."

"I can't sit," he said as he picked up pacing where Lauren had left off. "How long have you been in here?"

Lauren dug her phone out of her pocket and looked at the screen. It read 9:48 p.m. Could it be that she'd been at the hospital for less than two hours? She felt like she'd been there for days. "I think it was about quarter to eight when Reese—I mean Shane—pulled onto Beyer Place. I've been in this room since I got to the hospital."

"And you haven't tried to find out what's going on with my son?"

"Peter." Sandra's voice sounded weary. "She knows as much as we do. Come sit down."

He spun to face Lauren, pointing his finger at her. "No. She knows more. She was there."

"Mr. Reese," Lauren said, getting up. "I'm going to find out what's going on. My commissioner ordered me to stay here, but short of handcuffing me, they can't keep me prisoner." Lauren headed for the door, ready to fight her way through the blockade if necessary.

"Lauren!" Sandra called after her but didn't get up. Instead, Peter sat down with her and she sank back against his chest, his fingers threaded through her dark curly hair.

As Lauren grabbed the doorknob, it turned under her hand. As she stepped back, an impossibly young-looking doctor walked in. She retreated toward the couch to give him some room. He was chubby and pasty pale with short, neat blond hair parted on the side. A plastic ID badge was clipped to his white coat.

"Hello, everyone," he said in a tight voice. "I'm Dr. Kowal." He directed his gaze to Reese's parents. "You must be Mom and Dad."

Of course, they waited until his next of kin showed up, Lauren realized, sizing up the doctor. *I'm not his next of kin. I'm nothing to Shane Reese.*

"Was my son shot in the head?" Peter asked, tightening his grip on his tiny wife, who was leaning forward like she was about to pounce on the doctor.

"Shane suffered a deep grazing wound to the right side of his head." He took his index finger and pointed from just above and behind his left ear, dragging it along his scalp to almost the temple. "He was very, very lucky. The bullet didn't penetrate the skull."

Reese's mom exhaled a relieved sob.

"However," the doctor continued, "he fell forward and his head struck something solid." Now he looked at Lauren.

"The sidewalk. His forehead hit the sidewalk."

The doctor nodded as if that confirmed his suspicions. "The fall caused a fracture to his skull. He has what we call an epidural hematoma. He's heading into surgery right now to evacuate the hematoma."

"Evacuate?" Sandra choked out. "What does that mean?"

"It means we have to do a craniotomy. When that's completed, he'll be moved to the ICU to monitor him for increased cerebral pressure." He hooked his thumbs into the front pockets of his khaki scrub pants. "The gash looked bad from the outside, but it's what's going on inside the brain that we need to worry about."

"Can we see him? Talk to him when he's out of surgery?" Lauren asked.

"He's been intubated and there's no predicting how long his recovery from the surgery will be. He's strong, but he's in critical condition right now. The next twenty-four hours will yield more answers."

"What's a craniotomy?" Sandra asked, her face streaked with tears. "I don't know what that means."

The doctor hesitated for a second when he saw Peter tense up. "It's when we remove a portion of the skull to evacuate the hematoma. We'll store that portion of the skull in his abdominal cavity until the swelling has gone down and we can replace it."

"Oh my God," she wept, burying her face in her husband's tan Carhartt jacket. "A piece of his skull? Oh God, please."

Lauren bit her tongue. She wanted to ask straight out if Reese was going to make it, but the doctor had already answered that question in not-so-many words. And Reese's dad had picked up on it as well and was trying to shield his wife from it.

The doctor didn't know.

36

Nolan came to the hospital late, after midnight, looking tired and drained. Reese's mom had passed out on her husband's shoulder. He just stared straight ahead as Lauren got up and exited the comfort room. "I'll be right back," she told him. He gave an almost imperceptible nod and hugged Sandra tighter to him.

The hallway was still choked with cops. Lauren and Nolan just walked right through them, ignoring the well-wishers and concerned co-workers until they were outside on the emergency room ambulance ramp.

It was now deserted, except for a few police cars parked at the far end. The chaos of those first few minutes was fresh in Lauren's mind. A used latex glove sat on the ground. Some cigarette butts were scattered under a NO SMOKING ANY TIME sign. The light overhanging the ramp buzzed. It was too cold for mosquitoes or moths yet, but the noise reminded her of the swarm of people who came at the ambulance. The raw memory of what went down only a few hours ago blazed in her brain.

"How are you holding up?" Nolan asked.

Without her jacket, she wrapped her arms around herself to keep warm. Lauren had managed to hand off her bloody coat to one of the Homicide detectives who had showed up at the hospital looking for it. It was evidence. She hoped the thing was gone for good; she never wanted to see it again. "I'm better now that the doctor came in. And a nurse just stopped by. She said Reese is out of surgery. I can't be out here too long, in case the doctor comes to give an update."

"I can't find him," Nolan ground out between his teeth. He leaned against the concrete wall. "I had car crews at David Spencer's house within minutes of the shooting. His car is gone and he's missing. His crazy girlfriend doesn't know where he is. The bastard is in the wind right now."

He won't get found until he wants to get found, Lauren thought, rubbing her arms up and down to stave off the cold. "If he doesn't turn up in the next twelve hours, we need to bring Melissa in."

"You let me worry about that. Stay here with your partner." His hazel eyes were clouded over with concern for her, not for Reese, and it pissed her off.

Shaking her head, she told him, "No. I can't. I'm the reason Reese is in the hospital right now. I'm the reason he's in critical condition. Me." She slapped her palm to her chest. "Me. And I have to be the one to find David."

"Every cop in Erie County is looking for him right now. He won't get far."

"He has access to multiple vehicles, multiple properties, and cash. Believe me, he thought out exactly what he was going to do before he did it."

"Okay." He was placating her now. Trying to keep her calm, like the first two cops who had shuffled her into the comfort room. "Okay. Let me walk you back now. Try to rest your eyes a little." He reached out to put an arm around her shoulder. She walked on, leaving him hanging as she pushed through the double doors.

I don't need your pity right now. Lauren plowed straight ahead, not looking back at Nolan, to get to the waiting room in case an update had come in. *I need Reese to survive the night.*

37

*H*ow *roles reverse*, Lauren thought. When the same male nurse finally came and said they could see Reese, Lauren let his parents go in first, without her. She chose instead to stand in the hallway, watching their feet move about under the curtain that encircled his bed, ignoring the whispers and stares of the hospital staff around her.

Four months ago, I was the one in the ICU and Reese was there for me. What have I done to repay him except lie, go behind his back, and drag him into all of my drama? Lauren glanced around. *These same people checked my tubes, watched my monitors, and wiped my ass. They must think I'm cursed.*

It was mid-morning. Close to eleven and she hadn't slept yet. She hadn't even tried. There was no way she was closing her eyes before she looked at Reese and made sure he was all right. Even now, just a few feet away from him, the curtain obscured her view, and she couldn't be certain. Not a hundred percent.

Another doctor, the surgeon, had come in during the night and told them that Reese had made it through the surgery and was in recovery. He looked as tired as Lauren felt, but he gave Sandra a reassuring smile, saying, "Your son is strong, and his surgery went off without a hitch. You should be able to see him in a couple hours, after they move him to the ICU. He's intubated, but that's standard in these cases. Right now, the most important thing is to monitor for any swelling."

Lauren repeated those words in her head throughout the night, over and over as she waited in the comfort room. After Nolan left, she asked the cops outside that no one else be allowed in, unless it was one of Reese's relatives. Both Sandra and Peter had huge families, but apparently the hospital staff had set up another room for them. At one point during the night the couple had gone over to see their family, only to come back a half hour later, exasperated. "This is why we go on cruises for holidays," Peter had said, with Sandra giving an agreeing nod.

Peter came out of the ICU curtain first. "Go ahead in, Lauren. I need a minute." His face was flushed, his eyes rimmed in red. He stuffed his hands deep in the front pockets of his jeans and walked down the hall.

Taking a deep breath, Lauren steeled herself before walking in, but it wasn't enough. Reese was lying on his back, face up with a plastic tube down his throat and a huge white bandage wrapped around the top of his head. His eyes were closed, and his chest was rising and falling, but his skin had a pallor to it that made him look unreal, like a wax dummy in a museum.

Sandra was by his side, holding his hand, careful of the IV lines, looking down at her son. She wasn't crying, but she was on the verge, just barely holding it together.

When Lauren came in, she looked up. "Come over," she told her, then said to Reese, "Your partner's here, honey. And the whole police department, it seems. Our entire family. Your friends from baseball. I told you, everybody who loves you is with you."

She moved aside a little to let Lauren in next to her but didn't drop his hand. Lauren gripped the metal rails of the hospital bed, looking down at Reese. A thin blue hospital sheet covered him to the chest, leads and wires snaking out, attaching him to beeping monitors. She tried not to think about the piece of skull the surgeons had put in his abdomen.

"Talk to him," Sandra said softly. "Let Shane know you're here."

"Reese." Her voice broke at the sound of his name coming from her own mouth. She cleared her throat and tried again. "Reese, you did good. The doctor said you came through like a champ—"

Sandra pulled at Lauren's hand and put Reese's in hers.

It was warm and dry and unexpectedly soft. Lauren stared down at their hands, rubbing her thumb over his palm. "—and I made sure someone went and got Watson. I told the commissioner where your spare key is, and she said she'd have one of the Homicide guys go in and take him until I can grab him for you. So don't worry about that."

She turned her eyes upward, blinking back tears. The heart monitor above his head showed a steady rhythm of spikes and drops. *I won't cry*, she told herself. *I have to show him he's going to be okay.*

"You just rest and get better. That's all you have to do."

Her hand was cramped when she finally let go of Reese's. His mom gently scooped it back up, holding it near her heart. Lauren watched his chest rise and fall, the way she'd done in the ambulance, listening to the sound of his breathing, hoping his eyes would flutter open.

Minutes ticked by.

They didn't open.

Leaning forward, she bent over Reese's bed and whispered in his ear, "I'm going for a walk. You go ahead and wake up now. This whole unconscious thing you got going on is getting old."

Sandra gave her a half smile, still clutching Reese's hand. "I'll be back," Lauren told her, stepping away from the bed.

"I know you will," was all she said, and she turned her face back to Reese's.

After I go out and hunt down the son of a bitch who did this to him.

38

"What are you doing here?" Nolan dropped the folders he was holding down on his desk. "Have you even slept yet?"

Lauren closed the door to his cubicle in the task force office, not that it would do much good in giving them privacy since the walls didn't reach the ceiling. She hadn't seen any of the other officers' cars out front, just Nolan's Explorer, but you never knew who could be lurking around.

"Have you found David Spencer yet?"

"Is your shirt on inside out? Come over here and sit down."

She stayed where she was. "Did you find David yet?"

He shook his head. "No sign of him. We have guys sitting on his house in Clarence and on his mother's house in Garden Valley."

"Weren't we supposed to have surveillance on him when the shots were fired? Wasn't Kencil supposed to make sure someone was sitting on his house?"

"From what we can figure, the unmarked car outside his house saw him leave for work and tailed him. Sat on him all day at the office in the Ward, then tried to follow David, but lost him and his Lexus in rush-hour traffic around five o'clock."

"And the surveillance car didn't report that? Didn't call it in to the rest of the task force?"

Nolan hesitated for a second, then said, "It was Cam Bates. He thought David was just heading back to his place in Clarence, so he tried to catch up with him there. By the time he realized he fucked up, Reese was shot."

Lauren sucked in a breath. "That son of a bitch—"

Nolan cut her off. "He knows he messed up. He actually feels terrible about it."

"My heart is breaking for him," Lauren shot back, pissed Nolan would even try to defend Bates to her. "Reese took a bullet because he dropped the ball. No wonder he and Perez didn't come to the hospital. I should have known."

"He's out there now, searching for David Spencer like a man possessed, if that makes you feel any better."

"It doesn't," Lauren snapped. "Why would it? It's the least he can do. The very least." It was a good thing he wasn't in the office. The days of Lauren Riley holding back her temper were officially over. She'd take a couple suspension days for one good punch to Bates's face.

"Agreed," Nolan said. "It's too little, too late, but we still have a job to do, right?"

"Exactly," Lauren told him. "That's why we need to bring Melissa St. John in. Right now."

"Are you sure that's a good idea? Shouldn't you go home, get some sleep, and then get back to the hospital? I'll let you know what's going on."

"No." There was no room or time for arguments. "I need to sit down with Melissa St. John, right now. Me."

Nolan looked at Lauren, really looked at her, in her backwards blood-encrusted shirt, dark circles under her eyes, and blond hair coming undone from her ponytail. She knew she looked a mess, but she'd never been more determined to do anything in her life. And she *was* going to do it, whether Nolan tagged along or not.

"Okay," he said, walking toward her. "I've got an old button-down shirt in the back of my Explorer." He held the door open for her. "How did you get here anyway?"

"I called an Uber when no one was looking." She passed by him, back into the hallway. "Ain't modern technology wonderful?"

39

"This is what we know about Melissa St. John." Lauren produced a large box from under her desk and dropped it in front of her and Nolan. She'd had Nolan take her back over to headquarters and had marched him to the Cold Case office. She answered as many questions as she could about Reese to her co-workers, then got on the radio and had a patrol car go and grab Melissa and bring her there. The surveillance team stayed, just in case David Spencer decided to make an appearance after his girlfriend was put into the marked patrol car. Hopefully, this team would do its job correctly.

Lauren called Kencil from the Cold Case office and let him know what they were planning to do. He sounded surprised to hear from her. "Just an interview," he clarified. "I don't want you throwing the cuffs on that woman."

"This isn't my first interview," she said. "I know what to do."

"Does your commissioner know what you're up to? Is she even aware you left the hospital?"

"I'm sure someone will tell her soon enough." Lauren clicked the end button and stuffed her cell in her back pocket. "All set," she told Nolan, as she reached into the box and pulled out several files she had amassed over the last few months on David Spencer and his girl-friend, Melissa St. John.

"When did you have time to get all this?" Nolan began sorting through the neatly tabbed folders.

"I've had my eye on David Spencer for a long time." She fished around in the box until she found the specific folder she wanted. No need to tell him the details of her illicit surveillance. "Melissa St. John used to be morbidly obese. She was in an accident involving a ride at an amusement park and received a multimillion-dollar settlement. That's how she met David, through her lawyer, Frank Violanti."

"I thought he was a defense attorney?"

"Defense, personal injury, some disability claims. I guess when you're a one-man law firm, you have to be a jack of all trades. Any-way." She opened the folder to a printout of street addresses. "It seems that Melissa and her two brothers were in the business of flipping properties before and after her accident settlement. Obviously when she got awarded the cash, she made higher-end buys, but fewer of them. According to the city records, her limited LLC owns twenty-two properties. Seventeen residential, five commercial." She handed the paperwork to Nolan, who scanned the addresses. "She's bought and sold twenty-seven more in the last four years. She buys them under her name, usually at city auction, her brothers fix up the prop-erty, and then they sell for a nice profit."

"Seems like a good deal if you can swing it." Nolan handed the folder back to Lauren.

"Spencer also has access to their so-called office." She grabbed another folder out of the pile, pulling out a Google Maps picture of the front of a business, along with several pictures she had taken from across the road, under a railroad bridge. An eight-foot fence surrounded the square-shaped building. Two vehicles loaded with tools sat parked in front, safely enclosed by the gates. "I know we've driven by there about a hundred times, but this is where they keep their building supplies, tools, and work vehicles. Obviously, I've done a little surveillance. When one guy takes a work truck, he leaves his personal car." Tugging the three-sizes-too-big white button-down shirt Nolan had given her back into place, she tapped the photo. "You can't see it from the picture, and they've never been outside when we've driven by, but there are two huge Rottweilers in there. David working for Melissa means he has access to multiple properties, vehicles, and cash."

"You sure about the Rottweilers?"

She let out a hard breath. "I'm sure."

Nolan studied the pictures. "The profile he used with Brianna said he was working in the construction business."

"Fill your big lies with little truths," Lauren replied.

"Access to multiple vehicles, numerous properties, cash," Nolan repeated. "This guy fell into a pyscho killer's dream."

"And Melissa St. John has a pistol permit. It's the perfect freaking storm for David Spencer." She flipped the files down onto the table and ran her hands through her hair. It felt greasy and limp.

"Are you ready to do this?"

Lauren glanced at the monitor. Melissa was sitting in the interview room staring straight ahead; not playing on her phone or leafing through the files they had purposely left in there with her. She was just staring at the caged-in window that held a view of the brick wall of the church building next door. Lauren's mind flipped back to Reese lying in the ICU with his head bandaged and tubes snaking every which way out of his body.

"Yeah," she breathed, "let's do this."

40

Melissa St. John sat with her chin up, pointed towards the window, and her arms crossed. She barely blinked when Lauren and Nolan came in. Ben Lema had read Melissa her rights, leaving the white printed card on the table next to her.

"Let's get this over with," Melissa said as they settled into their seats across from her. Her sparkly green eye shadow glittered under the overheard light. Combined with the cream-colored sweater she had on that was generously sprinkled with tone-on-tone sequins, she reminded Lauren of some half-assed, overaged fairy princess wannabe.

"You don't have to talk to us," Nolan reminded her. "This is a voluntary interview. You can get up and leave whenever you want." Lauren and Nolan had agreed before the interview started to only concentrate on the dead and missing women and only talk about Reese's shooting if Melissa was the one who brought it up.

"What I want," she said enunciating every word, "is for the police to stop harassing me and my boyfriend. He came in, voluntarily. I've come in, voluntarily. After today, you better lock me up if you want me to step foot in this building, because I'm done."

Lauren launched right in, before Melissa decided to revoke her cooperation, such as it was. "Do you know where David Spencer is?"

"Right now? At this very second? No." She locked eyes with Lauren. "He went to work yesterday and he never came home. I'm worried sick that he's okay. I don't know where he is."

"Would you tell us if you did?" Lauren asked.

"Sure, I would. If I knew, which I don't. Why wouldn't I? Has he done something wrong?" The corners of Melissa's lips turned up in a hint of a smirk. "Nice shirt, by the way."

Not rising to the bait, Lauren pressed on. "David doesn't have a job. He's gone at all hours of the day. He switches cars all the time. Doesn't that seem suspicious to you?"

Now she gave Lauren a full sharp smile, as if her answer itself would cut her. "He does have a job. He works for me. And that requires him to switch out vehicles and be out all hours of the day. And night."

"He works for you?" Lauren wanted her acknowledgment of her employing him clarified for the camera, so there was no doubt.

"Yes. Off the books." She threw her hands in the air in mock surrender. "Okay. I've confessed to tax evasion. Call the IRS and have me put away."

"What does David do for you?" Nolan asked. He was obviously going to try to play the good cop in this scenario.

Melissa leaned back in her chair, slouching a little. "Whatever needs to be done. If a tenant has a leaky pipe, he goes over to the property. Electrical problems at four in the morning? I send him along."

"Now David's a plumber and a master electrician?" Lauren asked.

Melissa's eyes narrowed. Her voice got tight. "No. But he can call one on his cell and wait at the property for them to show up. Some things he can do himself, like install new batteries in all the smoke detectors or winterize certain unoccupied properties. It's not rocket science."

Lauren wasn't convinced. "And you pay him for this?"

She nodded. "Cash. In my business, flipping properties, a lot of transactions are strictly cash."

"How convenient."

Melissa didn't even bristle at the sarcasm in Lauren's voice. "I know you want to believe David is some criminal mastermind," she countered, "but the fact is he's just a young guy, working odd hours for his girlfriend, and trying to get his college degree. I wish our lives were more exciting, but they're just not."

Lauren wasn't willing to accept that answer. "Oh, come on. David never came home late? Maybe with weird stains on his clothes or smelling like another girl? He doesn't shut his laptop when you walk in the room? You've never seen him with a strange phone, maybe a burner phone, and thought 'What's up with this?'"

"What my partner is trying to get at," Nolan swooped in, trying to rescue the interview with his calm, even voice, "is whether you've seen anything in the last year that's made you suspicious?"

"That's a broad statement. You keep saying the word *suspicious*. What's considered suspicious? He's never come home smelling like sex. I've never seen a strange phone. Does he tell me every move he makes? No. But I don't nag him about it, either."

"Ever see him on a computer cruising online dating sites?"

She snorted back a laugh. "Oh, please. Do you think he'd still be in my house if I found out about something like that?" She leaned forward toward Lauren and told her, "And I'm a jealous person. I admit that, okay? So I do check."

Lauren reached under her chair where she had stashed a folder before the interview started. She produced four pictures: Katherine Vine, Amber Anderson, Isabella Colon, and Brianna McIntyre. "Have you ever seen any of these people before?"

Melissa took the glossy 8x10 pictures from her and looked at each one. "Only on the news," she replied, handing them back.

Lauren took a deep breath and circled away from her attack mode. "You know what he went to trial for, right?"

Melissa's mouth pulled into a tight smile. "You got him off on a murder charge. A jury of his peers looked at all the evidence and found him not guilty. Thank you for that."

"That jury didn't know about his dead girlfriend, Amber Anderson." It was Nolan again, with the soft touch. "Did he ever talk to you about Amber?" At Amber's mention, Lauren held up her picture.

Melissa's hand flew to a beaded, crocheted rose pinned to her shoulder. "We talked about that. She ran away all the time. They weren't going out anymore when she took off. And you guys don't even know how she died." Her fingers plucked at the beads.

Lauren tried to match Nolan's tone. "She was too decomposed."

Melissa's confident mask slipped for a second as both of the detectives sat silent, letting her absorb that last statement. She pulled so hard at her flower one of the beads popped off. "I don't know what you want me to say." Her voice sounded small as she tried to stuff the bead in her front pants pocket.

"We want you to be safe," Nolan was leaning in, forearms on his knees, hands clasped together in front of him. "You have guns." It wasn't a question.

"Legally. I have guns legally for my protection, and I've had them since before I knew David Spencer."

"You have a pistol permit." Nolan held up the document. "Do you also have long guns? Rifles or shotguns?"

She scratched at the side of her nose with one long, manicured nail. "Two rifles. Those were my father's. My dad was a hunter and so are my brothers."

"Is one a .22?" Lauren asked.

"I think one is a .22, but you can go into any sporting goods store and buy one of those without even having a permit."

"Do you carry often?"

"Not really. Some of my properties aren't in the best neighborhoods. Only when I know I'll be dealing in cash."

"Does David take them with him when he goes on jobs?" Nolan asked.

"No, he doesn't take them with him on jobs. That would be illegal. And we both know someone who'd love to catch him carrying without a pistol permit." Her eyes slid sideways to Lauren, then back to Nolan. "And yes, before you ask, we've both shot them at a shooting range. My brothers belong to a rod and gun club."

"Where are your guns now?"

"In my gun safe. Like I said, I only take one out with me when I'm going to collect rents. I'd tell you that you're welcome to come in my house and look, but I think I'd rather have you get a search warrant."

"With all these bad things happening and his name coming up"—Nolan inched his chair as close as he could to her without actually touching—"you don't wonder if David might be involved?"

Tears should have been welling up in her eyes; Melissa should have tearfully shaken her head and told them in a tiny voice she couldn't believe he'd ever do such a thing. Instead, Melissa seemed to rally her strength. "If you had any evidence, you'd arrest him. You don't have shit if you're talking to me."

"A lot of people around David seem to get hurt," Nolan said.

"No," she shot back, pointing a glittering nail at Lauren, "a lot of people seem to get hurt around *her*. Now her partner is shot. So let's pin that on David too. Right? This is bullshit." She stood up.

"Sit down." Lauren's last nerve snapped. She jumped from her chair, partially blocking Melissa's way.

"No." Melissa tried to maneuver around to get out the door.

"Where is David Spencer?" Lauren demanded.

"I don't know," Melissa hissed, then looked up into the camera. "I want a lawyer. I don't want to talk to any cops, now or in the future. Let me get out of here."

"Relax. You can go." Nolan got to his feet, reached past Lauren, and opened the door for Melissa.

They followed her out into the main Homicide office, where Melissa grabbed her coat off the rack and headed for the door. Lauren's anger bubbled up as they trailed behind her all the way to the elevator. Melissa stabbed the down button five times with her ridiculously long fingernail.

"I just want you to know," Lauren told her as the doors bonged open, "that I think it's pathetic, the way David uses you to get his rocks off."

235

Nolan gripped Lauren's shoulder as Melissa stomped onto the elevator. She turned to face them with a snarky smile as the doors slid shut. "Saved that last one for off camera, huh?"

The doors slid shut in Lauren's face.

41

"Lauren." Captain Maniechwicz stuck his head out of his office and motioned for her and Nolan to come inside. "We need to talk."

Lauren's pulse was still racing from her confrontational interview with Melissa. She had swiped back into the Homicide office ready to punch something or someone when the captain summoned her into his inner sanctum.

Nolan had never dealt with the oddities of the Invisible Man yet, but he didn't get the full measure of his kookiness because his shrine to the Buffalo Bills was packed away. All that was left in the office was the captain's desk and three chairs. Boxes sat stacked to the ceiling on the far wall. She wondered if his cherished Buffalo Bills flag was stashed away in one of them. Or if he knew that Reese had stolen his Jim Kelly bobblehead.

"Yes, sir?" Lauren asked.

"The hospital detail assigned to you was quite concerned when they couldn't find you."

"I'm sorry, sir." She wasn't sorry. "I had to get on this. We have to track down David Spencer. And Melissa is playing games. Isabella Colon might still be alive. I think he shot Reese because we were getting too close—"

The Invisible Man held up a hand silencing her. "David Spencer's Lexus was located in West Seneca about two hours ago, parked on a residential side street. We've impounded it."

"So he's in West Seneca?" Nolan asked. West Seneca was a first ring suburb that butted up to the city and to Cazenovia Park.

"We don't know." The captain shifted his bulky belly against his empty desk. "The district attorney says we don't have enough for a search warrant of his car, let alone his house, or his work place. Carl Church says we have nothing to tie David Spencer to either Isabella Colon's disappearance or Shane Reese's shooting. And he's right."

"But Captain—" Lauren sputtered.

"Right now, we have every cop, every detective, every resource we have focused on finding the person who shot Reese. The Evidence techs found no fingerprints on the gun, and even with a rush order at the lab, I doubt they'll find any DNA."

David would be too smart to leave any evidence on the gun, Lauren knew. And rifles didn't have to be registered in New York State. David could have ten of them he bought at a local hunting store, and if he paid cash, there'd be no record.

"What I want from you right now is to take another Homicide car and go to Reese's house. Grab whatever you think he's going to need and head back to the hospital. Or go home. No more interviews unless I approve them."

"Where's his dog now?" Lauren asked, ignoring that last statement. She wasn't interested in his approval.

"Joy Walsh went and grabbed him. She turned him over to Reese's buddy in K9, Evan Harold, for now. Evan said he'd get ahold of you."

She nodded. Evan was a good guy and she knew he and Reese had been friends since the police academy. When she was done with the captain, she'd check her phone to see if Evan had called her. After she grabbed Reese's things, Lauren needed to arrange a pick up. She wanted Reese's dog, Watson, staying with her, even if Dayla had to watch him while she was at the hospital. Evan was a nice guy, but he was still a stranger to Watson.

Her phone had been blowing up since the shooting. The only messages she'd returned were her daughters' and her parents', and those were very brief conversations, just to let them know she was okay and Reese was still alive. If Evan had called, his message was probably buried in her inbox somewhere.

"I want to head out right now, so I can get back to the hospital," Lauren told the captain.

"No more leaving without telling anyone where you're going," he admonished. "We're trying to protect you. That's why I want a car crew with you at Reese's house, in case the nut job who shot him is still lurking in the park."

She wanted to protest that she didn't need a babysitter. Couldn't he see Nolan standing right next to her? But she bit her tongue. It was time for her to pick her battles very carefully. "Who's working?"

"Garcia and Anthony are going to go over there with you."

It figures, she thought, *the two people in the world I least want to be around right now.*

Lauren looked over to Nolan. "You want to take a ride over to Reese's house with me?"

"I am your ride," he replied. "Let's get his stuff and we'll go back over to the hospital together."

"It sounds like we're all on the same page." She turned to the Invisible Man. "Tell Garcia and Anthony we'll be in the Cold Case office finishing up the paperwork for the interview we just did."

The captain nodded. "They're on their way back to headquarters now."

"Good," Lauren said. "Are we done?"

The captain's voice took on a softer tone. "We had to rein Reese in when you first got stabbed, even though there was no clear suspect at the time. Then he wouldn't leave your side. So I get it, Lauren. I do."

You don't get anything. The thought was bitter and poisonous in her brain. *Things have changed.*

"And one more thing," he called as they turned to leave.

"Yes, sir?"

His frown followed his eyes as they traveled her up and down. "Change that shirt."

42

Despite her less-than-stellar relationship with both Garcia and Anthony, they stifled their disdain for Lauren for the moment to help out Reese. Reese and Vatasha Anthony had always gotten along, and Craig Garcia was just afraid of him. They saved their passive-aggressive animosity for Lauren, and they made no secret that they both had always considered her a know-it-all and a glory hound. Driving back over to Beyer Place in Nolan's truck, Lauren had to appreciate the irony of those two being the ones to "protect" her from the phantom menace that had become David Spencer.

"How are you feeling?" Nolan asked, hands at ten and two on the wheel, staring straight ahead.

"It's amazing what a diet that consists solely of black coffee can do for you." She glanced in the side mirror, checking to make sure the detectives were still following in their vehicle.

"I'm taking you to get something to eat, and to change before I bring you back to the hospital."

There were still traces of blood smeared on her khaki pants, near the knees, but Nolan's button down hung low enough to cover those. "There's a café inside the hospital. I can get a bite there," she told him. "I'll grab one of Reese's sweatshirts when we get to his house. I'm sure he won't mind."

Nolan didn't answer, his face screwed up in a look of concern, eyebrows drawn together into a V-ed pucker.

As they pulled up, Lauren noticed a strip of crime scene tape lightly flapping from the trunk of a small tree in front of a neighbor's house. The fire department must have hosed down the sidewalk, but the dark patch where Reese had fallen was still visible. His unmarked car was parked on the street where he had left it. No one had thought to come back and grab it. Someone had left a bouquet of blue carnations wrapped in clear plastic on the concrete. It, too, fluttered with the slight breeze.

They parked the Explorer on the street, waiting for Anthony and Garcia to pull in behind them before exiting.

Anthony had on a brown windbreaker with a tan scarf knotted at her throat and matching gloves. That was the one thing the two women did have in common; they were constantly cold. "How's Reese doing?" she asked as she came around the front of the un-marked green Chevy.

"He's alive," Lauren said, stepping over the flowers. "He's still critical, but stable." She felt totally exposed out there in the open, with the park at her back. If David Spencer was out there, he had a clear shot at her. And everyone she was with.

"We combed this entire place last night. Didn't we, boss?" Garcia asked Nolan, motioning to the tree line. "Whoever did this made sure he got out quick."

"I don't remember hearing a car engine starting," Nolan said. "But then again, I was expecting to get shot."

Lauren reached into her pants pocket and pulled out her keys. She had a spare for Reese's back door that he'd given her months ago, so she could check on Watson from time to time. Lauren had told Joy Walsh last night where Reese's hidden key to the front door was so she could grab Watson. Joy had taken the spare key with her, along with the dog. Lauren made a mental note to grab some of Watson's things as well.

To get to Reese's back door, the four of them had to walk single-file between his house and his next-door neighbor's. With only about three feet to maneuver, Anthony reached out and let her fingers trail over the siding as she walked ahead of Lauren and Nolan, while Garcia brought up the rear.

"Is this it?" Anthony asked, coming around the back of the small cottage.

"It should be the only door back there," Lauren replied, trying to keep the snark out of her voice. The other detective didn't want to be there as much as Lauren didn't want her there. Lauren walked past her, sticking the key in the doorknob and twisting.

"Let's do this the right way," Garcia said from behind. "Tactical. Let's clear the rooms one by one. There's still a shooter at large out there."

That was the one suggestion Craig Garcia had made in a long time that she was willing to take.

Reese had painted the door a cheerful red but neglected the trim, which was peeling off in whitish strips. *He was going to get the whole house resided this summer,* Lauren thought, pushing her way into his back hall. *That was his plan. I was going to help him redo his bathroom and.*

kitchen. When I got around to it. But of course, something was sure to come up and I'd put Reese off, like I always did.

The back hall was cluttered with coats, shoes, boots, and shopping bags filled with odds and ends he never unpacked after he moved in. Lauren and Nolan swept it quickly with their guns. It was too cramped for the four of them, so Lauren, Nolan, and Anthony moved into the kitchen while Garcia made his way inside.

"Double check the hall," Nolan yelled to him. "We'll clear the kitchen."

As Lauren checked her corner, something caught her eye. One of the plates Lauren had bought Reese as a housewarming gift was sitting on the kitchen table, sprinkled with crumbs. It had a cheery red and brown rooster painted on it and she had thought the pattern would brighten up the dimly lit room. Anthony was at the doorway to the living room, gun drawn, checking her corners before they entered.

Lauren broke protocol and went to the table. Instead of yelling "Clear!" to let Garcia know the room was safe to enter, she found herself picking up the plate. She couldn't help herself. She was about to brush the crumbs into the garbage can when she heard Garcia yell, "Everyone stop."

Lauren's head swiveled to where Garcia was standing, still in the back hall. He was crouched down, looking at something wedged between the door trim and large canvas bag with baseball equipment sticking out of the top, flush against the wall.

It was a tire iron.

About thirty-six inches high, it was the long bar kind, not the four-way type she had in the back of her car. It was exactly the sort that had been used to bludgeon Joe Wheeler to death in November.

Garcia was peering at it closely, then he let out a low whistle and said, "There's what looks like blood and definitely hairs stuck to this. We need to call Evidence and Photography and get this down to the lab."

"Garcia, come on." Lauren dropped the plate into the garbage can and tried to get back into the hall. "That can't be what you think it is."

"Stop her!" Garcia called, blocking her view of the tire iron.

Nolan grabbed her by the shoulders. Anthony pushed past them to back up Garcia. "No. You stay in there," she told Lauren. "Both of you stay put. Don't touch another thing."

She jerked out from under Nolan's grip. "Let me by," Lauren warned, trying to push past her.

"Or what?" Anthony asked, squaring herself to Lauren. "You don't really want to go down this road right now with me."

"What's going on?" Nolan asked. "Who cares about a Goddamn tire iron?"

"Sorry, Mister Sheriff, that Riley here didn't bring you up to speed, but her ex-boyfriend, who she tried to get fired, got his brains beat in with a tire iron four months ago," Garcia said. He reached for his portable radio and added, "And the murder weapon was never recovered."

"I am up to speed," Nolan snapped back. "I have a tire iron in my garage at home. Does that make me a suspect too?"

Garcia ignored him, keying his mic. "Car 1272 to radio?"

"This is bullshit," Lauren hissed, turning toward Nolan. "Anyone could have picked the back door lock and planted that there. Especially David Spencer, if he knew he was going to wait for Reese to come home."

"Really? That's your theory?" Anthony asked. "David Spencer is a criminal mastermind who killed your ex, planted evidence, laid in wait, and shot your partner? For what purpose?"

Lauren opened her mouth to argue, then snapped it shut.

Anthony wasn't done. "You really think this kid is capable of all these things? Killing cops and kidnapping girls and tampering with crime scenes?"

"I'm leaving," Lauren announced, turning toward the door from the kitchen to the living room.

"No way," Garcia yelled after her. "You need to stay. Vatasha, stop her. I'm calling for a supervisor!"

Lauren crossed the living room, past Watson's crate near the window, and opened the front door. She wasn't wasting one more precious second of time arguing with either of them.

"Let her go," she heard Anthony say from behind. "It's only going to cost her her job."

Coming out on the front step, she noticed for the first time that day that the sky was dark and overcast. *Fitting,* she thought, making her way along the path to the sidewalk. *It's like some comical, cosmic practical joke is getting played on me. It wouldn't shock me right now if a plague of locusts started raining from the sky.*

"Lauren?" Nolan came out of the door after her. When she didn't stop, he reached out and caught her by the arm.

She turned on her heel, an eye out for any stray media vehicles that could be lurking nearby looking for a sound bite. "I want to go back to the hospital."

Nolan let go of her. "What about Reese's things?"

She looked past him to the front picture window, hung with a yellow curtain she had picked out for him. "It's a crime scene now. That's the murder weapon used to kill Joe Wheeler. David Spencer has been one step ahead of me since we found Brianna's body. And the more I point it out, the more irrational I sound."

246

"So you're just going to give up? On David Spencer, on Isabella Colon, on Reese?"

She shook her head. "Hell no. I'm not giving up on anything except the bullshit going on right here. I'm going to go to the hospital. You can give me a ride, or I can call for a car. But I'm going now."

43

Nolan drove her to the hospital.

She was silent the entire ride, staring out the window, watching the sky grow more ominous. Nolan attempted to make conversation, but she ignored it. *This is what I'm good at, isn't it? Taking advantage of the men in my life. Using them and being ungrateful. Maybe it's time I showed my gratitude in a different way.*

In the hospital parking lot that faced Grider Street, Lauren could see news vans with their antennae sticking up from their roofs, like the remote-control cars she bought the girls for Christmas when they were four and five. Reporters and their cameramen were trying to get the best shot of the Erie County Medical Center in the rapidly deteriorating light.

After Nolan flashed his badge, the guard allowed him to drive up the emergency room ramp. Someone had hand-lettered a sign and stuck it on the wall of the guard shack that said, EMERGENCY VE-HICLES OR EMERGENCY DROP OFFS ONLY! ALL OTHERS WILL BE TOWED/FINED! Nolan pulled over in front of the ambulance bay. Thankfully, there were no other emergency vehicles there at the time. "What do you want me to tell Kencil? Or your boss?"

"Tell them I'm with Reese. Anything else, I don't care."

"Lauren—"

She opened the door and hopped out. "Thanks for everything, Nolan." She let the door fall shut behind her and walked toward the double doors without looking back.

She made her way to the elevators, got off on the right floor, then followed the correct colored line to the ICU. Her body was on autopilot, but her mind was a blizzard of jumbled thoughts. David Spencer was barely twenty years old. Could he be sophisticated enough to pull off this elaborate scheme of murder? Obviously, Reese had hit a nerve, maybe the biggest nerve, when he questioned a sexual relationship with his mother. Those were fighting words to just about any guy. But David had proven time and again he wasn't just any guy.

As she rounded the corner of the ICU, she noticed a flurry of activity around Reese's room. Nurses, orderlies, and white-coated doctors were rapidly coming and going. Quickening her pace to just short of an all-out run, she was intercepted by Peter Reese, whose red-rimmed eyes confirmed what she had suspected.

"You can't go in," he said, holding onto her by the shoulders.

"What's wrong?" She bounced on her toes, trying to see over him into the room.

"The doctors say there's swelling on his brain. They're taking him to relieve the pressure now."

Fear knotted her stomach. "How?" she demanded. "How are they going to do that?"

"You folks have to clear a path all the way to the nurses' station," a nurse wearing blue scrubs told them, motioning them back with her arms.

Peter retreated, still holding onto Lauren. "Sandra went to the chapel to pray as soon as they kicked us out." Swallowing so hard Lauren could hear it, he stopped shoving her when Lauren's rump hit the desk. "It's not good." A tear rolled down his face. "They asked me if we had a priest or a pastor."

A chill ran through Lauren's body. Down the hall, a cluster of people wheeled Reese out of his room on a gurney. Another nurse pushed his IV pole along with the group and together rushed him toward the rear elevators.

"They said they were going to try to remove the breathing tube just after you left." Peter was speaking to her but looking at the elevator bank as the doors closed on his son. "They said everything was looking good. Then ... this."

"He's going to be okay," Lauren said, just because it was what she was supposed to say. They both knew what the doctors meant when they asked for clergy. Doctors had asked her to do it for them in the past. She'd played it as if it was meant to comfort the family members, but that was just to soften the blow.

Peter wiped his nose on the back of his jacket sleeve. "He's strong, right? That's what the doctor said. That kid is strong. He'll pull through. He will."

He crumpled forward into Lauren's arms, weeping as quietly as he could manage. She held onto him the way she'd held her daughters during the most traumatic moments of their lives, knowing that nothing she could say could help them, that she could only hold them and hope for the best.

After a few seconds Peter straightened up, rubbed his eyes with the heels of his hands, and took a deep, stuttering breath. "I have to go talk to the rest of the family, tell them what's going on. Will you find Sandra in the chapel and tell her that's where I went?"

She nodded stiffly. The last place she wanted to be was the chapel. "Whatever you need me to do, Peter."

He looked up at the ceiling, as if trying to stave off more tears. "I know cops get shot. I know they do, but I really never, ever was afraid for Shane. He made it back from the Gulf in one piece. What could happen to him here? This is America, right?"

Before she could answer, he broke away and headed for the bank of elevators that had just taken his son away. He punched the down button, stuffed his hands in his pockets, and stood facing away from her, shoulders slumped. His despair was palpable from where she was standing. He radiated it like a cold, dark sun.

She felt it all the way into her bones and should have blinked back tears. But no. There weren't going to be any tears. Not from her. Not ever again.

Peter Reese stepped inside the open car door and was gone.

As she crossed the corridor, she spotted Kencil coming toward her. She knew by the way he was charging towards Reese's room that he had found out about the tire iron and was looking for her. The State Attorney General's Office handled all cases of police misconduct. The Buffalo Police Department wouldn't be allowed to investigate Reese as a suspect in Joe Wheeler's death; Kencil's office would.

She ducked into an empty room and quietly pulled the curtain around her, peeking out of the split in the fabric. She watched Kencil question an orderly who pointed toward the elevators. He nodded, straightened his jacket, and stalked back that way. She waited until he had hopped on the elevator and slipped out into the hallway

44

Lauren knew there was a chapel on the second floor of the main building, but she'd never been inside it. Turning around, she headed for the stairs. She hoped to avoid the throng of concerned police officers and overzealous reporters who were surely roaming around. But more importantly, she hoped to avoid Kencil.

Taking the stairs two at a time, she hit the exit bar for the second floor and stepped out into the hallway. It took a second for her to orient herself before looking at the signs posted with arrows on the wall in front of her. She followed the color-coded stripe around a corner and kept going until she came to the cafeteria. Directly across was a set of large, white double doors marked CHAPEL. Next to the door frame, at eye level, was a listing of the various times of services offered.

She didn't know how long she stood outside that door. Time had lost all meaning to her sleep-deprived brain. She came to the hospital to be with Reese. To talk to him and tell him to stay strong, get better, they had things to do. A psycho to catch. Now that David had set both of them up, they could still work together. She would convince him they needed to stay together as partners. That she needed him. She'd done it before and he'd always come back.

But she wasn't going to get to say those things to Reese. She was waiting for him to die. This was not what was supposed to happen.

This can't be happening. This can't be happening. This can't be happening.

She repeated the mantra in her head over and over and over, stalling before she had to go in and face Reese's mother. Stalling because losing Reese was not in any of her plans. He was maybe going to dump her as a partner, not die on her. Not get ripped away from her. Not be erased from her life forever.

Finally, she took a deep breath and twisted the handle.

The door swung inward smoothly and silently, as if the maintenance people kept the hinges constantly oiled to preserve the solemnity of the place. It was a nondenominational chapel, but there was a small wooden crucifix over the altar in front of the rows of chairs. Flameless candles had been set around the room in strategic places and someone had laid a bouquet of yellow roses, petal edges turning brown, at the foot of the altar.

There was only one person in the chapel. Kneeling on the floor in the first row, head bowed to her hands, clutching a beaded rosary, was Sandra Reese. Her purple polka-dot dress was badly wrinkled and cheerfully out of place. She didn't look over when Lauren came in, or when she slid into the chair next to her.

"Peter went to update your relatives about Shane," Lauren said in a quiet voice. When Sandra didn't answer, she didn't know if she should get up, stay, or pray. She folded her hands in her lap over the shirttail of Nolan's button-down and shut her mouth.

"Did you know that Shane was almost engaged once?" Sandra asked, lifting her head a little, twisting the rosary beads between her thin fingers. Sandra had to be close to sixty-five, but she was still a beauty, with wide set brown eyes and high, sharp cheekbones, so much like Reese's. On a normal day she could have passed for twenty years younger. But now she had dark circles under her eyes and deep lines etched on either side of her mouth, aging her well past her years.

"No." Lauren was shocked to hear that. He had always claimed even his most serious relationships had never lasted more than six months and never mentioned anyone he had wanted to marry.

She nodded, not looking at Lauren, but at a spot somewhere above the altar. "When he was in the Army. Before he shipped out to the Gulf, he got very wrapped up in a girl. Her name was Stacey, and he was crazy about her. He met her after he enlisted but before he got his orders. Everything seemed so *immediate* then. All of his new military buddies were marrying their high school sweethearts, having babies. I hadn't been happy when he joined up, not at first." She gave a bitter laugh. "I thought something bad was going to happen to him."

"You were right to worry, but he came home safe," Lauren said, just to say something. The words sounded stupid, even to her own ears.

Sandra went on like she hadn't spoken. "He even bought Stacey an engagement ring. I helped him pick it out."

How did I not know this? "What happened between them?" Lauren asked, trying to keep her voice steady.

"My husband helped me hang some new curtains."

Lauren wasn't sure she heard her right and cocked her head. "Curtains?"

"Peter helped me put up some new curtains I bought on sale. That was when we didn't have a lot of money, and those big puffy drapes were popular, like hanging a prom dress across your window." A slight smile traced its way across her face. "Anyway, me and Peter struggled with those mauve monstrosities for two hours while Shane sat in the

255

recliner in the living room, just watching us, laughing the whole time. When I got home later that night, he was at the kitchen table, all by himself. I asked him how things were. He just let out a big sigh and said, 'We broke up.' I asked him why, when he'd just gone out and bought a ring? And Shane told me, 'I watched the way Dad looked at you when you were hanging those curtains together, and I realized I never, ever looked at Stacey like that. So I broke up with her.' And that was that. It was over between him and her."

Lauren sat back in the chapel chair, speechless.

"Do you know why I just told you that story?" Sandra asked, still looking at the spot on the wall where the crucifix was hanging.

"No." Lauren's voice was small and shaky.

"Because Shane looks at you the way Peter looks at me when I hang curtains."

45

"**W**here is he?"

"What? Hello? Wait one minute. The reception is terrible. I'm going to step outside."

It sounded like Violanti was at a restaurant. Lauren could hear busy sounds in the background: people laughing, the clink of dishes. He must have gotten out the door because suddenly the line was clear. "Riley? Are you still there?"

"I'm here," she replied. She was sitting in the backseat of a gray mini-van being driven by a thirty-year-old Asian man. Her ride share driver had tried to strike up a conversation with her when she first climbed in on Grider Street, telling her he made more money picking up fares than at his day job at a tech company in Amherst, but she'd immediately shut that down. She only needed to speak to two people, and she was on the phone with one of them.

"Where are you?" he asked. "Are you at the hospital? I'm so sorry about Reese. How's he doing?"

"Not good." She needed to keep this short and sweet. "Do you know where David is?"

"Melissa said he left yesterday morning for work like normal. Took the Lexus sedan and never came back. She's been frantically calling me every hour since you had her picked up. She said you bullied her in the interview room."

"She held her own," Lauren said, keeping her eyes on her driver, watching what she said. "She asked for a lawyer. Are you representing her?"

"No. I told her it would be a conflict of interest and referred her to a friend of mine, but that hasn't stopped her from hounding me over David. She thinks he's going to show up at my door."

"I think he has other plans," Lauren said then asked for the third time: "Do you have any idea where he is?"

"No. I told Melissa and I'm telling you—he hasn't called me, hasn't shown up here or at his mom's house."

"You'll call me if you hear from him?"

"Of course, I will. Riley—"

She hung up on him.

"Drop me off at the gate," she instructed her driver as the guard shack to her gated community came into sight. "I'm going to walk from there."

46

She froze the entire walk through her neighborhood to her house. Her driver had had news radio playing in the minivan and the forecaster was calling for a snowstorm to blow in from over the lake in the next twenty-four hours. He talked about low pressure systems in Canada and travel advisories. *It figures*, she thought bitterly, wrapping her arms around herself to stay warm. *Tomorrow is the last day of March and we get a snowstorm. Happy April Fool's Day to Buffalo.*

She hadn't seen any media vans parked outside her gate, so she assumed they were all still at the hospital. By now they'd heard Reese had taken a turn for the worse and Lauren could hear the sound bites flowing from their lips: *fighting for his life, clinging to hope, desperate attempts.*

She unlocked her door and slipped into her house. It was dark and quiet. She hadn't left a light on when she'd left for work yesterday. Had it really only been twenty-four hours since Reese had gotten shot? It seemed like days, like months, like years.

Reese.

She climbed the steps to her second floor, not caring about the mud she was tracking on the carpet.

These last few years we've been telling everyone there's nothing between us. What if we've been lying, even to ourselves, this whole time?

She couldn't imagine her world without Reese in it. His cocky attitude, his baseball hats, his jokes. She couldn't just wake up and go to work and him not be there. She couldn't fathom it. She'd taken him for granted for so long, lied to him, went behind his back, and yet he had stuck by her through everything. She'd never really asked herself why. What guy would put up with all of her bullshit for so long?

Or maybe she had asked herself and hadn't wanted to believe the answer.

She stripped off Nolan's white button-down and left it on the hallway floor in front of her bathroom. Her white bra was stained with blood. She left it in a heap with her pants and underwear. Piling her keys, Glock, and phone on the back of the toilet, she turned the shower on as hot as it would go and stepped inside.

She pressed her palms against the wall as the near scalding water poured over her body. She saw some pink run off her body and down the drain; Reese's blood. She was grateful for the burning sensation, it meant she was still alive.

After scrubbing herself raw with a purple washcloth, she stepped out dripping onto the bathmat on the bathroom floor. Wrapping a bath towel around herself, she stepped over the pile, careful to bring her phone with her. The clothes she was going to throw away. The phone she needed.

Grabbing her robe off the hook in her bedroom, she put it on and sat on the corner of her bed. Unlocking her code, she scrolled through her contacts until she found the one she was looking for; the one she used to know by heart.

"Mark?" she asked her ex-husband when he picked up the call. She used to love the sound of her ex's name when she said it. Now it was just a name of someone she used to know a million years ago when she was someone else.

"Lauren, I've been trying to reach you. I saw on the news what happened to Reese. Is he going to be okay? Are *you* okay?"

"No," she answered for both questions. "I need you to do something for me."

"Anything." Mark meant it. If only he could have stayed faithful, maybe they'd still be together. But maybe not.

"I need you to contact your computer guy. You know the one I'm talking about. I'm going to give you some names and I want him to track any credit card purchases in the last two days for all three of the ride sharing services here in Buffalo."

Mark was a lawyer who specialized in real estate law, but Lauren had found out when they were married that he kept an older friend's son, who had gone to college for computer science and gotten kicked out for hacking, on a cash retainer. Lauren and Mark had chosen simply not to speak of it while they were together. Mark liked to know who was buying what in real time and what his client's bank accounts looked like before he made a deal. Working homicides made you care less about corporate spying, and even though she'd been tempted over the years to enlist the man's services, the risk had never outweighed the reward. Until now.

"Are you sure about this?" he asked.

"Absolutely sure. And I need the information right away."

There was a long pause on Mark's end. He knew she'd never ask for this unless she was desperate. "You know anything you find because of this will get tossed out in a court of law. Fruit of the poisonous tree."

"Thank you for the constitutional law lesson. I'm hoping it won't come to that."

"What's that supposed to mean? Lauren, what are you planning to do?" The concern in his voice was genuine, so her dishonest answer didn't sound fake.

"I'm not planning anything. I just need some answers."

"Let me get a pen." She heard him rummaging around. *He must be at his new place with his son,* she thought. *I wonder how the second Mrs. Mark Hathaway fared in their divorce. Probably pretty good considering what I got after only a year.*

"Give me the names," Mark said.

47

Lauren hadn't planned on falling asleep, but her body must have just given up, because the next thing she knew she was lying on her bed in her bathrobe, still holding her phone and the morning sunlight was streaming through her window.

She had amassed twenty-seven emails, eight voice messages, and forty-two text messages while she was passed out. Ten texts and three emails were from Lindsey. Two emails and eight texts came from Erin. Seven texts were from Dayla. Four of the texts and two of the voice mails were from Mark. One text was from Peter Reese. It was two words long.

PRAY HARD.

It had come in at 4:38 in the morning.

It was 6:59 now. *A little more than two and a half hours ago, Reese was still alive,* she thought, *or maybe not. Maybe Peter wrote that because they were bringing in the priest for last rites. Maybe he's already dead.*

Instead of texting Peter back, Lauren bit her bottom lip until it bled as she listened to Mark's messages. All were insisting she call him.

Mark had always been an early riser, but she wasn't particularly concerned about waking him if he had chosen the luxury of sleeping in. He answered on the first ring.

"He's got your information, but he'll only give it to you in person, and he wants the cash up front."

"Whatever he wants." Lauren wiped her mouth with the back of her hand. It came away smeared with blood. "How much is he asking for?"

"He's my guy. I pay him. Just meet me in an hour at Teddy's Diner on Abbott Road in Lackawanna."

"Are you sure he'll be able to meet us on such short notice?"

"For cash, absolutely. You know the place I'm talking about?"

"Across from the plaza. Teddy, the Greek guy with the flowing black hair. We used to eat there when we were dating."

"That's the one. Eight o'clock."

"I'll be there."

She hit the end button and sat staring at her screen reflecting her mirror image back at her. She hadn't brushed her hair after the shower and it was a mess of tangles and snarls around her gaunt face. She clicked into her text messages and thumbed a reply to Peter. Just four words.

IS HE STILL FIGHTING?

Immediately three little dots started flashing under her message, signaling a reply was coming.

FOR NOW.

48

Lauren found zero relief in those words as she quickly dressed in a long-sleeve black thermal shirt and jeans. She clipped her holster to the waistband of her jeans, so that her gun sat in the small of her back. Ripping a brush through her hair, she pulled it into a tight ponytail and then gathered the clothing from the floor to throw away.

She was walking downstairs with the ripe, smelly, bloodstained pile when there was a knock at her front door.

She didn't have time to talk to anyone. She needed to be in her car and on the way to Teddy's. Wishing once again she'd had a window installed in her front door or at least a peephole, she opened up.

Wayne Kencil was standing there.

"Lauren, where the hell have you been? Half the city is looking for you right now."

"I'm surprised the guard at the gate let you in," she said, still clutching the pile of dirty clothes to her chest.

"We've been having patrol cars come knock on your door. I've been calling and texting you. Your commissioner has been calling and texting you."

"I saw. I just woke up. I'm heading back to the hospital now. I'll try to make it to the task force office later," she lied. She should have known better than to open the door after seeing him in the hospital. She should have known he'd come to her house. But she did know what was coming next.

"That's the thing." Kencil ran his hand over his forehead, shielding his eyes for a second. "You're off the task force. The tire iron in Reese's house tested positive for human blood. It looks like an exact match to the tire iron on the video."

Bullshit, she thought, *that video is so grainy every tire iron in the world looks like it would be an exact match. Don't try to trip me up with interrogation techniques so old we don't even use them anymore.*

"I know how to pick a lock. And so do you, I bet, but you'd never admit it. Can't you see what David Spencer is doing?"

"You have to leave David Spencer to us now." He'd taken on that patriarchal tone he used in the task force office. "Even if it's true he planted that evidence, it needs to be investigated properly. By someone other than you."

"I swear if you tell me I'm too close to this case, I'm going to punch you in the throat."

He seemed a little taken aback by that last statement because it was absolutely clear from the look on her face she wasn't kidding.

"Go to the hospital," he said once he gathered himself back together. "Stay with Reese. David Spencer will surface soon. He can't have gotten far, and once we grab him, maybe we'll be able to figure out what's really going on."

"Don't you dare let Bates or Perez search my house," she said. "I know you're going to apply for search warrants for Reese's place and mine. If I find out either one of those bastards was in here, I'm coming after you."

Any sympathy he might have had melted from his voice. "This isn't the time to be threatening people, Riley."

Lauren roughly shoved the pile of dirty clothes in his arms. He took a step down, off her front step, trying to juggle her pants and bra, almost slipping.

"Thanks for the heads up on the task force." Scooping her keys from the side hall table, she pulled the door closed behind her. "Do what you have to do. I gotta go."

She brushed past him, leaving him still clinging to her dirty underwear. "Lauren!" he called. But she was already in her Ford and backing out of her driveway.

49

She was late.

Wayne Kencil and his little pronouncement had made her late for the meeting. Mark was sitting in the far booth that backed to the wall, facing the door so he could see who came in. He looked rested and put together and handsome, as usual. A slightly younger guy was sitting across from him with his back to her. He was hunched over a breakfast plate, so all Lauren could really see was a long, scraggly pony tail trailing down his back. At least it wasn't a man bun.

Mark stood as she made her way across the diner. At the counter sat three elderly men passing sections of the morning newspaper to each other as they drank coffee. The familiar scents of bacon grease and onions filled her nose. "Where's your coat?" he asked as she slid into the cracked pleather seat of the booth.

"I didn't have time to grab it."

"Ethan, give the lady your jacket."

Ethan scowled. "What the hell am I going to wear then?"

Mark tossed a wad of bills down on the table in front of him. "Get yourself something nice." He reached over and snagged the olive-green army jacket from the back of the booth and handed it to Lauren. "Sorry it smells like convenience store burritos and his mother's basement."

"Hey! I got my own apartment seven months ago." Ethan protested as he scooped up the money, then held his coffee cup toward the waitress. "I've always said a man has to have his own place. My mom just really enjoyed me living there."

"You are a pleasure," Mark agreed. "Every time we meet, it's a delight."

Ethan ignored the sarcasm and shoveled some eggs into his mouth while still holding out his coffee mug.

Despite its odd smell, Lauren slipped her arms into the jacket. The weather was growing progressively worse outside. The morning sunshine had been covered over by ominous dark clouds and the temperature had plummeted overnight.

"Lauren this is Ethan. Ethan, Lauren." Mark motioned between them.

"That's not my real name," Ethan told her, glancing around as if someone might actually be interested in listening in on their conversation.

"Of course not," Lauren said. "Very clever. No one would ever look for a hacker named Ethan."

Ethan seemed undecided if she was messing with him or not. "Thanks?"

"Can you tell me what you found out?" she asked him. It was hard for her to look Ethan in the face. She was doing her best to ignore his attempt at growing a beard. He had to be past thirty, but it was sparse and patchy. It just made his round face look dirty to her.

"Yeah. Sorry about making you meet me like this, but I never give out my findings over the phone. Ever. If I can hack just about anything, so can a lot of other people, including cell phones."

"Your discretion is appreciated as well," Lauren said, accepting a cup of coffee from the short-haired waitress who came by to give Ethan a warm up.

"I'm all about remaining anonymous. And this assignment was easy. Almost too easy. I thought maybe you were trying to set me up."

He was met by Lauren's stony stare.

"I told you," Mark said. "This is just another job. Everyone walks away happy."

"You can't trust anyone, Mr. Hathaway. And the fact that you still use a smart phone after everything I've warned you about bothers me. A lot."

"How do you get your information, if you're not connected like everybody else?" Lauren asked.

"I build my own computers, for one thing. From the ground up. And I use this." He pulled a gray plastic flip phone, probably from the mid nineties, out of his pocket and put it on the table. "No GPS, no text messages, no photos with map coordinates imbedded in them. And I change out the actual phone as much as possible."

"They still make those?" Lauren asked, picking up and examining the big gray blob. It was the exact make and model of the first cell phone she'd ever used.

He snatched it back from her, rubbing it against his shirt, before stowing it away again. "No. But they're super easy to find. Just go to any flea market. These things are indestructible. Still, nothing's foolproof, which is why I have to dump them on the regular."

"Paranoid much?" she asked.

"I'm not stupid. I know who you are," he told her. "You're the one who stuck the fork in the dude's face. The one whose partner just got shot. And a cop getting credit card information this way is highly illegal. I think you've gone rogue."

Going rogue, she thought. *That's one way to put it.* "Then you know I'm in an awful hurry."

"So okay, then." He opened a little notepad at his elbow and read the first page over. "You wanted me to run three people's names for credit card transactions in the last two days on ride sharing companies operating in Buffalo. Of the three names, only one hit. Vernon St. John's credit card was used five times in the last forty-eight hours for rides."

Vernon St. John was Melissa's sixty-four-year-old father. Lauren figured David wouldn't be stupid enough to use his own credit card or Melissa's. She had Mark's hacker run Melissa's brothers' and father's credit cards instead. It had come to her during the ride back from the hospital when her driver was rambling on about how much money he made that David must be using ride sharing to get around once he dumped his car in West Seneca.

"This stuff is so basic. Why wouldn't you just get a search warrant or some shit like that?" Ethan asked.

"I might have been able to get one for the suspect's credit card, but there's no way I'd ever get one for his girlfriend's father," she answered. She motioned to the notebook. "Do I get to keep those?"

"Dates, times, prices. As well as all the pick-up and drop-off points. I wrote the drivers' names down too. I can get you their addresses if you want them." Ethan tore five small pages from the notepad and handed them to her. "Destroy these when you find what you need. I don't want anything lying around to tie me to this."

"Will do, boss," she replied, tucking the pages into her pocket.

Ethan sat back, seemingly relieved that he was not going to be busted and was going to get to keep all the money Mark had just given him. Lauren figured he'd be hitting the video game store on the way home. "I knew Mr. Hathaway used to be married to a lady cop. I figured it might be you who wanted this kind of stuff. He usually has me digging into people's real estate transactions."

"How very astute of you." She pointed to some buttered toast sitting on a plate next to him. "You gonna eat that?"

He pushed the plate toward her. "Be my guest."

"What are you going to do with this information?" Mark asked. His eyebrows pinched in concern for her over his stormy blue eyes. A few months ago, her heart would have been breaking.

She took a bite of Ethan's toast. "Whatever I have to."

50

The sky had taken on the dull gray color of a battleship's hull. As she crossed Teddy's parking lot, she saw other customers scurrying to their cars, leaning into the wind, clutching their coats around them. Lauren's new army jacket flapped at her sides, as she hadn't bothered to zip it. She went over in her head exactly what she had at her disposal: a gun with eighteen bullets, a flashlight in the glove box of her car, her portable police radio in the center console, twenty-two dollars cash, a credit card, and her police ID. Not exactly the arsenal she hoped she'd have.

The notebook pages listed five different addresses, all of which she knew from her research were owned by Melissa's family. All of them had been abandoned and bought at auction, but she was fairly sure none of them had been subject to any renovations.

She thought about calling Nolan. Apologizing to him for everything, the things that were her fault and even the things that weren't. She sat staring at her phone and knew that it didn't matter if she called him or not. They had no future together. It was best to just let things end with silence.

She took a minute to gather herself, then thumbed her screen, scrolling through her contacts until she came up with Lindsey's cell number. She knew it by heart but didn't trust herself to punch in the numbers correctly with the adrenaline flooding her system.

"Mom?" Lindsey answered on the first ring, her voice twisted in concern. "What happened to Shane? Is he going to be all right?"

"I need you to know something," Lauren said. Despite her spiking pulse, her mind felt calmed and steady because she knew exactly what was going to happen next. "I need you to know I love you and Erin more than anything in this world. You two are the loves of my life, and I am so proud of both of you."

"Mom!" Panic rose in Lindsey's voice. "What are you talking about? You're scaring me."

Lauren saw in her rear-view mirror Mark and his hacker exit the restaurant and jump into separate cars. "If you need anything, Mark will be able to help you. I'm sorry, baby."

She clicked off before Lindsey could say another word.

Lauren tried Erin but got her voicemail. She debated leaving a message as she watched Mark pull out of the lot, followed closely by Ethan, and simply said, "I love you."

That would have to be enough.

51

She needed her list of properties owned by Melissa's LLC, but those were at the task force office and she couldn't go back there. She pondered for a split-second calling Nolan but banished that from her mind right away. This was her fight, not his, and she'd dragged him into it far enough already. She was grateful he'd had the strength of character to turn her down and that nothing further had gone on between them. No matter what happened the rest of that day, any idea of a relationship they could have possibly had was effectively ended, for good.

She wasn't sorry about that.

All that mattered was David Spencer and Shane Reese. Everything else was background noise.

She'd have to drive to each spot, stake it out, and then move on to the next one. But she'd go in reverse order. Maybe she'd get lucky, and he was still at the last drop-off point. But in the time it had taken for Ethan to write down the list and bring it to her, he might have moved four times. She had a feeling in her gut these addresses were safe places to him, though. He'd be at one of them.

What she needed at the moment was a different car. David had surveilled her as much as she had surveilled him. He'd know her Ford from a mile away. And Reese's personal car, whose spare key hung on her ring.

Keys to each other's houses, keys to each other's cars. How had I not realized what was happening between us? she thought bitterly, but she pushed those feelings aside. It was time to go to work.

Stealing a car wouldn't be too hard, especially since she already knew of one that was going to be sitting idle all day and not missed for a long time.

She headed back toward her neighborhood.

Waving to her as she pulled up, the kid at the gate raised the wooden plank, allowing her into her gated community. He was a sweet young kid who loved wearing his security guard uniform and probably dreamed of being a cop like Lauren.

If you ever do become a police officer, don't be like me, Lauren thought as she gave him her fake smile. *Because everything you do catches up with you eventually.*

Lauren parked her car at the very end of her street. She wanted to, but she wasn't about to go back to her house for her spare gun and more supplies. For all she knew, Kencil had a car sitting on it while they typed a search warrant. She'd have to go into stealth mode. She slipped into the last house on the left's concrete patio and padded over to the hedge that separated the yard from the one next to it. Thankfully, most of her neighbors were at work, and the kids were still in school. Although, from the looks of the angry sky, they might be getting one last snow day coming.

The backyards in her neighborhood were empty and depressing this time of year. No one had been able to plant flowers yet because of the crazy weather, so only a few patches of purple crocuses poked through the ground here and there. All the lawn furniture was still packed away in her neighbors' garages; pools were covered.

She had to hop a small four-foot fence to get into Dayla's backyard. The ground had gone from muddy back to hard again with the previous night's frost, so her boots made a *whumping* sound when she landed.

Dayla's backyard consisted of an elaborate in-ground pool, complete with waterfall and hot tub. It was all covered over now in a thick plastic tarp. Black, brackish water had collected on top of the pool cover. She made her way around the kidney-shaped pool to the driveway.

Dayla had sent her a text the previous night saying she and her husband had a three-night function at a Las Vegas casino, and she'd get back as soon as she could. Her husband was a well-known plastic surgeon and was always going to medical conferences. Dayla only went with him if the hotel had a casino attached to it.

Dayla's dark blue Cadillac Escalade was big, but it wasn't flashy. It definitely did not resemble the tricked out monstrosity Violanti had acquired, even though it was the same make and model. Her husband's white Jaguar was much more noticeable. Both were parked one after the other in the long driveway. Thankfully Dayla's SUV was parked behind the Jag, so Lauren wouldn't have to move it.

Lauren didn't have a key to Dayla's Escalade, but she knew where she kept a spare hidden. She walked over to the side door and felt around under the awning. A bunch of keys fell into her palm, fastened together with a Gucci keychain.

Lauren went over to the SUV, hit the fob, and the door opened. Dayla hated keyless entry and made her husband special order her car without it. One morning she'd started her last car, ran inside to grab something, and hopped back in without realizing she'd left the keys on the hall table. She got all the way to her gym without keys and couldn't figure out why the car was bonging at her the whole way. That was the last of keyless entry for Dayla.

Lauren put the SUV in reverse and backed out of the driveway, looking for a surveillance car. She didn't see one, but that didn't mean it wasn't there.

The kid at the gate wasn't as interested in the cars leaving as he was the ones trying to get in, so Lauren drove right through. He'd copy down the plate, as he was now required to do since the great Joe Wheeler stalking incident that had taken place and gotten a couple of lazy guards fired.

By the time Dayla's Escalade was discovered missing, that would be the least of her worries.

She pulled the little white pieces of notebook paper out of her pocket and fanned them on the seat next to her. She'd go in order of the rides he took. Knowing David, he was likely to leave a vehicle somewhere and double back. The first address was close to David's office in the Ward; an abandoned warehouse for a defunct trucking company. She headed south on Delaware Avenue.

On the radio a meteorologist was announcing a travel advisory for all of Erie and Niagara Counties. "That polar vortex we've been talking about is sending an unusually cold air mass our way, bringing ice and snow with it. This is no April Fool's joke, folks. We're looking at six to eight inches of accumulation starting just after the evening commute. So if you can convince your boss to let you out early, go home and break out the shovels. It's going to be a bitter one, with temperatures dropping into the—"

She hit the channel button. A Metallica song popped on. *Fuck the weather and fuck the snow,* she thought, turning up the volume and letting the music thunder over her. *I'm coming for you, David.*

52

The first place turned out to be barely a burned-out husk. She imagined that maybe David had had another vehicle waiting there for him, because there was no place to hide in the shell of the building that was left. Maybe she would have been more suspicious if the fire had happened recently, but she could tell it had been a while. She tried to remember if the Google Maps pictures she'd pulled of all the properties showed one that was burned out.

Still, she checked around carefully. She even walked over to the next closest business, a small engine repair shop, and made sure nothing was out of the ordinary. The guy in the front office of the shop looked at her curiously for a second as she looked through their windows, then she waved to him and walked back to Dayla's Escalade. Whatever David had done there, it'd been quick.

The next place on the list was a defunct factory on the lower East Side. Snow had started to fall as she made her way across the city to Sycamore Street. The great brick building was enclosed by a chain-link fence topped with razor wire. She sat in front of the building and surveyed it. The enclosed parking lot was in front, exposed to busy Sycamore Street. There was no way he'd be able to park one of his white vans out front and drag a girl, living or dead, out in front of a main road and into the decrepit building. David was smarter than that.

But he had been there.

She caught a flicker of movement off to her left. A door was banging open and closed with the wind. Lauren checked her gun and exited the car. David had come there for a reason. Maybe he'd been the one to kick in the door.

Maybe he was still inside.

She crept along the fence, looking for an opening. Just as she passed a NO TRESPASSING sign she saw the jagged hole cut in the fence. If any of the cars inching along on Sycamore Street saw her climbing through, no one beeped or stopped. Motorists would be intent on not sliding into the car in front of them, not the background scenery.

Lauren waded through the inch of accumulation to the stairs that led to the open door. If there had been any footprints, they had since been covered over. She grasped the rail tightly; the stairs were dusted in snow with an underlying layer of ice. *That'd be just my luck, wouldn't it, Reese?* she thought as she made it to the landing. *To break my ankle on some fucking unshoveled steps?*

She paused for a second at the edge of the doorway, listening.

Nothing but the wind and the creaking of the rusty door hinges.

Holding her gun with both hands, but down by her thigh, she slipped through the entrance.

That part of the building housed the now abandoned offices. A hallway stretched out before her, lined with doors on either side. Homeless people had set up camp inside at one time or another; black spots on the floor with matching soot on the ceiling gave away their indoor cooking fires. Beer bottles, empty fast food wrappers, and discarded clothes lay scattered around. Lauren carefully picked her way through the trash, checking and clearing each empty office at gunpoint until she got to the end of the hall.

She stopped and listened again.

Nothing.

Lauren cut to the right of the door of the last room in the hallway, sweeping the interior with her Glock before she stepped inside. The smell of piss assaulted her nose immediately upon entry. In the center of the windowless room, two square plastic crates were stacked on top of each other, forming a makeshift table. An upside-down white bucket with grayish-taupe spackling still stuck to the sides made up the chair. A brown paper bag lay wadded on the floor next to it.

Lauren walked over to the do-it-yourself dining set. There on the crate were two cheap-looking black cellphones sitting next to an empty Chinese take-out box with a pair of chopsticks sticking out of it. A fortune cookie, still wrapped, was placed neatly on top of a white paper napkin. She nudged the chopsticks with the barrel of her gun and the box tipped over, sending the wooden utensils sailing onto the floor. David had been there, all right. But how long ago?

Lauren had no way to know if David had access to another credit card. All she knew for sure was that he'd gone to the addresses Ethan had given her in the time since Reese was shot. David had come to each of the properties for a reason. Had he stashed a gun at one? Slept at another? Obviously, he had eaten dinner here, despite the urine smell, and dumped two cell phones. It was possible that he had already doubled back to the first property she'd visited, but she had to go through the entire list before she started backtracking. She had to be methodical.

The fact was, David wanted Lauren to find him. But just like she couldn't be one hundred percent sure which property he was located at right then, he couldn't be sure when she'd show up. Her passing out on her bed the night before had either thrown David's game off or given him enough time to set a trap. She could only hope for the former rather than the latter. He was bouncing from place to place, on the run, with every cop on this side of the state looking for him. Even if he'd prepared these little nesting places ahead of time, there was no way he was immune to lack of sleep, stress, and pressure. The things that were working against her were also working against him.

She gave the room one last glance before exiting. David was long gone from that location. It was time to move on.

53

The next two places were just as much a bust as the first two, the only difference in her surveillance being that the weather had gotten steadily worse, slowing her to almost a crawl. The visibility continued to deteriorate as the storm crept across the lake.

Dayla's windshield wipers beat furiously against the blowing snow. The two yellow beams of her headlights didn't even reach as far as the next car ahead of her, which was only discernable because of the red taillights against the whiteness. If she had been worried about David recognizing her vehicle, she hadn't needed to. The snow was taking care to camouflage everything.

The last property was off Fuhrmann Boulevard, backing to Lake Erie itself. Lauren knew the building; she passed it every time she drove on Route 5 into the southtowns. It sat next to a small marina, shuttered up until the weather broke. Driving by, she'd see the boats taken out of the water for the winter, lining the parking lot, set high on trailers with what looked like blue Saran wrap over them. Next to that was the parking lot for the warehouse.

The warehouse itself was huge; giant compared to the other businesses scattered around it. Unlike most cities on the Great Lakes, Buffalo's waterfront property wasn't developed into high-rise apartments or cute retail shopping strips. Old factories, abandoned grain elevators, and random boat launches made up much of the coastline just south of downtown.

She tried to make out the outline of the building as she turned down the access road into the parking lot that spread out behind the building, which should have had a spectacular view of the lake. Instead, all she could see was a great expanse of churning gray water topped with blowing white snow.

This had to be the place.

It was the only place left.

Lauren hoped she parked far enough back that her headlights would be obscured by the snow. The wind surely would cover the sound of the engine.

Putting the Escalade in park, she patted herself down: cell phone, flashlight, and gun. She'd leave her portable radio in the car. She had no intention of calling for backup.

Not now.

She pulled her cell phone out, fiddled with it for a second, and dropped it back in the front pocket of Ethan's jacket.

As Lauren got out of Dayla's SUV, the force of the wind hit her full in the face. The snow was blowing off the lake sideways, smacking into the old brick warehouse and swirling upward. Ethan's army jacket was as useful as tissue paper against that kind of cold. Still, she zipped it closed to the neck, tucked her head down, and tramped toward the side of the building.

It was time to end this game once and for all.

54

Lauren touched the smaller metal entrance door next to a row of overhead doors where she guessed trucks used to come in and out before the property was abandoned. It was ice cold. The lock had been busted off long ago, leaving a jagged hole where the handle should be. Using the pads of the first two fingers of her left hand she tested it. It swung open four inches, then caught on something. No light emitted from the gap. Above her, an ice-covered awning creaked and yowled in the wind.

She paused, listening for any movement inside. She inched forward, now nudging the door with her hip just enough for her to slip through, but not before unholstering her gun.

Lauren kept her little metal flashlight in her front jacket pocket as she crossed through into the warehouse space. No use making herself a visible target just yet. It took a second for her eyes to adjust. Looking up, she saw whole sections of the roof were missing.

She could see the snow swirling above her. Fat flakes drifted down, coating the floor in white. A crazy maze of zig-zag footprints snaked across the ground, some older than others. Some were already disappearing under the new snow, others looked fresh and newly stamped.

Someone with work boots was in the warehouse. And from the frantic pattern, they'd been busy.

Thankfully, the snow was reflective. Between whatever light was filtering in from the ceiling between the gusts and the broken windows that lined the walls, she could make out the immediate ground floor around her without the flashlight. But there were still plenty of dark spaces and voids to hide in. If David was in that warehouse, he could see her already. She might as well have put a bullseye on her back.

He wanted to draw her in. All these games and clues David had left scattered like breadcrumbs in the forest had all led up to this. He'd done everything perfectly, orchestrated how every scene would play out and choreographed every move. The only thing Lauren had on her side was his desire to keep playing with her. If she could string that out, he might make a misstep.

Maybe.

She crept forward, snowflakes catching in her hair, eyes sweeping the area in front of her from left to right and back again. Old machinery of indeterminate use littered the huge open space, like the former owners had dumped broken-down equipment from other plants inside this warehouse in the hopes that their parts might be useful one day, only to have them rust and decay with the rest of the building.

She spotted a metal staircase threading up the back wall, leading to a rickety catwalk that seemed to ring the room, as far as the dimness would let her see.

When she got to the approximate center of the room, an oddly familiar box shape caught her eyes. It looked out of place among the boat hulls and engine guts dumped haphazardly around the space. She tried to take a measure of cover here and there, shielding herself with the debris as best she could, as she crossed the warehouse floor.

Lauren recognized the shape as an old-fashioned newspaper box once she got within twenty feet of it. The wood was painted a faded brown color. It looked a lot like the one her uncle Bob had kept in his garage when she was a kid. Her uncle's had been an ugly blue-green and had been stuffed with wrench sets and saw blades and car parts he had every intention of using one day, but never did. It had sat next to an old generator and served as a table from time to time, depending on the project he was working on. Lauren would play with the heavy padlock on the front when her aunt would babysit her, pretending to pick it open to get to the pirate treasure inside.

Her aunt had told her that back in the old days, paper trucks would leave newspapers in those huge boxes and the carriers would have a key and come get their papers for their routes every morning. When paperboys went the way of the dodo bird, the boxes ended up in garages and basements, fossils of a bygone age.

Five feet long and three and a half feet wide, the box's bleached-out brown color contrasted with the bright snow like a coffee stain down the front of a crisp white shirt. It was raised up on raw wooden pallets stacked on the floor, which brought the top to just above Lauren's waist. She could see that the lid would open upward. The rusty latch was still there, but the lock for it was long gone. Two large holes perforated the front, and Lauren recognized them immediately for what they were: bullet holes. Someone had pumped two rounds into the box, leaving behind a pair of splintered wooden stars.

Then she noticed the red metal dolly propped against the wall next to the chest. With its two thick, black rubber wheels, it looked like a shiny new toy sitting among the garbage. A shiver of revulsion ran through her. A dolly moved heavy things. Maybe dead things.

This is what he wants, she thought as she approached. *He wants me to open it, to see what's inside and be shocked. He wanted me to see the dolly. David wants me to react. He's watching his little play being acted out exactly how he scripted it.*

Still, she was drawn to the box, like going over to it was an inevitability. Boot treads led to and fro in either direction from the chest; someone had come and opened it several times, checking on something.

Or someone.

Could Isabella still be alive in there?

Her footsteps echoed only slightly in the cavernous space, drowned out by the squall overhead and softened by the snow underfoot. She closed the distance slowly: ten feet, eight feet, six feet. The chest was sitting against the far wall, positioned directly under a huge gaping window. The busted-out pane had jagged pieces of glass sticking up from the bottom and thick, twisted icicles hanging from the top, like a frozen great white shark's mouth.

On the lid of the box was the Murder Book. Its distinctive olive-green cover was lying open flat, the three metal rings in the binder still holding a few pages in place. Lauren saw that the remaining pages and ends of the plastic cover were charred around the edges.

She didn't realize her hand was shaking until she reached for the metal handle.

David's voice echoed through the warehouse from up above her somewhere on the catwalk. "I interrupted Ricky Schultz as he was trying to burn the pages in a little metal ashtray in his basement. I don't know what he planned to do with the cover. It looks like he tried to set that on fire too, but the ashtray just wasn't going to cut it."

Don't show him he's getting to you. Lauren's mind raced as she traced her gun around the catwalk. She noticed an elaborate pulley system above her, heavy chains sagging down from what was left of the ceiling. *Don't play into it and give him what he wants.*

"He was so annoyed when I started pounding on his door. I yelled to him that I was from his lawyer's office. I wish you could have seen the look on his face when he opened the door and I stuck Melissa's .45 in his gut. I swear he almost pissed himself." David let out a joyful laugh at his own cleverness.

Lauren pivoted and scanned the space behind her. She tried to find a target in the uneven light.

"Why don't you open the chest?"

She spun around, her gun tracked the metal catwalk as far as she could make out. He had to be up there somewhere.

The only thing that moved was her cloud of breath with each exhale.

"Don't you wanna know what's inside?" His voice was mocking now, but playful, like they were two kids playing tag on the playground.

"Why don't you tell me?" Lauren replied, still searching the shadows.

"What would be the fun in that?"

"Is this fun for you?" she asked, trying to get a fix on where his voice was coming from. Above her the catwalk groaned and creaked, like someone was scurrying along it.

"I wouldn't use the word *fun*. It's actually kind of sad. Like I'm finally breaking up with you."

Now it was Lauren's turn to laugh. "That's some sick shit, that thinking right there."

"You think I killed Wheeler and Schultz because they hurt you. That's what's sad, you stupid bitch. I killed those guys to *frame* you."

David's voice lost its playfulness. It had taken on a cold, hard tone. "The first thing Wheeler did when he got back on the job was start asking questions about Amber again. I couldn't have him *and* you digging around my business."

The truth of what he'd just said hit her in the gut like a sledgehammer. He'd killed Joe Wheeler to get him off his trail, and when he saw the opportunity to draw any attention away from himself and onto her, he killed Ricky Schultz. But not before taking a few souvenirs from each crime scene, like the tire iron and the Murder Book, for future use against her and Reese.

"Your boy Ricky must have had a hiding spot somewhere. When I saw on the news he'd been questioned and released with no charges, I decided to do a little surveillance myself. I thought for sure your department would have had an unmarked car watching him. You folks really dropped the ball on that one."

She knew David was creeping along the rickety catwalk almost directly above her, but the echoes in the cavernous warehouse made it hard to pinpoint his exact location. She waited, heart pumping, finger on the trigger, tracing along with his voice as best she could in the swirling snow and gloom.

"Schultz must have thought the coast was clear to drag out your book to try to get rid of it. Man, did I get lucky on the timing with that one." His obnoxious laugh filled her ears. "I kept the tire iron after using it on Wheeler. I knew it would come in handy someday. Every police car in Buffalo is probably over at that asshole Reese's house right now, searching for more evidence."

Suddenly, pages from the Murder Book began to rain down from the ceiling, scattering around the floor. A single burnt page came to rest on the toe of her boot. She kicked it off, sighting her gun at the spot from where they seemed to have been tossed, but no one was there.

"I have to admit," David's voice fell down on her from above, "that I was a little obsessed with you when I first met you. Uncle Frank always thought I had a problem with women in general. I know now that he was right, just not in the way he thinks."

Now his voice seemed to be coming from one corner, and then the opposite. Lauren wondered if he had set up some kind of wireless speakers along the catwalk to confuse her. Hell, he'd thought of everything else.

"I finally found my sweet spot. I like the whole process of luring them in, watching them get pissed when they think they've been stood up, and then the look on their faces when they find out I really did show. That look's better than sex. It really is. But Wheeler was a problem, and I took care of that. Then I knew you'd be a problem, so I thought killing Schultz would take care of that. But it didn't."

His voice was coming from everywhere now. Lauren moved with each new location, spinning like a top.

"I need to wrap this up so I can get on with my life."

Lauren snorted, aiming into the far-left corner. "You think you'll kill me and you'll be able to just go on with your life, like some model citizen? You think that's how it works?"

"I need to able to function without looking over my shoulder all the time. You should have just let it all go."

"You're a killer," she spat, not caring that she was out in the open anymore. He could have already taken her out the minute she stepped in the building. "There's something wrong with the way your mind works. You need help."

"I need help? Are you going to help me? Hell, you're the one who followed me here. Who came to my work? Had me picked up for questioning? That was you."

"You attacked me in the park."

"Oh, please." He was starting to sound bored. He was done playing around with her. "I was just trying to make you seem more crazy than you already looked. I gotta say, you've done a good job of that on your own, though."

Lauren took a step backward, trying to keep him talking. "You don't need to do all this."

"What I need is a clean shot, so I can be done with this and you forever."

She caught movement on the catwalk to her left. As she raised her gun, a beer bottle smashed on the floor next to her, the sound thundering through the building like a bomb going off. She jumped, let a wild shot off, and the figure was gone.

He's trying to disorient me, get me to move, she thought, *but something's blocking his view of me. The pulleys?*

Seventeen bullets now, she thought as she backed up, toward the brown box, keeping a huge hulk of a machine to her left. The echo of the shot rang in her ears. She wondered what he could see from his perches, if the snow and chains really were obscuring his view, and as soon as he had an opening, a single shot would end it all.

The wind whipped in through the mouth-like window frame above the old chest, blowing against her neck. She checked her back. She was inches from the box now. The icicles, three feet long and six inches wide across the top, came tapering to sharp points, almost meeting the broken glass left sticking up from the bottom. Snow had started to collect on the lid, dusting over the Murder Book.

"Are we done talking?" David asked as her calf banged into the big wooden chest. He sounded closer this time. She scanned the room left to right, but there were too many hiding spots, too many areas hidden from her sightline.

She pressed herself backwards against the box; the rough, cracked wood tore into her pants like little barbs. *Isabella could be inside,* she thought.

But was she alive?

Turning her back to the danger, she had to know for sure. Lauren faced the chest and, still holding her gun in her right hand, grabbed the rusted metal handle and pulled.

The heavy lid made the same squeaking noise she remembered hearing every time her uncle had opened his tool box. Only she wasn't looking for a ratchet set or old jumper cables.

There was Isabella.

She'd been placed face-up, arms folded over her middle, legs bent at the knee so they almost touched the lid. Her face had taken on a blueish tinge, her eyelashes frosted with ice droplets, frozen in place. Lauren reached in to touch her throat but drew her hand back; she knew Isabella was dead. She was a beautiful frozen doll that David had stored away until he was ready to dump her, like the others. Rage bubbled like molten lava at Lauren's very core.

She let the lid slam down and turned to face the darkness, arms spread wide in an invitation. "Here I am!" Lauren screamed into the swirling snow. She took a step forward so he could get a good look. "Come and get me, you fucking coward!"

Silence.

"Nothing to say now, little boy?" She laughed out into the warehouse. "It figures. Gonna go run home to Mommy?"

The attack came from the side, her bad side, sending a shocking bolt of pain through her body as she was crushed against the box. David grabbed her gun arm with both hands and brought it smashing down on the chest's lid, sending her Glock flying, clattering to the floor.

She reached up and clawed at his face with her free hand as he bent her backwards, drawing deep, bloody furrows in his cheek as she tried to hook her finger in his eye socket, but she couldn't manage it.

A blow hit her in the head, stunning her for a second.

David's face swam before her eyes as he hoisted her onto the box, sending the Murder Book sliding off the side. The ancient wood snapped and moaned underneath her, threatening to cave in. David clamped his hands around Lauren's neck, pushing her body back until it was flush with the wall and her head hit the bottom of the windowpane.

Lauren could feel the butt of a gun in his waistband digging into her stomach as he wedged himself between her legs to get better leverage. "I could have shot you, but I want you to see me do it. I want you to know what I'm doing to you."

His brown eyes were hard and narrow and cold as he brought his face close to hers. She could feel his hot breath on her mouth. "I'm going to take my time strangling you, and then I'm going to leave your body in here and call the media, so the cameras get here first and the whole world can see what's left of you."

His fingers dug into her throat, closing off her airway. Black spots floated before her eyes.

The choking, the darkness, the panic. Lauren remembered this feeling on the floor of the Cold Case office when she got stabbed and her lung collapsed. This was how it was supposed to end for her then.

No, the thought raced through the anger blooming in her brain. *This is not how it's going to end.*

With every ounce of strength she had, Lauren brought her knee crashing into his groin, making him double over in pain.

David let out a wounded howl as his grip loosened, like it had on the walking path, allowing her to gasp half a breath, but he didn't let go.

Reaching behind her, her fingers searched for one of the icicles hanging in the window. A three-inch tip broke off in her hand while the rest came crashing down, just missing her head. It fractured and broke into chunks on the wooden lid.

"You gonna stab me in the eye with an icicle?" David laughed, doubling up on his grip, squeezing harder. "I saw that in a movie once too. You pathetic old hag." He wasn't wearing gloves this time. He wanted to feel it, skin on skin.

Good, the thought raged through her, *I want you to feel it too.*

Her hand slapped back to the window, reaching lower as he throttled her. She wrapped it around one of the shards of glass jutting from the bottom of the frame, ignoring the searing pain as it cut into her hand and snapped it from the windowpane.

She jammed the triangle of glass into the side of his neck.

His brown eyes looked down into hers, turning from mocking to questioning as hot, thick blood pulsed from his throat.

She shoved harder, deeper. The glass sliced into her palm as it carved through his neck.

His hands went to his throat, releasing Lauren as he slipped down to his knees. The glass was at least four inches into him, his blood soaking into the black hooded jacket he was wearing.

"I'm going to do to you what you did to Ricky Schultz." She coughed, jumping off the chest, crouching next to him. She watched as he fell to his right side, hands grasping, trying to pull the slippery shard out, making the blood spurt even harder.

Kneeling on the frozen floor next to him, she leaned over him. David was gagging, choking on his own blood as his eyes desperately darted around, searching for some kind of help.

"Look at me," she said, then grabbed his chin, finger and thumb digging into either side of his jaw and forced his face to hers. "Look. At. Me."

A gurgling noise came from somewhere inside David. His mouth was opening and closing as if he was trying to say something.

"I want you to see my face. Because it doesn't mean anything if you don't know who did this to you." Her voice was the raspy whisper it had been after he'd choked her in the park. But it was audible, and she knew he heard her. "I want you to know that *I* did this to you."

She let his face go, leaving gory, smeared fingerprints behind.

"I did this to you."

She watched as his lifeblood pumped out onto the concrete floor, spreading around his head and upper torso, melting the icy accumulation. She cradled her injured palm in her other hand just above David, her own blood dripping down, mixing with his. More snowflakes blew in from the window, disappearing as soon as they hit the dark pool.

A minute ticked by. Maybe two. It seemed like an eternity, but she had to be sure.

David took one last ragged breath, his chest rising, then stopping abruptly, collapsing in on himself. His eyes glazed over, and his head tilted forward, staring at the ceiling.

She regarded the shell of his body for a moment: the handsome face, the dark-colored clothes, the dyed blond hair. Everything about him had made him a predator.

So what did that make her?

She turned around and heaved open the lid on the box again. Blood from her injured hand ran down along the wooden side. Looking in, she whispered a small prayer above the broken girl. Lauren wished she was strong enough to lift Isabella out, but that would have to do for now. Leaving the lid open, she turned, stepping over David's body. Random pages from the Murder Book tried to stick to the bottom of her bloody boot, but she kicked them off.

Pulling her cell phone from her pocket, she made sure it was still recording as she walked toward the exit door. Twenty-seven minutes of audio inside the warehouse had been captured. She hit End and a text message from Peter Reese flashed across her screen: THEY GOT THE SWELLING DOWN. HE'S GOING TO BE OKAY.

She should have been flooded with relief, but she was numb. Numb to David, numb to everything that had happened in the last forty-eight hours, numb to the pain in her throat and hand. Maybe later she'd cry for Isabella and for Reese too. But for now, she had one last thing she had to do.

She headed toward the entrance, scrolling through her contacts, pausing in the doorway when she got to the one she was looking for. She hit the call button and put the phone to her ear. It picked up on the first ring.

"Violanti," Lauren said, hovering just inside the warehouse. "I think I'm going to need a good defense attorney."

Then she stepped out into the storm.

Acknowledgments

First and foremost, I'd like to thank God for blessing me with this new journey. I have traveled all over the country in the last two years and met the most amazing and wonderful people. I will be forever grateful.

I'd like to thank my husband, Dan, for supporting me through thick and thin. You have always been here for me and none of it would have been possible without you.

Many thanks to first readers/editors: Stephanie Patterson, Michael Breen, Ruth Robbins, Patricia Carrington, and Joyce Maguda. Also, everyone at the writer's group at the Dog Ears Bookstore in South Buffalo for reading my pages and being fair and honest. You help me to be a better writer!

Thank you to Tom McDonnell, Karen Adymy, Maura Krause, Sharon Kysor, Maureen Lynch, Alyson Krause, Brian Ross, Missy Sullivan, Nell Kavanaugh, Karen Quinn-Higgins, Peg and Dan Redmond, Mollie Redmond, and Galen Kogut for all your unwavering love and support.

Mom, Lorri, Lenny, Myles, and my entire family: thanks for putting up with me!

Thank you, Terri Bischoff, for being a tireless supporter of your authors. And thanks to Nicole Nugent for all you've done.

Thanks to my agent, Bob Mecoy, for taking a chance on me.

To all the book clubs, bookstores, and libraries that have invited me in, listened to me talk, and read my book; thank you! Your warmth, enthusiasm, and generosity has amazed and humbled me.

Natalie and Mary, you two are the reason I get up in the morning and my last thought before I fall asleep at night. You both surprise and inspire me every day.

© Short Street Photographers

About the Author

Lissa Marie Redmond is a recently retired Cold Case Homicide detective with the Buffalo Police Department. She lives and writes in Buffalo, New York, with her husband and two kids. *A Means to an End* is the third novel in her Cold Case Investigation series.